Twisted Tales
from the
Torchlight Inn

10-Year Anniversary Edition

Ty Schwamberger
Thom Erb
Dean Harrison

JOURNALSTONE
YOUR LINK TO ARTIST TALENT

ISBN: 978-1-68510-025-4 (sc)
ISBN: 978-1-68510-026-1 (ebook)
Library of Congress Catalog Number: 2021949045

First printing edition: October 22, 2021
Published by JournalStone Publishing in the United States of America.
Cover Design and Layout: Thom Erb
Edited by Sean Leonard
Proofreading and Interior Layout by Scarlett R. Algee

JournalStone Publishing
3205 Sassafras Trail
Carbondale, Illinois 62901

JournalStone books may be ordered through booksellers or by contacting:
JournalStone | www.journalstone.com

Contents

Afterword
203

About the Authors

Twisted Tales
from the
Torchlight Inn

10-Year Anniversary Edition

Last Night Out
Ty Schwamberger

Chapter 1

It was only the beginning of May, but the air already seemed to be blowing in that old familiar excitement of the approaching summer. In the months ahead there would be odd jobs that needed done, working internships (if that was your thing), factory work, or that ever-stable standby – a fast food restaurant, where by the end of the summer your skin would pay the price of having to stand over a disgusting vat of boiling grease while you toss in and pull out basket after basket of still-soggy French fries. Sometimes you would be lucky and get griddle duty, where you would be frying up a meat that you could never quite identify – even if the sign did say "one hundred percent all-beef patty." You knew it was a shitty job, but you did it anyway. Besides, a shitty factory or restaurant job would last less than three months, and more often than not, you were back to school before you knew it. Sometimes that was a plus; other times, not so much.

In Gabe's case, he knew it was going to be another summer standing over the boiling grease, and was dreading every minute of it. He wished he could draw the lucky straw this time and be able to fry up some burgers or the occasional chicken sandwich, but when it came down to it, he knew his luck just wasn't that good. He was doomed to be a "fry guy" for the rest of his natural-born life. Or at least until he graduated with the rest of his friends from Southpoint State University – nestled in the middle of the beautiful town of Miller Falls – and went on to law school.

A grin stretched across his face.

His smile turned upside down when he was elbowed in the ribcage.

Gabe grabbed his side and half bent over as he continued to walk through the quad. Gone were his fantasies of one day being a high-powered attorney with money to blow on hookers, booze, and fast cars.

"What gives?" he managed to huff out.

Erin just shrugged her shoulders, winked, and quickened her pace.

With the pain quickly dissipating, he jogged and caught up with Erin.

"What the hell was that for?"

"Nothing."

"What do you mean nothing? You could have broken a rib back there."

"You're such a pussy sometimes, Gabe."

He was still muttering to himself about Erin's comment when they came to the door of the student union. Even with her almost breaking one of his ribs, he was going to be a gentleman and open the door for her to enter first, but she beat him to it, flinging the door open and quickly pulling it closed behind her. It banged shut in Gabe's face.

"Bitch."

Erin smiled, knocked on one of the glass windows embedded in the thick wooden door, then turned and walked away.

She might be Alan's girl or whatever, but God how I would love to sock her in the nose one of these times.

Gabe knew he would never do such a thing, but liked to think about it sometimes. The truth of the matter was, he liked Erin. Hell, he loved her. As much as you could love the girl your roommate was dating, anyway.

Gabe pulled the door towards him and stepped inside.

The school must have been anticipating the heat wave, because as Gabe stepped inside a cold gush of air swept over him.

The hair on the back of his sweaty neck stood on end as he spotted Erin getting a Diet Coke out of a vending machine. He walked over to her and smacked her on the back of her jeans.

"Owww! Watch it, buster! What if Alan saw you do that?"

"After what you did to me outside, he would probably say you deserved it."

"Dick."

"Bitch."

They smiled at each other as they heard Alan yell out to them from the other side of the student union.

Side by side they walked over and joined him on one of the soft leather couches that an alumnus had donated at the beginning of the school year.

Erin popped her soda open and took a long drink. She handed the can to Alan, who took a swig and then passed it to Gabe. He nodded thanks and then handed the cold can back to Erin. She winked at him, then took another drink.

"That final was a fucking killer, man," Alan said, dropping a book into his backpack and zipping it up. "I don't know who this bitch thinks she is. None of the questions were from the review materials she handed out last week. Not. A. Single. Fucking. One. Can you believe that shit? I probably bombed the fucker."

Erin laughed.

"Dude," Gabe said, "you say that shit all the time, and every single time when the test comes back you aced the fucker. You damn well know it's gonna be the same this time around."

Erin laughed again.

"Bullshit. Don't you remember mid-terms?"

"Ohhh...*riiight*," Gabe said, laughing. "What? When you got a B-plus on your Advanced Chemistry exam? You're full of more shit than a goose, Alan."

This time Erin laughed so hard soda came shooting out her nose. She started to choke and cough, trying to expel the liquid from her burning lungs. The two boys just pointed and laughed.

She managed to get out "Assholes" before running off in search of the girls' restroom.

When she was gone, Alan said, "What got up her butt?"

"I don't know, man. Maybe she's on her rag or something."

"Shit. She better not be. She was just on it last week and I want to get me some before we blow this pop stand tomorrow morning."

"You know it'll probably be a rough day to pack and move out, don't you?" Gabe asked.

"Probably. But that's what makes it that much more fun."

"Can't say I agree with you there."

"You don't have to, my fine fellow. All you have to agree with me on is the fabulous bar I picked out to get our drink on for our last night out before break."

"Oh, yeah. I remember you saying something this morning that you heard of a cool place to check out. You sure you don't just wanna go back to the Clover Club like every weekend?"

"Nah. That place has become a dump. Now, this place that I have lined up for us tonight should be a real beauty."

"Do tell."

"All in good time, my man. All in good time."

Gabe and Alan got up from the cushy leather couch and went to make sure Erin was okay.

Chapter 2

By the time Gabe and Alan left Cooper Hall and started to walk across campus to France Hall, where Erin lived, the warmth of the day was gone. A cool breeze blew through campus and wrapped around Alan's bare arms.

He shivered.

"I told you to wear a windbreaker, dumbass."

"I didn't think it'd be as cold as a witch's tit out here, man."

Continuing to walk, they passed a few students going this way or that. Some were probably headed to their respective partner's dorm rooms, to a friend's place, or starting their trek to a local watering hole.

Alan jogged ahead of Gabe and stomped up the front steps to the all-girl's dorm. He gritted his teeth together as he pulled the door open and motioned for Gabe to go inside. Alan followed behind him.

"Damn. It really did get nippy out there. Where'd the sun go, anyway?"

"Down with the day?"

"Don't be a smartass, man."

Gabe laughed.

Soon they came to Erin's room. Alan pressed his ear up to the old wooden door. Gabe nudged him with his elbow and remembered earlier in the day when Erin hadn't given just a friendly *hey* nudge but had really laid into his ribs. He winced at the very thought of it. He put his hand on his side to make sure his ribs weren't tender. It hurt a little bit as he pressed but not too much. He'd live.

Gabe tapped on Alan's shoulder again.

Alan turned his head and gave him a *what the fuck* face and then pressed his ear back against the door.

Gabe didn't know what Alan was doing. He couldn't hear any loud music playing or Erin on the phone, so there could be only one other reason Alan was trying to be so sneaky and not just knock on the door and wait for Erin to come open it for them.

He thought she was cheating on him.

Again.

It had happened at the beginning of the current school year.

Gabe remembered it like it was yesterday.

The three of them had gone to Sigma Tau Nu's "Here's to Another Year" party. There was plenty of booze, beer, and babes to go around. There was even weed, if you were into that sort of thing. But the three of them had mostly gone to the party because everyone on campus knew that if you wanted to party – *really* party and have a great time – that was the frat house to do it in. So they had walked to the house, paid their three bucks to get inside, and went straight to the bar to have one of the fraternity guys pour them a cold beer. Gabe could recall how the beer had been Coors Light. It was always Coors Light as the Sig House. Some good shit. At least all the Sigs thought so.

So, they had their beer. Hell, they drank a lot of beer as the night wore on. Alan had even sampled some weed in the upstairs of the house. So he, to say the least, was feeling no pain when *it* happened.

He and Alan had been sitting on one of the Sig's beer-soaked couches when Erin told them she had to take a piss and would be right back. Of course, the two of them being guys, they could have cared less at that point. They were half crocked out of their skulls anyway. So if Erin said she needed to take a piss, by God, you go girl and take the best piss of your life. Gabe recalled Alan saying something along the lines of "Have a good one and don't fall in" or "Have a mighty fine piss and make sure to wipe after 'cause I wanna tap that ass of yours later and don't need no piss getting on my dick."

It had been something along those lines.

Alan could be a prick sometimes, to say the least. But the two of them had been roommates for three years already, so if he wanted to be a prick to other people, even someone as sweet as Erin, far be it from Gabe to stand in the way.

The two of them were sitting on the couch, nursing what was left in their cups of the five kegs of beer the Sigs had bought for the party, when Alan suddenly jumped up and started running across the room. Before Gabe could even make half the distance that his friend had just run, he saw Alan straddling some guy and pounding the shit out of him. With each impact the guy's face was exploding with splashes of blood. After watching for a few seconds, Gabe ran over and pulled Alan off the guy, who was now lying on the floor and not moving. Blood was running from his nose and mouth. His cheeks had been turned into valleys of gore. If Gabe hadn't been struggling to hold Alan back from pummeling him some more, he probably would have vomited right then and there at the very sight of the poor bastard that just got his ass kicked.

Soon after, Gabe and Alan were walking back across campus towards their dorm.

Erin didn't come with them. Gabe didn't know where she had run off to.

"What the hell was that all about, man?" Gabe asked.

"You didn't see?!"

"No. What the fuck, man? Spill it. Why did you cave that dude's face in?"

"He was fucking with my woman."

"Huh? Who, Erin?"

"Yes. Ya dumb shit. Erin. He had her pinned against the wall and was slobbering all over her."

"I didn't see her doing that."

"No shit. You were half zonked out of your skull. You couldn't have seen a cow with fairy wings fly into the room."

"Hey. I was no more shit-faced than you, man."

"Okay. True. You got me there. But I still saw it."

"You sure?"

"Damn tootin', I'm sure. I saw her sucking his face right back."

"Whatever you say, man."

The two of them walked in silence the rest of the way back to their dorm room. They passed out the moment they hit their pillows and didn't speak of the incident again. The only other time that Gabe knew the subject was brought up was when he was in their adjoining bathroom taking a dump and overheard Alan and Erin on the phone. Alan was yelling at her about "making out with some random dude" and "how could you do such a thing" and "you slut" and "I don't give two shits if you were drunk or not, you shouldn't have been sucking face with any dude but me." It went on like that for a while. So long, in fact, that Gabe had finished his business and was just sitting on the john wondering if he would ever be able to re-join the living again.

After the phone call finally ended, Gabe finished wiping his ass for the umpteenth time, washed his hands for several minutes, and walked out of the room. Something flew at his head. He snatched it mid-air, popped its top, and took a long drink.

The beer tasted just as good as the Sig's beer had a few weeks earlier.

Gabe knew then, even though the Sig House was "the place to be" that Alan would never want to go through their doors, whether Erin was with them or not, ever again.

He could respect that.

Alan stood up, seemingly satisfied with the knowledge that no one else was in the room with his girl, and knocked on the door.

A moment later the ever-beautiful (though sometimes sinful) Erin opened the door and welcomed them in while she finished getting ready for the last night on the town before their junior year ended.

The last time as juniors that they would walk into a bar.

Just the three of them.

For a night filled with good times, laughs, and many many drinks.

Gabe hoped that this night wouldn't end up like it did back at the Sig party.

He hoped this place, the Torchlight Inn, was a cool place for three college kids to hang out and have a good time.

He really hoped.

Gabe and Alan plopped down on Erin's bed and waited for her to finish doing her makeup.

Chapter 3

They exited Erin's dorm and started walking. Gabe looked past Erin, who was walking in between the two of them. Alan was wearing one of Erin's sweatshirts to shield him from the chilly night. It looked sort of funny on him since it was obviously too small, but Gabe was glad he was wearing it anyway. It would keep him from bitching as they walked to the bar.

They had a two-mile walk in front of them.

It would have been a hell of a lot easier to just hop in Alan's car and drive there, but after being stopped by the town's shitty police earlier in the school year, where they were both asked to "please step out of the car, gentlemen" and perform a variety of tests, they hadn't driven when it involved drinking. Probably a smart thing to do every time, but they were college students, therefore not the sharpest tools in the shed.

As they continued to walk through campus, the wind started to pick up. It was very unseasonable for it to be so chilly at the beginning of May, so the three of them made do by placing their hands in their pockets and putting their heads down some of the time and folding their arms in front of their chests the other half of the time.

As they passed Laird Hall, which was the second to last building before leaving campus, Erin must not have been able to take the wind any longer because she snuggled up next to Alan. Gabe wasn't really paying attention. He was too busy thinking about the place they were headed.

The Torchlight Inn.

I wonder how it got a name like that... Alan didn't say much about the place except that we'd like it. Shit. What am I thinking? I could give a rat's ass what the place is called as long as they have beer. Cold beer. Hell, cheap cold beer.

Gabe smiled.

He was still immersed in his thoughts when Alan reached over and punched him in the arm. It only hurt for an instant, but it startled him anyway. It was the same side of his body where Erin had elbowed him earlier. He was glad it was his arm this time and not his still-tender ribs.

"Owww… What the hell did you do that for, man?!"

"Thought you could use a little wake-me-up. You seemed half out of it. What gives?"

"Nothing. I'm walking. The same as you, jackass."

Alan reared back and punched him again. His fist connected with a bullseye where he had struck Gabe just a few seconds before. Erin laughed.

"It's not funny, bit– Hurts like a motha!"

"Sissy."

Now Alan was laughing.

Two fucking comedians, Gabe thought, and turned his head away.

They didn't say much else as they walked past the library and off college property.

Left behind were the safe confines of their campus where everybody knew their names. Sure, they were only juniors, but they had been to quite a few off-campus parties over the past three years and even had a couple parties in their room as well. Gabe and Alan thought of themselves as celebrities. Big Men on Campus. Top Dogs. The Big Cheeses.

The reality was they were nothing more than two average guys that liked to have a good time when classes ended during the week. On weekdays they would do what most college guys would do – drink a few beers, play video games, talk shit, gawk at chicks wearing nothing more than a small towel wrapped around them as they strolled past their open dorm room door on their way to the showers, talk about how they would bang this girl or that one, and sometimes even do some homework if the right mood struck them. Luckily, they were both reasonably intelligent, at least for the majors they had chosen, and could get by without having to put forth much effort.

Now, when the weekends came, that was a different story. That's when they would spend as little time as possible in their dorm room doing the everyday college student activities. Instead, they would either find a few guys to go outside and play some sort of sport together, usually frisbee (it only takes one hand to play and you don't have to move around too much to catch the damn disc, and therefore could use your other hand to hold a beer), while listening to some sort of new age hippie music. That was during the days, anyway. During the nights, they would either go to a frat house that was having a party (any one of them besides the Sig House) or to their favorite watering hole – the Clover Club.

But it wasn't the Clover Club that Alan had on their agenda tonight. Oh no. It was a place called the Torchlight Inn.

Gabe snapped out of his daze, thinking about what a great year it had been (besides the fight at the Sig House, of course), looked over to the snuggling couple walking next to him, and asked, "Hey, Alan. So you gonna tell us about this place we're going to tonight or what?"

"Good question, my fine fellow," Alan replied, taking his hand off Erin's shoulder and giving her a quick smack on the ass.

"Let me tell you the legend about a little place they call the Torchlight Inn." Alan was laughing as he said it.

Erin didn't laugh this time, but gave Alan a strange glance.

Gabe's bowels tightened.

Alan started his story.

Chapter 4

When the story was finished, Gabe turned to Erin and said, "He is full of more shit than a goose."

She laughed at the remark and replied, "I agree. Alan… That is one of the most bullshit-filled stories I have ever heard."

Then she laughed some more.

Gotta admit, Gabe said to himself, *she does have a pretty cute laugh.*

Ahhhh… Quit it, man! She's your best friend's girl. You can't think like that.

Gabe quickly wiped the thought from his head and turned to Alan, who had a shit-eating grin on his face.

"What?"

He started laughing. Really busting a gut. At one point he had to stop walking altogether as he bent over and clutched his stomach. Gabe wanted to sock him one. Erin did the honors with a slap to the back of his head.

"HEY! Watch it! You'll put my eye out with those things."

Gabe looked over at Erin's hand. She really did have some daggers at the end of her fingers. She held her hand in front of her face and waved it back and forth. The light from the moon glistened off her clear nail polish.

"What, these?" she asked. "These here are beautiful. Hell. Alan, I don't hear you complaining when I use them while we're in the sack and I'm clawing the hell outta your back."

Alan's face dropped and then he said, "Well. Yeah. But that's different. You're not poking around my head where my eyeballs are at. You're scratching and shit on my back and ass. Hell. That's the good stuff right there. I especially like it when you take a finger and insert it in my..."

Erin smacked Alan again. It was a lot harder this time, and not on the back of the head where his hair had cushioned the previous blow, but straight across his left cheek.

He bellowed out a scream.

This time it was Gabe who was doing the laughing.

After Alan recovered from the blow to the face, they continued walking. From what Alan had told Gabe earlier, before they had gone over to Erin's dorm to pick her up, it was around two miles to get to the Torchlight Inn. Gabe estimated that they had walked about halfway at this point. He looked over at Alan, walking a safe distance from his girlfriend, and noticed the welt that was forming on the left side of his face. It was a raised bump and looked red and itchy. Gabe wanted to reach over and give it a poke but resisted the urge.

Damn. She really walloped him a good one. Serves the dick right, talking all that shit about the bar being haunted and shit. Hell. Who gives a rat's ass about it being haunted anyway? We're not going there on a flippin' ghost hunt. We're going there to tie one on and see what the night brings.

Gabe really hoped the night wouldn't bring any ghosts. He had seen enough of them, or what he thought looked like ghosts, in his room back at his parents' house when he was a little kid, and didn't really care to see another one anytime soon. The truth of the matter was, he was scared shitless of them.

There had been one ghost in particular that had haunted him throughout his entire childhood, and ever since then he always found himself checking the closet and under the bed before slipping under the covers and going to sleep. He knew it was silly being twenty-one and still scared of ghosts, but he didn't give a shit. Even Alan made fun of him their freshman year for always checking under the bed before lights out, and it had always bugged the shit out of him. He wanted to tell him so many times back then to shut the fuck up, "You don't know what you're talking about," but figured he wouldn't quit giving him shit about it no matter what he said and therefore would just be wasting his time. Gabe was glad that when sophomore year rolled around and Alan caught him doing the same things as the year before, checking under the bed, in the closet, etc, before lights out, he didn't give him any more shit. Gabe figured Alan just took it with a grain of salt and with an *it is what it is* attitude and left it at that. There were also times back during freshman year that Alan would intentionally try to scare the shit of out him.

There was one time in particular when Alan knew Gabe was asleep and he crept out of bed and snuck into their adjoining closets. To this day, Gabe had no idea how long the fucker stood in there, just waiting for the right moment (even though any moment would have been just as good as another since Gabe *was* sleeping the entire time – *the dumb shit*) to throw open the closet door and jump out, shining a flashlight in his eyes and yelling like a banshee. Gabe had jumped out of bed, clearly disoriented, and started running around in circles screaming, "Help me, help me!" He pissed his pajama pants in the process. Out of all the dumb shit that Alan had pulled through the years – getting into fights at fraternity houses and doing countless other semi-legal and downright illegal activities – Gabe never gave a shit. That was all in good fun. It was making him piss down his leg and laughing about it that made Gabe never forgive Alan for that particular incident. Hell. Truth be told, Gabe still held a pretty large grudge about the whole thing.

That's what made seeing Erin bitch-slap him all that much more enjoyable.

The bitch of it was, Alan could be a major prick, but also a hell of a good friend when it came down to it, and Gabe knew in his heart of hearts that Alan would always be there for him when the shit really hit the fan.

Something that Gabe hoped didn't happen tonight at the new-old bar they were walking towards.

Only a half-mile away.

Gabe could almost taste the ice-cold beer gently sliding down his dry throat.

He couldn't wait.

As long as the ghosts stayed where they should be.

Hidden under a bed or locked away in a closet, never to escape.

Or, as Alan told them, hiding in the dark recesses of the Torchlight Inn's basement.

Chapter 5

The sign to the Torchlight Inn extended away from the old brick building and hung by two rusty chains. One chain was longer than the other, making the sign tilt to one side. The sign itself was made from wood and had the name carved into it in Old English lettering. It was dull, cracked, and faded.

The three college students walked under the sign and started up a few steps that led to the bar's door. Gabe, bringing up the rear, looked up at the sign. It looked so old that Gabe didn't doubt one day a gust of wind would make the sign flap so much the chains would break, and it would fall onto some unsuspecting victim entering the bar. He didn't want to be the person that happened to, so he brought his foot up to the next step. His shoe came down on the back of Erin's ankle. She yelped out in pain, lost her footing, and started to fall backward.

Arms flying through the air and her legs out from under her, she toppled and crashed against Gabe's chest. Gabe, still on the first step, lost his balance and went crashing to the ground. Erin's rump landed on his stomach.

The air bust out of his lungs.

He was coughing as Erin scurried off him and sat down on the sidewalk. Alan jumped off the top step of the bar, landed on two feet, and then crouched beside Erin. He asked, "Are you okay?" as he started to help her to her feet.

Gabe was still on the ground. He looked over at the two lovebirds.

"Don't worry about me, asshole. I'm just fine and dandy over here," Gabe said, clutching his stomach with one hand and pushing himself up with the other. He sat on the ground, trying to take deep breaths, but it hurt his lungs to do so. He was wheezing.

"Prick."

"What?"

"You heard me, asshole. I'm fucking hurt over here. Your chick is the one that crashed into me, remember? She didn't hit the ground. I did. I cushioned her fall. You should be asking me if I'm all right instead of her, for christsake."

"Pussy," is all Alan replied, pulling Erin the rest of the way up. She swayed from side to side a few times but stayed on her feet.

Fucking asshole.

Gabe pushed himself up and tried to straighten his back. He cried out and bent over. His back felt like it was on fire. He wondered if he was bleeding.

Gabe looked over in time to see Erin push Alan away and take a step towards him. She came by his side and put a hand on his back. She had done it gently, but it still was enough pressure on his wounds to make Gabe want to cry out.

He didn't.

Instead he looked up at her and asked her if she was okay. She nodded and asked him the same.

"Feels like it's on fire," Gabe said, reaching around and pointing to his back.

"I'm so sorry, Gabe," Erin replied. "Here, let me take a look and see what the damage is."

"Okay," Gabe replied as Erin slowly lifted the back of his shirt.

The cool breeze made his back tense up, and gooseflesh popped up all over his bare skin. He shuddered and looked back at Erin.

He raised an eyebrow, asking, "How bad is it?"

"Yikes," Erin replied.

"What? How bad?"

"Doesn't look pretty."

Alan walked over and looked at Gabe's back.

"Damn. Looks like you were clawed by Bigfoot or something."

"Thanks."

"Don't mention it. But seriously, man… Your back is jacked up."

"How bad is it?" Gabe asked again, as he turned his head from Alan to Erin.

"Doesn't look good. There are some deep scratches that are bleeding pretty good. That and your garden-variety bumps and scrapes. Hell. We should probably take you back to the dorms and get you patched up. I think I've got a First Aid kit in my room that my parents bought me a while back."

Gabe really didn't like the idea of having to make the two-mile hike back to campus, but didn't see much way around it. Especially since Erin had said that some of his injuries were fairly bad and bleeding. More than likely he had already bled through his shirt. He didn't want the blood running down his back and into his jeans. Then he'd have two articles of clothing, depending on the severity of the spots, to either wash or throw out. He really didn't want to deal with either of them, but he knew he didn't have much of a choice. It was either hike back to the dorm now, when the blood on his back and clothes was still fresh and easier to clean, or sit around all night inside the bar until the blood dried and adhered itself to the inside of his shirt. Sure, he probably wouldn't feel much of anything after drinking a few, but just the idea of either peeling the sucker off when they got back to the room or ending up passed out after a long night of drinking and having to do it in the morning didn't sit well with Gabe.

He took a deep breath and looked over at Alan.

He was staring at the two of them, eyebrows raised, lips curled, and shaking his head back and forth.

"Like I said. P-U-S-S-Y." He actually spelled out the letters of the word.

"What the hell is your problem, Alan? You need to shut the fuck up, you sonofa—"

"Don't tell me to shut the fuck up, you motherfucker. You almost break my girl's ankle by stepping on it and then go crashing to the ground. She could have broken her ass when she landed on you."

"Alan. Chill. It was an accident, for heaven's sake," Erin said.

"Don't give me that shit, Erin. He probably stepped on your foot on purpose so you would fall on top of him and land on his dick or something. Don't even tell me you'd put it past him either. You've told me yourself that you've caught him giving you the eye from time to time. I'm sure there is nothing he'd like more than for you to fall on his stick and impale yourself."

Erin screamed, "You rotten bastard!" then lunged for Alan.

She was in mid-stride when she felt something on her arm and she was being pulled backwards.

She crashed against Gabe's chest. This time his arms were wrapped around her so she wouldn't fall. Once she was steady, he released his grip, stepped in front of her, and looked Alan in the eye.

"Listen, man. I don't know what the fuck your problem is, but I don't want your woman. I mean… She's great and all. Hell, you know I think that. But she is *your* woman, and I'd never think of her in that way. It was an accident. Plain and simple. There was no ulterior motive or anything, man. I accidently stepped on her foot or whatever and that caused her to fall on top of me. And no, it wasn't so I could feel her ass against my dick or anything like that. Like I said, it was an accident, plain and simple. It was nothing more than that. You know me, man. We've been roommates for three years now. Do you really think I'd hit on Erin, let alone right in front of you? I don't know what your problem is, but you need to chill. We came here to have a good time. Yeah, the accident sucked and everything, and my back feels like it was raked with a cheese grater, but big whoop. Let's just put this stupid misunderstanding behind us and go inside and have a few rounds. Hell. I'll even buy the first, if that'll make you feel better and show you there is no ill will towards you or any sexual desires towards Erin. All right? Now, whaddya say, man? Let me buy you a round or what?"

Alan just shrugged his shoulders and said, "All right. Whatever," and started back up the bar's steps.

Erin rolled her eyes and followed him.

Alan's temper was beginning to worry Gabe, and it could become an even bigger problem if he lost it again while they were inside the bar tonight.

As he started up the steps, he really hoped that he was wrong and that everything would go smoothly.

That his friend wouldn't snap again and start shit with one of the bar's patrons.

That they would have a fun last night out together before summer break started.

He'd worry about his jacked-up back later; he knew it was nothing that a few drinks wouldn't cure.

Alan grabbed the brass handle on the huge door and swung it towards him.

Gabe and Erin followed him inside.

Chapter 6

The music stopped when the door thudded shut behind them. Well, it didn't actually stop playing on the jukebox, but it sure seemed that way to the three college kids, as all eyes in the bar turned and looked at them as they entered the establishment.

The air smelled of stale beer and cigarettes.

They looked at each other and quickly walked over to the bar and took their seats next to one another. From left to right it was Gabe, Erin, and then Alan. Gabe was glad that Alan was sitting so far away from him. He hoped that if his friend did start shit with some big dude, he would be able to just slip away and pretend he didn't even know the guy. For all Gabe cared, Alan could get the shit kicked out of him and it would probably do his attitude a world of good. He was still concerned about what was going on inside his friend's head. Not that he really wanted to find out, though. As far as Gabe was now concerned, the more distance between him and Alan, the better.

The burly bartender, a guy wearing a red-and-black plaid long-sleeved shirt, hole-covered jeans, and work boots, shambled over to them. He didn't say anything, just nodded and smiled. He had a wide gap between his two front teeth. Gabe couldn't tell if the guy had just grown up with the gap or if maybe one of his teeth had been knocked out by an unruly bar patron one night. Gabe quickly looked away. Alan ordered three beers and a shot for each of them. The bartender nodded, then walked away.

"What the hell is his problem?" Alan asked, entirely too loud. Gabe turned his head and looked at the still-walking away bartender to see if he had heard the remark. The two-hundred-and-fifty-pound (at least) man didn't seem to hear, as he continued on his way to the beer taps at the other end of the bar.

"Shhh. You're going to get our asses kicked," Erin whispered.

"Ah. He don't scare me. You know what they say: the bigger they are, the harder they fall," Alan said with a snort.

Gabe wanted to lean over Erin and ask Alan what his problem was, and to tell Erin to tell him to knock off his shit, but thought better of it. The last thing he needed was for Alan to get pissed at him. Again. Especially since they were now inside the bar and could easily be overheard by anyone that happened to be sitting around them. With Gabe's luck, one of the patrons in the bar would mistake Alan talking shit at them instead of him and a fight would break out. Gabe didn't want that to happen, so he kept his mouth shut and waited for the burly bartender to bring their drinks. He was thirstier now than ever.

As they waited for their drinks, Gabe took a look around the bar itself.

They were sitting at a straight bar that extended from one end of the room to the other. The shellacked mahogany structure was probably fifty feet long and had thirty or so flat chairs sitting in front of it. Half the stools were taken by a variety of odd-looking characters. They were mostly older men, with a few haggard looking women thrown in between a few of them. None of the women were sitting together.

Behind the bar sat the normal variety of liquor bottles, with the good stuff on the top shelf and the well drinks towards the bottom. Gabe recognized most of the brands.

The wall behind the bottles was a mammoth structure of old-looking ornate wood of some sort. Gabe figured it was probably mahogany like the bar itself. It also had a large mirror. It, too, extended from one end of the room to the other. The mirror was cracked in several places and was dull, more than likely from the thousands of cigarettes and cigars that had been smoked in the place over the years. It probably hadn't been Windexed in God knows how long. If the place was Gabe's, he knew he would have given it a good scrubbing years ago to retain its once-beautiful shine. He had no doubt that at one time it had been just that – a sight to behold.

Turning his head, Gabe looked behind him. There were fifteen or so tables scattered throughout the place, only a few with people sitting at them; two pool tables that looked like they had seen better days; a jukebox in one corner, and an old-fashioned bar-style bowling game in the other.

Besides the once-fabulous mirror structure behind the bar, the rest of the walls were mostly bare. There were no windows – which Gabe thought was a little strange and something he hadn't noticed when they were outside – only a few dusty beer ads, most of them torn in at least one place, and a single dart board. Gabe didn't see if there were still darts or not; there weren't any stuck into the board itself. Perhaps later he would ask the bartender if they had any darts so the three of them could play a few games.

Gabe figured if the bar didn't still have a supply of darts, they could always just play pool. Though for some reason, he had a feeling that the rack would be missing a ball or two, so it would end up being useless to try to play anyway. He made a mental note to at least check if they still had the two through nine balls. A round of nine-ball is better than no pool at all. Gabe had always been a fan of bar-type games. He felt there was nothing better than a mix of alcohol and things that could either stab you or crush your balls if you were standing too close to the respective playing area.

He turned his head around just in time to see the burly bartender stride up to where they were sitting with three frosted (shocking!) mugs of yellow liquid and three small glasses filled with an amber-tinted liquid (ah, whiskey!).

The bartender, who finally introduced himself as T-Bone, set the six items down and immediately turned and started walking away.

Alan leaned past Erin and said, "Jesus on a rubber crutch… Did you get a look at that guy, man?"

Gabe smiled at Erin and was about to reply with a smart-ass remark about the bartender when he caught a glimpse of something out the corner of his eye.

T-Bone was coming back towards them.

We haven't even taken a sip yet. What the hell does he want?

Gabe had a feeling he didn't want to know.

He widened his eyes at Alan and then faced forward just as the man stopped in front of them.

"Yes…sir?"

"Forgot to ask you kids something."

"Ah. Sure. Okay."

Gabe's bowels tightened. This wasn't going to be good. Sure, they were all twenty-one and were legally able to drink in a bar, but that didn't mean they were *allowed* to be in this particular bar.

Especially with how the clientele looked.

Gabe had a bad feeling about what the man was about to ask.

But then he relaxed as the bartender asked, "You kids want to pay as you go or start a tab?"

In unison, the three college kids replied, "Tab, please."

The bartender didn't say a word, just nodded and walked away.

A feeling of relief washed over Gabe as he, Erin, and Alan raised their drinks and toasted to their last night out on the town before summer break.

One last night to let it all hang out and get a little crazy.

Perhaps this place won't be so bad after all, Gabe thought, taking a long drink from his frosty mug of beer.

Chapter 7

After ordering another round, Gabe got up and started walking to the jukebox on the other side of the room. Passing by several occupied tables, he could feel the eyes of the bar's patrons following him.

He kept his eyes on the wooden floor and quickened his pace.

As he neared the machine, he turned his head around to see if Alan and Erin were watching. They weren't. Instead, they seemed to be staring into each other's eyes as they took turns moving their mouths. Gabe wondered what they were talking about. Was Erin still pissed at him for the sexual comment from earlier, or were they making up? He couldn't tell. Then he saw Erin raise her hand and place it on Alan's left arm. She started rubbing his arm up and down. It made Gabe think about other things that she rubbed on Alan.

Looks to me like they made up. Damn.

Gabe couldn't help but wonder what it would be like to be with a girl like Erin. She had always been way too nice to Alan, even with him being a prick most of the time these days, and he wondered how much sweeter she would be with a guy that treated her right.

A guy like me.

Gabe stopped in front of the jukebox and took a look on both sides of him. No one was sitting at the nearby tables. There were a few empty beer bottles on one and a still-lit cigarette in an ashtray on another. The smoke from the cigarette looked like bands of white ribbon drifting up to the ceiling. He looked up and noticed the ceiling of the bar had a dull yellow hue to it. At one point it had probably been beautiful, with all the ornate designs that had been carved into it years ago.

He looked back down to the jukebox and pressed the right arrow button. The cards inside the machine started flipping from one side to the other. Most of the albums were from the late sixties and early seventies. It didn't surprise him much in a place like this. It didn't look like they had kept up with the times in any regard. His dollar's worth of quarters would buy him three songs. He punched in his selections of "Yellow Submarine," by the Beatles, "Mustang Sally," by Wilson Pickett, and "Sherry," by Frankie Valli.

"Yellow Submarine" started playing over the bar's raspy speakers as he pressed down on the arrow buttons, returning the cards to their original position. He then turned around and started walking back to the bar to join his friends. He tried to keep his eyes on the floor and couldn't see if anyone was looking at him, but he had a feeling they were.

He got back to the bar, pulled back his stool, and sat down.

Apparently finished with their conversation now that he was back, Erin leaned over and gave Alan a kiss. Gabe could hear their lips smack apart as Erin sat up straight, grabbed her shot glass, and placed it on her bottom lip. Then she opened her mouth and tilted her head back. The amber liquid drained from the small glass. Gabe watched her throat move up and down as she swallowed.

Dear Lord! I bet it feels great when she's going down on you and–

Gabe quickly picked up his whiskey and threw it back. It burned on the way down but tasted wonderful. He chased it with a swig of beer. He belched.

"Nice choice," Alan said, and then downed his own shot.

"Thanks. The jukebox doesn't have much of a selection though. Mostly old stuff."

"Sounds all right to me," Erin said.

As Gabe was thanking her for the kind remark, T-Bone came back and asked if they wanted another shot.

They must have all been thinking of the same scene in the classic college movie, *Animal House*, when a guy is taking swats from one of his fraternity brothers, because they replied in unison, "Thank you, sir. May I have another?"

They started laughing.

T-Bone must not have gotten the joke, as he scrunched up his face and shook his head from side to side.

They laughed even harder.

If it weren't for their laughter, they would have heard the bartender say, "Fucking college kids," as he started walking away to get their drinks.

Chapter 8

The beer and whiskey continued to flow even as the lights dimmed and Happy Hour came to a close.

Gabe figured it had to be at least eight o'clock at this point, but he had forgotten to put his watch on before he and Alan had left to pick up Erin, so he didn't have a way to check. He almost felt naked without it. It had always been funny to Gabe, that once you got used to wearing a watch all the time, when you did forget it, your whole day seemed out of whack.

He looked over to Alan and Erin. Neither of them was wearing a watch either. Gabe thought he had seen one on the bartender's wrist, but based on the shear look of him, he didn't plan on asking him the time.

"So," Erin said, "are we just gonna sit here all night getting shit-faced, or are we gonna do somethin'?"

"Getting shit-faced was the general idea, wasn't it?" Alan said.

"Well, yeah. But don't you guys wanna do *something* besides just sitting here? I mean, we could go over and play some pool or something. What do you say, Gabe?"

"Sounds like a plan to me. But I wouldn't be surprised if the pool tables don't have all their balls."

Alan started laughing.

"What?"

"You said *balls*. That's funny stuff right there."

"Huh?"

"Balls. Nuts. Fruit in a basket. Ya know. Then again, maybe you don't. When was the last time you got laid anyway, Gabe? Five…six months now?"

Erin slapped him across the back of the head. Gabe muttered, "Dick."

"HEY! What did I do now?"

"You know what you said, Alan," Erin said. "Why do you have to be so crude all the time? I swear, the only thing on your mind anymore is sex stuff."

"Do you blame me?" Alan asked.

"What is that supposed to mean?"

"You know what it means, babe. You don't give it up much anymore, not since the miscarriage and all. I mean, I guess I don't blame you for wanting to take a week or two off from doing it. But damn…it's been, what…one or two months now. You should be over it by now."

Erin slapped him again. Hard.

"Ouch! Damnit, woman! What did I tell you about hitting me?"

"I wouldn't have to if you just kept your mouth shut about our sex life."

"It's just Gabe, babe. Why do you care so much? We tell each other everything."

Gabe wondered if *everything* included Alan telling Erin about him pissing his pajama pants their freshman year. He hoped it didn't. But he wouldn't be surprised if Alan had told her about it. She was a good friend and all – hell, probably his best friend outside of Alan – but he still felt uncomfortable with her knowing such personal things.

Speaking of personal stuff… I didn't know Erin had a miscarriage. I wonder why Alan never told me that. Probably hurts the shit out of him and he just uses the joking around defense mechanism to shield his true feelings about the matter. I'll have to ask her about it sometime.

Erin just shook her head at Alan and got up from her barstool. Gabe figured she was just getting up to go use the john, but then she was grabbing at his arm and telling him *come on* without actually saying the words. Alan frowned at Gabe but didn't say anything.

The look said it all.

Gabe knew that Alan thought he was screwing around with his girl. It was the farthest thing from the truth, but from the look on his friend's face, Gabe knew that was what he was thinking. It didn't make much sense, but not much did anymore when it came to Alan's behavior or way of thinking. Gabe was just glad that Alan wasn't swinging at him, trying to take his head off.

T-Bone walked over and set three more mugs of beer and three more shots on the bar, then wandered away.

"So what do you say, Gabe? Do you wanna?"

I sure do wanna *with you, Erin. You have no idea how much I wanna take my hard–*

"GABE!"

That snapped him out of his perverse thoughts about his friend. His best friend's girlfriend.

What the hell am I doing?

"Now, what?"

"Do you wanna go play pool or something?" Erin asked again.

"Oh. That. Sure, why not. Might as well do something in here. This place is kind of the pits."

Gabe saw Alan frown at that comment.

But he didn't let it phase him.

One way or another, *he* was going to have a good time tonight.

Their last night out together.

Even if it didn't include Alan for the rest of the night.

Him and Erin, that's all Gabe needed.

Standing up from his stool, and just to be a dick back at him, Gabe winked at Alan. Alan mouthed "You motherfucker" and then threw back his shot of whiskey. He motioned for T-Bone to bring him another.

Gabe let Erin grab him by the arm and lead him away from the bar.

Chapter 9

To Gabe's surprise, one of the pool tables did have all its balls. He and Erin spent the next few hours playing eight- and nine-ball. At first they had been keeping score, flaunting each win in the other person's face. It was all in good fun; nothing like the shitty remarks that Alan had been making throughout the night. They were having a hell of a good time together.

Just the two of them.

In fact, the only time they stopped playing was to take a drink or order another round from T-Bone, who kept coming by every so often, asking if they needed anything. They were having a grand time.

They didn't even notice some of the bar's patrons paying and leaving during their time together.

Just the two of them.

It wasn't until Gabe felt like his bladder was about to burst that he said to Erin, "I've gotta go drain the main thang or I'm gonna explode," that they really took a break. Erin didn't smack him after he made the comment. She just smiled and said, "Yeah, that does seem like a good idea. I'll join you." That really set Gabe's head spinning. But he knew what she meant by the remark. She wasn't actually going to join him in the men's restroom. No. She was simply saying that she had to use the facilities as well and would walk with him until they reached the restroom doors and each went their own way. In any regard, it still sounded great to Gabe. He smiled back at Erin and said, "Okay. Ladies first," and watched the back of her jeans rise and fall with each step she took. Soon they were at the restrooms. They smiled at one another, pushed open their respective doors, and walked inside.

After Gabe finished at the urinal, he washed and dried his hands, then walked out of the restroom. He figured that Erin would be waiting for him outside, but she wasn't. He also knew there was a good chance that she had gone to check on Alan, since it had been hours since they last spoke with him, but since he had to fetch his drinks by the pool table, that is where he went first.

It didn't surprise Gabe that Erin wasn't by the table. He noticed that her drinks were gone, so he picked up his mug and empty shot glass and started walking back towards the bar.

A fat bald man jumped up from a table he had been sitting at and stood in his way.

"Excuse me, sir," Gabe said, trying to be polite and not insult the huge man in any way.

The man stood his ground. He didn't even blink.

"Excuse me," Gabe said again, louder this time. The music was blaring over the bar's speakers, so he didn't doubt that the man hadn't heard him the first time.

The large man still just stood there. He had a hard-nosed look about him. He was now staring into Gabe's eyes. Gabe blinked, trying to ease the burning sensation.

"How 'bout you buy me a shot, boy," the man finally said.

"Huh?" Gabe thought he heard what he said, but wanted to make sure before he replied and inadvertently insulted the man.

"You deaf, boy? I said BUY ME A SHOT!"

Gabe didn't know what to do. He thought about just handing over his own mug of beer to the man, but there were two things wrong with that idea. For one, the man asked for a shot, not a beer. And two, Gabe was afraid that if he didn't just say yes, the man would pound him senseless and leave him lying on the floor in a puddle of his own blood.

Gabe definitely didn't want the bloody part to happen to him. He knew if it did, not only would he have an even shittier hangover tomorrow morning when he had to pack up his stuff and drive home, but when he got there, his parents would be asking him all sorts questions like, "What happened to your face?" and "We told you not to drink all the time" and "You're turning into your old Uncle Pete." Gabe didn't need any of that. So instead of saying something stupid to upset the man, he replied, "Yeah. Okay. What ya having?"

The man gave his order to Gabe and then stepped out of the way.

As Gabe was walking away, he heard the man shout over the loud music, "And make it snappy, boy. I'm as thirsty as a bitch in heat."

Gabe was glad that Erin wasn't around to hear that. She had already smacked the shit out of Alan for inappropriate sexual comments, and he didn't need her trying to do the same to the big, bald, fat man as well.

Even though the guy looked hardcore, he more than likely wouldn't hit a female. You were the scum of the earth if you did that. So it would be Gabe that would end up getting pounded for Erin's response to his sexual comment.

If the man wants a shot, Gabe thought, *that's what he'll get.*

He walked up to the bar and motioned for T-Bone to bring him two shots and a beer – one of the drinks for the big man and two for him.

The bartender nodded and then walked away.

Gabe looked down the bar to where his two friends and him had been sitting together earlier in the night.

He noticed that not only was Erin still nowhere to be seen, but Alan was now gone as well.

Chapter 10

Gabe walked back over to the scary big man and slid the shot glass across the table. The man caught it in his big hand and, in one quick motion, picked it up and downed it. He belched. Gabe, not wanting to offend the man, asked if he wanted another. The guy replied with a grunt and bobbed his head up and down. As he walked back over to the bar to order another shot, he scanned the room for his friends. He didn't see them anywhere. The bartender came up and asked what he wanted. Gabe slid the shot glass towards him and said, "Another for the big man, please." T-Bone nodded and then walked away.

Standing at the bar, Gabe felt a gust of chilly wind on his back. He looked to the right and saw a group of bikers entering the bar. Most had on what you would imagine a biker wearing – leather, and lots of it. Even the pieces of cloth wrapped around a few of the men's heads were made of leather. Some looked shiny and new and some of them looked dull and well-worn. Like most people do when they enter an establishment that serves alcohol, the bikers made a beeline to the bar. The six (three male and three female) bikers crowded around Gabe. He felt like a pea in a pod. He couldn't help overhearing the conversation taking place all around him.

"So," one of the male bikers said, "I take him by the hair and then pound his face against the sidewalk. Shit, fucker… You should have seen him when I was done with him."

The remark was met with a chorus of hoots and hollers. Two of the men high-fived one another. The one that had been telling the story nudged Gabe with his elbow. Gabe whirled around and came face to chest with the biggest son of a bitch he had even seen dressed in leather. The man looked like he was six-two, two-fifty. He had a long mop of black hair on his head and face and gray eyes. His neck was as thick as a tree trunk. His massive arms were covered with tattoos. Gabe took him instantly as the leader of the pack since he was the biggest hard-nosed guy he had ever seen. The two other men looked like mice compared to the king of the asphalt that was standing in front of him.

"Hey, boy."

"Uh, yes, sir?" Gabe asked, staring up at the big man.

"How 'bout you tell me your name."

"Huh?"

"Huh? I said… How 'bout you tell me your name."

Scared as all get-out and feeling like this might be the second time in three years that he was going to piss his pants, he opted to take the road more traveled and tell the man his real name. Sure, he could lie and it might possibly protect him and his family in the long-run from being hunted down by a bunch of crazed biker loonies, but if the man found out later that he had lied, things might get even worse. Gabe had no idea what could be worse than being hunted down and run over by a pack of biker-wolves, and he didn't feel like finding out.

"Name's Gabe."

"Ah, Gabriel. That was my old man's name."

Gabe smiled.

"Damn, was he a sketchy fucker, though. Beat the shit outta me and my mom all the time. I hated that fucker."

Gabe's smiled turned upside down. He looked down at the floor to see if a puddle of piss was forming around his shoes. It wasn't. At least, not yet.

"Don't be scared, boy," the biker said, slapping Gabe across the back. "I took care of him long time ago... You don't have to worry about him comin' in here and beatin' your ass or nothin'."

"Thanks," is all Gabe could manage to get out.

Gabe and the biker stared at each other for what seemed like hours but was really only a few seconds. God was Gabe scared. He felt like if he blinked the wrong way the big man would hit him on top of the head with one of his huge fists and drive him into the floor like in the cartoons. He sure as shit didn't want that. The thing he most wanted now was to find Erin and maybe even Alan and get the hell out of Dodge.

"Aren't you gonna ask me my name, Gabriel?" the big man finally asked.

"Oh. Right. Sorry about that, sir... Ya see, I'm here with a few friends and I can't seem to..."

"Hey," the big man said, stopping Gabe mid-sentence. "I didn't ask for yer life story, man. All I asked was, 'aren't you gonna ask me my name'. I don't need all that other shit you're trying to shoot on me. Hellfire. If anyone is going to be doing some shootin', it's gonna be me." With that, the three men busted out in laugher. The three biker women just looked at one another, rolled their heads around in circles, and looked towards the ceiling.

"Oh. Yeah. You are absolutely right, sir. What may your name be?"

The big man turned to his friends and said, "Get a load of this kid... He's trying to be all proper around us to make us feel stupid. Now, Gabe... You wouldn't be tryin' anything like that, would ya?"

"Ah, no, sir. No way."

"Okay, then. Now... How 'bout you try one more time and don't act like a smartass there or I'll have my buddy Razor," he said, pointing over his shoulder to one of his biker friends, "cut your gullet and feed ya to the fishes."

Gabe wanted to correct the man when he said "feed ya to the fishes," that it was more of a mafia saying than an American biker one, but he kept his mouth shut. He wanted to be careful not to upset the big man. He already looked unstable enough as it was.

"Okay. So, what's your name, man?"

"Ah. Much better, my fine chap," he replied. His buddies and their female companions started laughing and pointing at Gabe, saying things like "dumbass" and "he really showed you up" and "yeah, fuckin-a, man." Those sorts of things. Gabe just shrugged his shoulders and attempted to move forward. He hoped their name calling and laugher were enough to distract their feeble minds enough that he could make an escape. But he was soon stopped dead in his tracks when the biker put a hand on his chest.

"I'm sorry… I'm sorry," the biker said in between laughing. "How rude of me. The name's Erb. Tommy Erb."

The biker took his huge right hand off his chest and thrust it forward. Gabe teetered backwards and started falling. The bar broke his fall by hammering into the middle of his back. He let out a grunt and then limped onto a nearby barstool. Even with the pain raging up his already-damaged back from earlier in the night, he could see out the corner of his eye that the bartender was walking towards him. Now he was really in for it. Between the two men they probably tilted the scales at five-hundred pounds.

The bartender didn't look happy.

Coming up to the other side of the bar, T-Bone crashed a fist against the bar and shouted, "Now what the fuck is going on here?! You guys are gonna have to quiet the fuck down or there are going to be some fucking skulls hitting the floor tonight!" He hammered his fist against the bar again.

Through his watery eyes, Gabe looked up at T-Bone.

And noticed he was smiling.

He'd been had.

The bartender and the lead biker, whom T-Bone called Tommy Guns, were apparently friends.

Gabe still felt like he might piss his pants.

Chapter 11

As the hours rolled on and the drinks continued to be poured, Gabe started to feel more and more out of it. He had a good buzz going. Normally this wouldn't be a problem and he would be loving every minute of being in a bar with his friends and pounding some drinks. The only problem was that his friends were still nowhere to be found, and the pack of bikers were sitting on either side of him at the bar and had *insisted* that they and Gabe were now friends, and as all good friends do from time to time – they take turns buying rounds. What worried Gabe was that he didn't see any money being laid out on the bar when it was the bikers' turn to pay. He hoped that they had started a tab of their own, though he didn't hear Tommy Bones, as T-Bone had called him, say anything about one.

Gabe didn't feel all that bad for buying them *one* round.

Besides, he was still scared shitless of them, even though they had been acting fairly nice to him ever since they had exchanged introductions.

But Gabe also knew that without Erin and Alan around to split it three ways, if the bikers continued to put their drinks on his tab, he wouldn't have enough money by himself to pay T-Bone at the end of the night.

It worried him.

A lot.

Swallowing what was left in his mug, Gabe excused himself and started towards the restroom. He heard Tommy Guns shout, "Hey, Gabriel. Remember: If you shake it more than twice, you're just playing with it!" and then he was laughing. Soon, his two buddies and their whores were laughing right along with him.

Halfway to the restroom, Gabe's head started to spin. Some vomit rose up into his mouth. He choked it back down and continued on his way.

He figured it was from a combination of drinking too much and worrying about his bar tab at the end of the night. Well, that and wondering where the hell his friends had run off to.

If only Erin and Alan hadn't run out on me to go screw back at the dorms, I'd be able to pay T-Bone and get the fuck out of here, he thought, bringing a hand up and placing it on the restroom door.

He pushed.

It opened a few inches and then stopped.

What the fuck?

He tried pushing the door open again.

Nothing.

What the shit is going on here?

He felt the bile starting to rise up into his throat again.

Feeling like he was going to spew all over the place, which he knew T-Bone wouldn't think too highly of, Gabe put his weight behind him and pushed with all his might.

The door suddenly swung open.

His feet got tangled together and he started to fall. He tried to hold onto the door, but without it having a handle, his fingers just scraped at the old wood like a bear on a tree in the woods marking his territory. He sure as hell was about to mark *his* territory all over the place if he didn't catch himself in time.

His shoes played Slip n' Slide over the wet cracked tile floor. They were going this way and that.

And then his feet went completely out from under him.

His back hit the floor and the air burst out of his lungs. His head bounced off the floor like it was being dribbled down the court by Michael Jordan.

Finally he came to a rest.

He stared up at the cracked ceiling through blurry eyes. The back of his shirt was wet and clinging to his skin. He pushed himself up to his elbows and took a look around. He felt okay for a brief moment, realizing he was still alive, but then turned to one side and vomited. The brown and yellow liquid splashed on the floor and back up onto the front of his shirt and pants. After heaving a few more times, he spit out the last few chunks that were in his mouth and tried to sit the rest of the way up. His head was still spinning but he didn't feel as bad as he had a few moments ago.

Hopefully that'll get me through the rest of the night. You know what they say: if you feel like you're gonna have a hangover in the morning, or if you don't give a shit about that and just wanna keep binge drinking, you make yourself throw up, and everything will be all right after that.

I sure as shit did that. I threw up all over the fucking place.

Shit. Look at this mess. I better clean this shit up or T-Bone is gonna take part outta my ass.

"Half is better than nothing at all," Gabe remembered his grandmother telling him.

Yeah, right. Bet ol' grandma never had a guy like T-Bone that she owed a shitload of cash to.

I'm so fucked.

Standing up, Gabe staggered to the first stall and opened the door. The smell of fresh shit wafted over him. He felt like he was going to vomit again. He quickly shut the door.

He walked to the next stall, said a little prayer, grabbed the handle, and pulled the door towards him. This stall still smelled like shit, but it wasn't as bad as the first. He took a few steps and shut the door behind him. It thudded, twice.

What the…

He shook the door. Nothing. It didn't rattle at all.

He pulled his pants down to his knees and sat down on the toilet seat. It felt wet and slimy against his buttocks, but at this point he was wet all over anyway so it didn't really matter. He released his sphincter muscle and his ass exploded into the toilet. He felt a sense of relief.

Damn. If I lose any more liquid from anywhere else, my body isn't going to have anything left. Once I'm done in here I better go out and order another beer…

No! That's what got me into this situation in the first place.

Once I'm finished taking a shit, I'm gonna wipe my ass, wash my hands and the vomit chunks off my shirt and pants, go back out to the bar and pay my tab (he was still worried he wouldn't have enough, especially if the bikers were still drinking like fish) *and get the hell out of this place. The hell with Erin and Alan. They fucked me* (or are back at the dorm fucking each other) *so I'm not gonna worry about leaving without them. What do they expect me to do, just sit around here all night and drink by myself when they're God knows where, doing God knows what? Fuck em'. I'm out of this place. Gonna blow this puppy. Gonna pay my bill and take the next train outta Dodge. I'm gonna pay the piper and ride a magic carpet out of this place and never...*

Gabe's thoughts were cut short as a deep voice yelled, "What the fuck is this horseshit!"

The thunderous voice was followed by the lights in the restroom going out.

Chapter 12

When Gabe woke up, the restroom was still dark. He felt something hard pressing against his buttocks and figured it was still the toilet seat. His head was spinning. He felt like he was going to vomit again even though he knew there wouldn't be much left in his stomach.

He tried to sit up, but his legs wouldn't work.

Shit. They must have fallen asleep when I passed out on the shitter.

He tried again.

Nothing.

No problem, Gabe thought, *I just gotta sit here a little while longer and let the feeling come back to my legs and then I'll be able to stand up* (he couldn't remember if he had wiped his ass before passing out) *and then go back out to the bar, pay my tab, and get the hell outta here.*

He knew the next order of business would be to find Erin and Alan and really give *him* a piece of his mind for leaving him behind at a shady bar to drink with a bunch of lunatic bikers. Okay, the lunatic part wasn't really the case. Overall, they seemed like an okay bunch of people, besides letting Gabe buy their drinks the whole night, but it was still just another crazy part to a night he just wanted to forget.

Bottom line: he needed his legs to work again so he could pay T-Bone and get back to his dorm room.

Bitching at Erin and Alan might have to wait till morning, thought Gabe. *I just want to get the hell out of here and pass out in my own bed and not on some piss-covered toilet in a run-down bar in a bad part of town.* Okay, the part of town really wasn't that bad. But it was bad enough to allow a biker gang to frequent the establishment.

Shit.

Starting to feel a tingling sensation in his legs, Gabe tried to stand up again.

He was able to stand a few inches and then something around his legs pushed him back down.

Damn.

No wonder I can't stand. I still got my pants around my knees.

Gabe almost wanted to laugh at his oversight.

Almost.

Gabe lifted his ass off the toilet and tried to reach down to pull his pants up.

He couldn't move his arms.

What the fuck? Did my whole body fall asleep or what?

He tried again.

Nothing.

Sonofabitch.

Gabe's head started to spin with the simple question of how long he was going to have to sit on a piss-covered toilet seat, with his pants around his knees and drying shit in the crack of his ass, until his limbs regained some blood flow so he would be able to pull up his pants, go pay his bar tab, and get the fuck out of the Torchlight Inn.

I'm sure as shit *never coming back to this place...*

Then two things happened at once; he remembered someone coming into the restroom sounding eerily like T-Bone's voice, and he heard a scuffling sound next to him.

It sounded like the noise was coming from the stall next to his.

Chapter 13

Gabe felt a puff of air against the right side of his head. The breeze tickled his ear and the hairs on the side of his neck. He shook his head back and forth and then stretched his head to the right and rubbed his cheek on his shoulder.

And noticed his shirt was gone.

What the...

Another puff of air blew against the side of his face.

"What the fuck?" Gabe muttered to himself, and rubbed his face again on his bare shoulder.

Where the hell did my shirt go?

That's when Gabe's mind started to wander. He thought about the chances of not remembering already paying his bar tab, walking back to his dorm room, and passing out in his own bed. He thought about the chances of having picked up a girl at the bar (maybe one of the biker chicks?) and taking her back to his room and fucking the hell out of her. The problem was he couldn't remember any of it. Sure, he wished the part of picking up a girl were true (even though the biker chicks were sort of skanky looking) but he couldn't remember doing it. Then again, he couldn't remember much of anything after puking on the floor of the restroom and struggling into one of the stalls. There was a thudding sound after that, a deep voice echoing off the restroom walls, and then the lights went out. The next thing he remembered was waking up and not being able to stand up because his pants were still around his ankles. That didn't explain why he couldn't move his arms (though they very well could be asleep if he passed out on the toilet in an awkward position) or the puff of air that kept blowing against the side of his face.

Yeah... What the fuck is that all about...

The puff of air came again.

"All right, fucker," Gabe shouted through his growing headache. "Whoever is in the stall next to me better quit blowing in my fucking ear like some woman or I'm gonna kick some ass."

After the feeling comes back to my arms and legs and I'm able to pull my pants up, Gabe thought.

Nothing like getting your ass kicked with your pants down.

Shit.

"You're never getting out of here, no matter how hard to try."

The puff of air on the side of his face turned into a raspy voice whispering in his ear. Gabe tried to jump back but he still couldn't move his arms and legs.

"Who…who the fuck are you?" Gabe stammered.

"Ah. You will find out all in good time, my dear cellar-mate. But until then, feel free to call me Berta."

"Huh?"

"I said my name was Berta," the voice said, a little louder this time.

"Oh. Hi."

"Aren't ya gonna introduce yourself, sonny?"

"Oh. Yeah. Sorry about that…" Gabe replied, still confused why he was talking to a woman in the men's room.

What the fuck? Maybe I'm dreaming or something. You never want to be rude to someone in your dream, cause the next thing you know, they might be coming after you with a knife or something.

Just the thought of being chased by a wife or an old hag sent chills over Gabe's bare chest and down his back.

"My name is Gabe."

"Ohhh," cooed the old woman's voice. "I really like that name."

"Uh…yeeeah. Thanks, Berta. Nice to meet you."

"Nice to meet you too, Gabe. It's been a long time since we've had a guy come down here to visit us. Well, unless you count T-Bone. But he's a real horse's ass, if you know what I mean. Pardon my French, but he is. Oh, shoot. I almost forgot that we did have what sounded like a young man come down here a few hours ago… Well, it seemed like hours anyway, though I'm not too sure of time these days, being down here as long as I have, ya know. Anyway. I didn't see where he took that guy. Oh, yeah. Almost forgot. There was what sounded like a girl with the two of them as well. Though, can't be too certain, ya know. Not with how dark he keeps it down here and being down here for so long and all. But, yeah…I do remember…"

Gabe tuned the old lady out. There were some things she had just said that really confused him. Just a few moments ago when Berta started to talk to him, he was certain that he was still passed out on the toilet in the restroom of the Torchlight Inn, but now he wasn't so sure. There are times when dreams can pull real-life events into them, but this sounded a little too realistic. The fact of the matter was it scared him. It scared him a lot.

Okay, Gabe thought. *If this isn't really a dream, and I am still in the restroom of the bar, then why did Berta say "down here" and "he keeps it so dark" and "you never know time anymore when you're down here for so long"?*

It just didn't make sense.

He realized that Berta was still talking, so he put his wandering mind on hold and leaned closer to her shaky voice. The puffs of air on the side of his face, neck, and ear started again.

"...so, that's how I ended up down here, Gabe. I remember it as if it was yesterday, ya know. Though, at the same time, it does seem like I've been down here for an awfully long time, so I don't know if my saying 'yesterday' is really accurate or not. You know what I'm saying?"

Gabe had obviously missed the majority of the old lady's story, but he sure as hell couldn't be rude by asking her to repeat what she had just said, so he just nodded.

"You know what I'm saying?" the old lady repeated.

Gabe realized that it was so dark that she couldn't have seen him nod his head. He replied to Berta's question with, "Yeah. Sure. I know what you mean." Though he really didn't.

Gabe had no idea what the old lady had just told him and had absolutely no idea what the fuck was going on inside the dark recesses under the Torchlight Inn.

Chapter 14

As the feeling came back to his legs, Gabe could sense he was sitting on something cold. He remembered when he had first sat down on the toilet inside the restroom that it had indeed been wet and cold. But that didn't explain why it had remained that way. Not after sitting on it for what seemed like hours now. Though, if what Berta said was right, he might very well have a misconception of time anyway.

Gabe stretched his legs out in front of him and finally realized there was no way he was still sitting on a toilet seat.

His legs went straight out in front of him instead of down and out, the way they would if you are sitting on the toilet when you stick your legs out. No. Instead, they had skidded along a rough surface (definitely not a tile floor, even with as many cracks as the one in the restroom had) he was sitting on and stuck straight out in front of him. Gabe felt a mixture of wetness and roughness under his bare legs and feet.

Sonofabitch! The fucker not only stole my shirt, but my pants and shoes too? Fucker!

He was naked.

Just the thought of being naked in an unknown dark place with someone other than Erin (*shit, I gotta quit thinking about her like that*) made gooseflesh pop up all over his skin and made his penis pull back up into his body. It felt warmer there. Thank God.

Gabe tried to recount the night's events.

He remembered having to buy some big fucker a few shots and then the group of bikers coming into the bar and instantly becoming his friends, whether he liked it or not. He remembered constantly looking around the bar for any sign of Erin or Alan the entire time he sat with the bikers, but never found them anywhere. He remembered excusing himself and walking to the restroom where he had to force open the door. He remembered falling and vomiting. He remembered staggering to a stall and not being able to go inside because of the putrid odor of shit that was coming from it. He remembered walking to the next one, holding his breath from the somewhat-better shit smell, pulling his pants down and dropping a deuce in the toilet. And he definitely remembered a loud deep voice yelling "What the fuck is this?" evidently after seeing the mess he had made just inside the restroom's door, and then the lights going out. The part that was bothering him the most was that he couldn't remember what happened next. Was he ambushed inside the stall by T-Bone and taken somewhere? Did he pass out on his own and, after the bar closed, get taken somewhere by T-Bone to sleep it off until the morning? He couldn't remember jack shit. That's what worried him the most.

He had no idea where he was.

He had a feeling though, with what Berta had said, that T-Bone had something to do with it.

Gabe was dreaming of fields of amber waves of grain when he suddenly woke up to something warm running against his leg.

He snapped his eyes open. It was still completely black all around him. He was obviously still in the same place as he was before when Berta had been talking to him and he was recounting all the night's events inside his head.

"Sorry about that," a raspy voice said next to him.

Berta.

"No prob–"

Gabe smelled the distinct scent of urine from a female – musty and fruity.

Berta's pissing on my leg!

Gabe tried to lurch to his left, but he was pulled back by whatever had been wrapped around his stomach, arms, and legs.

His rump and the back of his legs splashed down into the puddle of piss.

"Sorry," he heard Berta whisper again.

Gabe didn't know what else to say, so he just muttered, "It's okay. Don't worry about it."

Obviously, wherever he and Berta now were, they weren't even allowed to get up and relieve themselves in private. Instead, they just had to piss all over the person next to them. Just the thought of it made Gabe want to vomit.

But he didn't.

He choked the thought back down and wondered what else they had to do down here, wherever they were, in the dark, with the person next to them.

Chapter 15

The third time Gabe regained consciousness was when his head was finally clear – as clear as his head could be, anyway, after several hours of drinking a combination of beer and liquor with friends and new *friends* alike. Well, that and being secured God knows where to a wet and grimy floor.

Gabe tried to push himself up again.

As expected, he wasn't able to stand.

Exhaling with despair, he leaned over to Berta and said, "So, you really don't have any idea how long you've been here, huh?"

There was no response.

Gabe tried a second time.

Nothing.

What the fuck is going on now...

Something crashed. It sounded like it was coming from above him.

A few seconds later he could hear the distinct sound of footsteps.

Coming towards him.

He was too petrified to speak, so he said nothing. He knew if he could, if whatever it was that was holding him to the floor would release him, he would curl into a ball and play dead. That was what his biology professor had always said in college: if you're ever in fear for your life in the wild, just curl up into a ball, protect your head, and act like you are dead. He wasn't sure if the adage even applied to his current circumstances, but it was the first thing that came to his mind, so if he had been able to do so, he would have. Instead, he just sat there with his legs out in front of him and his eyes closed tight. He figured it wouldn't make that much of a difference at this point, but it was better than doing nothing at all.

Gabe could hear the footsteps getting closer.

A few moments later, they stopped.

He could hear heavy breathing, like someone had just run a marathon and was now trying to catch their breath. Whoever it was, their breathing was obviously labored by coming from wherever they had been.

"Well...well...well!" boomed the strangely familiar voice. "Look what we've got here."

Gabe didn't reply. He only shut his eyes tighter. If he would have been able to move his arms, he would have covered his ears from the deep voice.

T-Bone.

"Yup. Looks like I got ya right where I want ya," T-Bone's voice boomed.

This time Gabe let out a whimper. T-Bone obviously heard it, because he started laughing. It was a deep, thunderous laugh that echoed.

Through his bellowing laughter, T-Bone said, "So, you thought you college twerps could come into my fine establishment, puke all over my shittin' room, and not have to pay your tab, eh?"

"Uhhh..." is all Gabe was able to get out.

"Yeah. That's what I thought. The three of ya will pay for what you did to T-Bone's bar. This fine establishment here was built by my great-great-great grand pappy, and was passed down to me through the generations. I don't take kindly to those that come into my place – especially some shit-for-brains kids – and try to take away all the hard work that generations of Vandersmoot's put into this here place. No sir-ree-bob, I don't!"

"Sir–" is all Gabe managed to get out. The word came out as a mumble.

"Don't 'sir' me, you piece of shit," T-Bone said. "You and your friends here will pay for what you did. Hellfire. I saw what your one friend tried to do. The little shit stain. He tried to walk out without paying his tab. But I got him. Oh, yes I did. Snuck up on him about halfway down the street and bagged his ass. Didn't take much to take him down and make him start crying for his mommy, neither. Nope, sure did not. Just thumped him once on the head and he went down like a ton of bricks."

"I tell ya," he continued. "You college kiddies are a bunch of pussies these days. Hellfire. At least back ten or fifteen years ago I'd get a little fight out of you little shits that came into my bar and tried to drink my shit for free. Yup, I sure did. There was one time in particular that these two whores drank a shitload and then at the end of the night they told me that they didn't have any money. I told them that they better find some way to pay their tab, whether it was calling their rich daddies for money or whatnot. I didn't give a shit. All I wanted was for my great-great-great grand pappy's bar to get the respect it deserves, and that means that everyone, and I do mean *everyone*, pays their fuckin' bar tabs. Shit ain't free here, ya know."

"Yes. I know that, sir," Gabe mumbled.

"Don't talk, boy, unless you're told to!" T-Bone snapped.

"Anyway," the crazed bartender continued. "I saw your friend there try to sneak out of the place and I just knew that I had to protect my great-great-great grand pappy's investment. So, like I told you, I snuck up behind him and conked him on the noodle. Still can't believe how little it took for him to start pleading for his life. Shitfire. Anyway, I drug the little shit back by his hair to the bar. He was all crying and shit. Hell. I even think he was trying to point to you and your whore girlfriend when you guys were across the bar playing with my stick-n-balls, er, 'pool,' as you college pussies say.

"But I didn't give a shit. I go by what my grand pappy used to say: 'If you can't pay for yourself, then you're no better than a bum that sleeps on the street and begs for change.' That's what I've always lived my life by. I pay for myself. I don't rely on anybody else's money or bullshit. I do it myself. It would be wise if you college kiddies would learn the same thing."

"Sir," Gabe interrupted, "we were gonna pay our bar tab. I had just lost where my friends were and tried looking for them when that biker gang came into the bar and made me start to drink with them. Really. I would never disrespect you or your great-great-great grand pappy by not paying what I owe. I can afford it, believe me."

"Uh huh. And?"

"And... Well, I didn't even notice that our friend Alan was gone until I got outta the restroom the first time. But that's also when my friend – Alan's girlfriend, not mine – disappeared on me. That's when Tommy Guns and his friends came into the bar and started making me drink with them. Seriously, sir. I'm really sorry for whatever Alan did and all, but I swear that I personally would have never walked out of your bar without paying the tab."

Gabe still didn't understand why T-Bone didn't just ask him to pay for Alan instead of beating the shit of him and dragging him to God knows where, but figured he would keep that part to himself. There was no need to aggravate the mammoth bartender unless it was necessary to do so. Gabe knew now definitely wasn't the time to try and act like a smartass. He kept his mouth shut and waited for T-Bone's response.

"Uh huh. Can't say I believe you, boy."

"Sir. Honest to god, that's the truth."

"I don't think you're gettin' what I've been saying, boy. You need to learn to pay for yourself in life and not rely on someone else. It should be you and you alone that pays for your tab. Why do you think that I made three bar tabs, one for you and each of your friends, when you said to me, 'Tab, please,' and then started drinking like some fools that had been stuck on an island in the middle of fuck?"

Gabe was now starting to understand what the big man was saying. He finally understood why he had tracked down Alan and kicked his ass for leaving the bar without first paying for what he had drank that night. When Alan walked out (for whatever reason it had been – probably that he was shit-faced and pissed off at Gabe and Erin playing pool together), the bartender had taken that as him walking out on his tab as well. Gabe thought about telling the bartender now that he would have gladly paid for him if he had been asked, but he was pretty much certain that T-Bone wouldn't want to hear that – take care of yourself and don't rely on others in life – was his main point. Gabe could respect that. What he couldn't fully understand is why he wasn't asked to pay for Alan. Hell. It wasn't like they had come into the bar separately. They had come in together and were there to party together and planned on paying the tab together.

Gabe realized there was no understanding or questioning it now. It was T-Bone's way or the highway. He had to respect that. He didn't have much of a choice. Not since he was now bound to the floor of the Torchlight Inn and still had no idea of Alan or Erin's whereabouts.

The echo of a distant scream broke the silence.

Gabe heard T-Bone mutter, "Sonofafuckingbitch," and the sound of his heavy footsteps started up again.

Chapter 16

Gabe listened to the fading footsteps until he was certain T-Bone was a good distance away and then leaned over to where Berta had first spoken to him. He tried getting her attention again but there was still no response.

She could be sleeping, Gabe thought.

Either that or she's dead.

Ugh.

With the fog in his head finally subsiding and the numbness wearing off from his bound legs, chest, and arms, Gabe was able to wiggle his fingers a little bit. He felt cold, hard steel. They were woven to one another.

Chains.

Thick chains.

Shit!

I've gotta find a way to get outta here.

Gabe also knew that he would need to find his friends. But it was first things first. The first order of business was to find a way to escape from the chains that were preventing him from standing up and getting the hell out of there.

Arching his back until his shoulder blades were touching, he brought his elbows together, followed by his wrists. He put his hands together, forming a giant fist. There was just enough slack in the chain binding his chest and upper arms that if he could just shimmy his hands up above the chain, he would be home free. Then he'd have to find a way to get out of the chains around his thighs.

First things first.

Shrugging his shoulders up to his ears, he was able to get his elbows just past the chain. But it wasn't enough. After a few minutes of trying, he relaxed his shoulders and his elbows dropped below the border of the chain.

Maybe if I try leaning forward...I'll be able to shimmy out of this sucker.

Gabe bent forward until the chain grew taut against his chest. He felt the pull of it against his arms as well, and realized that the end of the chain had been secured to the wall behind him.

The steel links dug into his bare skin. He winced as a link pinched his left nipple.

Biting his bottom lip to stop himself from crying out in pain, Gabe once again touched his shoulders to his ears and started to pull his arms up behind him. The chain continued to dig into his soft flesh. He felt something warm running down one of his arms and the left side of his chest. He hoped the chain hadn't severed his nipple.

His elbows caught the chain again and made the section going around the front of his chest move up an inch. He could feel the cold steel links digging into his skin. It was scratching and pinching him. He could feel his skin start to tear and the warmth of more blood running down his arms and chest. He felt the blood pool in his belly button and then run down onto his groin. His penis grew wet. The blood started to make a puddle between his scrotum and the crack of his buttocks.

He leaned forward again. Felt the strain of the chains against his skin, the tearing of his flesh worsening as he was finally able to pop his elbows over the top of the chain.

He took a deep breath and relaxed for a moment.

In the distance, the footsteps started again.

Fuck!

Gabe took a deep breath and leaned forward against his restraints. His skin screamed in protest, but he pushed on. He had to escape. He knew this would be his one and only chance. He had to free his arms before T-Bone came back and did whatever he was going to do to him. It sounded like he had already discontinued one scream (Alan? Erin?) and he would probably end up doing the same to him.

That would make two – either Alan or Erin and Berta.

He was fairly certain that Berta was indeed dead at this point and not just sleeping.

No one could sleep through all this shit, he thought.

Keeping his hands locked together, he splayed his elbows apart. If someone had been looking at him from the front, he would have probably seemed to be growing a pair of wings.

The footsteps were getting closer.

Shit.

He brought his hands up and they bumped against the underside of the chain. They stopped.

The footsteps were closer still.

Taking another deep breath, Gabe gritted his teeth and pulled.

His hands popped from under the chain and cleared its top.

He was free.

Almost.

He brought his arms back down to relax his shoulder muscles for a moment and took a deep breath. He leaned back against the wall. The chain stuck to his chest for a moment and then popped free. There was a sucking sound as it released from the holes that it had formed in his chest.

It hurt like a son of a bitch.

He felt rivers of blood running down his chest, soaking his stomach, groin, and legs.

Almost there, Gaby-Baby.

Finally, he brought his arms around to the front of him. He touched the blood-covered chain. It was slack and hanging down against the bottom half of his chest.

He grabbed the chain, ducked his head forward a little, and drew the chain over his face. He released it and heard it rattle against the wall behind him.

Just gotta get this chain off from around my legs and I'm home free, Gabe thought.

He was so happy his upper body was free that he hadn't heard the footsteps stop and the return of T-Bone's heavy breathing off to his right.

As Gabe started to work the chain down the top of his thighs, T-Bone said, "Well, well, well... What have we got here? The little man is trying to run out on his bar tab again."

And then he started laughing.

Chapter 17

Gabe didn't fully understand how the bartender could see in such complete darkness, but how else would he have noticed Gabe trying to escape the clutches of the chains? He thought for a moment how T-Bone could have maybe heard the metallic clank of the chain that had been around his chest hitting the wall, but he doubted that was the case. At that point he would have been too far away, according to the sounds of his boots hitting the dirt floor, to hear anything that Gabe was doing. The more logical answer was that the bartender's eyes had grown used to the dark surroundings and could see what he had been up to. *That's probably why I didn't hear him running back to me,* Gabe thought. If the crazy bastard had heard me trying to get out of these chains, he would have probably come a-running just like when he heard the distant scream. Gabe still wondered if it was Alan or Erin that had screamed out. He wondered what their reason had been to do so. Were they hurt? Scared? A little of both? Gabe knew he had to find his friends and save them. Though, from what T-Bone had said before about people trying to run out on their bar tabs, which he assumed was one of the reasons *he* was down here, his friends (and Berta) had more than likely met the same fate.

"Sir, please..." Gabe pleaded, still working on the chain around his thighs. He was almost a hundred percent certain that T-Bone could see what he was doing but he had to at least try.

Fucked if I do. Fucked if I don't.

"Don't 'sir, please' me, you piece of shit. What you doin' down there, boy?"

Maybe T-Bone *couldn't* see what he was doing. Gabe didn't answer the bartender's question, but instead continued to work on the chain. It was around his knees at this point. He kept pushing it lower, and T-Bone continued to yell at him.

"I don't know what you kids are trying to pull on me. You try running out on your bar tab and now you're trying to get away from the pit, as my great-great-great grand pappy used to call it. You kids are gonna work off your tab if it's the last thing you do. Or should I say the *two* of you are going to work off the three of you's tab."

As T-Bone started to laugh, Gabe continued to push on the chain. He also began to think about what the deranged bartender had meant by using the word *two*. Did it mean that one of his friends were hurt and unable to work off the tab, or something else? Gabe wasn't sure that he wanted to know. He much rather preferred to believe that both of his friends were still okay and that once he got the chain off his legs and was able to stand, he would somehow take care of T-Bone and find them, and then the three of them would get the hell out of the pit and back up to the bar where they could escape through the front door.

"Sir, really..."

"What did I tell you about talking when you're not told to?" T-Bone boomed. "I ought to kick your teeth in so you're in so much pain you won't be able to talk...just work."

Gabe expected a boot to the chops, but it never came.

Listening to the bartender's breathing, Gabe estimated that he was probably fifteen or twenty feet away. *Just enough distance so he probably hasn't seen me, but figures I'm up to something since he left me all alone to deal with whoever was screaming*, Gabe thought.

Careful not to drag his bare feet across the dirt floor and alert T-Bone that he was indeed up to something, Gabe lifted his legs off the floor and brought his knees up to his chest.

He worked the chain past his ankles and feet and gently set it down on the floor. It didn't make a sound.

All right!

And then he heard T-Bone let out an ear-piercing roar and start running…

Towards him.

Letting out a high pitched *Yeeeee,* T-Bone leapt through the air.

Gabe jumped to the side. As he rolled out of the way, he felt dirt stick to his sweaty, bloody skin.

He kept rolling until he hit a wall.

He heard T-Bone's body collide with something. Gabe couldn't tell in the darkness if it had been the wall or the floor. The air exploded out of the big man's lungs. Gabe assumed he was now lying on the floor, trying to catch his breath. He could hear the bartender's labored breathing.

Serves him right…the big stupid sonofa–

T-Bone let out a moan. Gabe didn't hear him trying to rustle himself to his feet. The big man was then eerily silent.

Gabe didn't know if he had knocked himself unconscious or was simply playing dead, just waiting for him to move so he'd know his exact location and come charging at him again. Gabe didn't want that. Oh no. But at the same time, he knew he couldn't just lay on the floor forever. Sooner or later the big man would start coming for him again. He had to do something quick – and he had to be as silent as a mouse trying to steal a piece of cheese off a spring-loaded trap.

Gabe rolled to his stomach and slowly started pushing himself up to his hands and knees. His dirt-caked skin felt raw and itchy. He figured he'd have to bathe in a tub of hydrogen peroxide when he got back to his dorm just to make sure none of his numerous scratches and gashes got infected. He also knew that was the least of his worries for the time being.

First things first, Gabe thought again.

First things first.

Chapter 18

The big man was obviously out cold, because Gabe had no trouble when he finally got to his feet and was able to walk by him. He wanted to retrace the sound of the bartender's footsteps from when he had first come down into the basement in order to find the way out, but he knew he wouldn't be able to live with himself if he just got up and walked out of the bar without first at least attempting to find his friends. So he went the other way, the direction that T-Bone had run in when he heard the person scream. He shuffled his feet along the floor and kept one hand on the wall at all times. He couldn't see shit in front of him. It was complete darkness.

He walked another fifty feet or so and then the side of his hand hit something hard. At first it just felt like a loose brick breaking away from the wall, but as he inspected it more with his fingers he was able to tell it wasn't a brick at all.

It was wood.

Old splintery wood.

He felt along the wood with his hand as it came to an end and then started again over his head. He came to a second stop and then ran his hand down the other side. It was a doorway without a door.

All doorways lead somewhere, he thought, taking a step through the door.

His foot hit air and then he was tumbling forward. Gabe's arms and legs started flaying about, his body picking up speed, as he was shooting down the hill to nowhere.

Nowhere.

Shiiiiiit! he screamed inside his head.

And then at the top of each summersault down the dark hill he started to see flashes of light.

Again.

And again.

Faster.

And faster.

Brighter.

And brighter.

His head collided with something hard and sent a blinding pain through his skull and down the back of his neck. He came to a sudden stop. His body hurt all over. He didn't even dare to move a finger this time. He just laid there with his face in the dirt. His breathing was shallow, and he felt like he was going to die.

In his dream, that is exactly what happened after colliding with the wall and losing consciousness. At first his breathing was ragged, his heart thumping irregularly, until there was a bright flash of light and he was walking towards it. Everything was serene around him. Gone were the nasty people in the bar, gone was the bar itself and the pit underneath. He was walking through a field of grain heading towards the light. All his wounds were healed and he was no longer naked. He wore a dress of glowing white. It was almost as radiant as the light he was walking towards. He felt and looked wonderful, inside and out. And he was happy. He was happier than he had been his entire life – and that was an impressive feat. He had a great family growing up: a wonderful mother and father who loved him and took care of him for eighteen years before he went off to college to become a man; a wonderful sister (who, yes, had bugged the shit out of him most of the time, but he knew now she only did that because she looked up to him and wanted to be the female version of him when she grew up); he had good friends (Alan and Erin, with whom he had shared some great times) and a future that he already had planned out for after college (lots of money, a house, two cars, two dogs, two beautiful kids, and a wife – Erin).

Erin.

The wondrous white light suddenly turned into a yellow glow when his eyes snapped open and he realized where he was.

The basement of the Torchlight Inn.

Chapter 19

After coming out of a dead dream, Gabe gingerly pushed himself up to his hands and knees and then wobbled to his feet. He almost fell a few times, but was able to catch himself on a rock that was jutting out of the wall at the bottom of the steep hill he had just tumbled down. His body hurt all over. He had a splitting headache. A part of him he wished he could die just to stop all the pain he was feeling.

Keeping a firm grasp on the many jagged rocks coming from the wall, Gabe shuffled along the dirt floor towards the yellow light. It seemed to dim and then grow bright again with each step closer. He still didn't know what the hell was going on or where his friends were, but he was at least able to see now. Even though the light was faint, it was still bright enough for him to see two or three feet in front of him with each step.

He continued forward.

Soon he came to a dead end. The tunnel turned sharply to the right. It looked like that was the direction where the light was originating. He pressed his bare belly to the wall and sidestepped a few inches. Slowly, he peaked around the corner. He saw something move and it nearly jump-started his heart to an early death, but he quickly realized it was just a shadow of some sort cast by the light coming from God knows where.

Besides the shaky shadow there was nothing. No big burly bartender named T-Bone coming to crush his skull with his huge hands. No monster. Nothing.

Deciding the coast was clear, Gabe stepped away from the corner he had been hiding in and started down the tunnel. The light continued to grow brighter with each step he took.

After he walked another twenty or thirty feet, the tunnel dead-ended. There was a closed split-wood door to his right. He turned and faced it. The cracks in the door weren't big enough to see through unless you stuck your eye right up to one of them, but they *were* big enough to let beams of flickering light come through. The door looked very old. Gabe couldn't tell if it was painted or not. If it was, it was either brown or a dark green color. He looked down and noticed it had a knob. He said *fuck it*, reached down, and turned it. The door creaked as he gave it a hard push. It swung open and hit the wall behind it. A bright burst of light blinded him. He squinted and then started walking towards the light.

Once his eyes adjusted, Gabe couldn't believe what he was seeing in front of him. It gave new meaning to the name of the bar.

The Torchlight Inn.

Gabe wanted to scream out, but was afraid that the noise would somehow wake up T-Bone and he would come running before he had a chance…

To save the *nine* naked people who had been chained to the enormous pillars in the large hollowed-out room. One of the pillars stood empty. Gabe figured that was where he would have been tied.

He stepped into the large domed room and looked up. He finally was able to see where the flickering light was coming from.

On top of each pillar was a huge pit of fire.

Chapter 20

Gabe turned and closed the door behind him. He looked for a lock but there wasn't one. The closed door would at least provide him some level of protection if T-Bone woke up and came rushing into the room. It wasn't much, but it was all that Gabe had going for him right now.

Giving the handle a final jiggle, Gabe turned and walked to the center of the room. The ten pillars were now surrounding him.

He stood next to two metal tables, one much bigger than the other.

The smaller of the two tables had a variety of sharp cutting instruments on top of it. They looked shiny and new. Next to the tools were several syringes filled with an odd-looking green liquid.

The second table looked as if it belonged in an autopsy room rather than hidden away underneath a bar in the middle of a college town. He didn't see any blood on either the instruments or the tables.

Thank God for small favors.

He looked up from the larger table and slowly spun himself around in a circle. It was hard to believe the sight before him was real and not part of some horrible dream.

The people that were occupying nine of the pillars had chains wrapped around their chests and legs. They were all naked and sweaty. Gabe recognized two of them right away.

Alan and Erin.

Even though they had only been apart for a relatively short period of time, both looked thinner than they had earlier in the night.

Gabe had seen Alan naked several times over the past few years, not because they were gay, but because they had shared a dorm room ever since coming to college and it's inevitable that you'll see your roommate without clothes on from time to time.

Alan looked like he had been beaten very badly. There were cuts and bruises all over his body. Some of them were still oozing blood. He looked either unconscious or dead, Gabe couldn't tell which. He hoped it wasn't the latter.

He quickly looked away from Alan and moved his eyes to the next pillar. To where Erin was chained.

Her head hung down and her chin was resting against her chest. Her long brown hair was draped over her bare shoulders. She didn't look like she had been cut but did have several large purple bruises on her breasts, stomach, and arms. Like Alan, she wasn't moving.

Gabe quickly scanned the other seven people and noticed the same two things – all of them were naked and not moving.

Picking up a large, curved saw from the table, Gabe walked over to Erin.

He instantly noticed from the slight rise and fall of her breasts that she was indeed still alive.

Thank God, Gabe thought.

He took a step closer to Erin and looked her up and down. She was beautiful and just his type. She had curves in all the right places. He so badly wanted to reach up and squeeze one of her breasts just to see what it felt like. It had been such a long time since he'd had the opportunity to do that to a girl and here was one now, all naked and sweaty, and she was unconscious to boot. The situation couldn't be beat.

Maybe.

What would be even better than this, Gabe thought, *is if we were alone back in my dorm room and she was lying naked on my bed.*

He instantly felt guilty for thinking such a thing.

He looked behind him to make sure Alan was still out. He was.

Thinking of Erin in the past had only been in your head, Gaby-Baby, not right in front of you.

It was now or, maybe, never.

He reached out towards Erin.

Before now he had always thought about what it would be like to kiss, touch, or make love to Erin, and now was his chance. He had to take it. His hand hovered above Erin's left breast. All he had to do was lower it an inch or two and take her breast into his hand. He imagined that the white mound would be soft but firm. He thought how he could make her nipple grow hard by pinching it. He thought about running his hand down her stomach and touching her…

Gabe felt the strain of his penis against his jeans.

He looked over his shoulder again at Alan. Still out like a light.

Do it. Do it now.

He lowered his hand and squeezed. It felt every bit as wonderful as he imagined it would. Her skin was slippery under his hand. He moved his hand to her right breast and squeezed again,. a bit harder this time. He took her nipple in between his index finger and thumb.

Erin jerked awake and screamed.

Gabe quickly took his hand away and looked over at Alan. Still out.

He looked back at Erin. She was trying to blink the sweat out of her eyes. Gabe reached up and whisked the sweat away.

Their eyes met.

Now or never, Gaby-Baby.

He leaned in for a kiss and just as their lips were about to meet, there was a loud crashing sound behind him.

The door had been blasted from its hinges and was now lying on the floor.

On top of the door was T-Bone.

He scurried off the door and started running towards Gabe and Erin.

Gabe quickly put his right hand behind his back.

Right before turning around to meet his fate head-on, Gabe gave Erin a wink.

She gave him a strange look back.

Chapter 21

As T-Bone stopped at the smaller of the two tables, Gabe turned his head around and whispered to Erin, "Trust me." She gave him another funny look.

He quickly looked down and then back up to Erin's eyes. Gabe watched her eyes lower on his bare back all the way down to his buttocks. She quickly looked up. Her eyes were wide. She had seen what he was holding. He smiled and said again, "Like I said, trust me, Erin. I'll get us out of this alive. All of us." She gave him a wink and then looked past his shoulder. Her mouth formed a giant *O*.

T-Bone was obviously on the move again.

But this time he wasn't coming for Gabe and Erin.

No.

This time he was running towards a fat naked black man who had been chained to the furthest pillar. In the light from the fire, Gabe noticed an object glistening in the bartender's hand. It looked to be a large knife of some sort.

T-Bone ran up to the fat man and drove the knife deep into his belly. The man jerked his head up and howled out in pain. Obviously whatever the bartender had been injecting into the deadbeats from the bar wasn't enough to keep them passed out when pain was inflicted upon them. Gabe realized that was probably the reason that Erin had woken up the second he had pinched her nipple. It was pain that brought them back to reality.

Just what a sick fuck like T-Bone would do, Gabe thought.

Gabe watched as T-Bone pulled the knife out and stuck it in again. The man continued to scream, but was quickly silenced when T-Bone withdrew the knife the second time from his belly and slashed him across the throat.

T-Bone had obviously hit his jugular, as blood was squirting out of the man's neck. It hit the bartender in the face and chest. Gabe watched as T-Bone licked the man's blood from his lips and ran to the next pillar. A skinny naked woman was standing there. She was already awake.

Gabe felt sorry for the woman having to watch her own death coming for her. He wondered if she was Berta. But he didn't have the chance to yell out and ask her before T-Bone reached her and shanked her in the side. She screamed out, "No. Don't. Please. Heeelllppp meee!"

Gabe felt like an ass for not doing something. But when it came down to it, even if it was Berta, he didn't really know her all that well and he had to stay where he was and protect Erin. She was his friend and Alan's girlfriend (hopefully not for long) and it was his duty to protect the ones he loved. Gabe watched as T-Bone stabbed the woman in her left eye. She stopped screaming after that.

Then T-Bone was on to the next victim.

Gabe just stood there and watched.

Behind him, Erin started to cry.

Chapter 22

Gabe stood there and watched in disbelief as the bartender ran from person to person, cutting, slicing, and stabbing them over and over again.

When he finished gutting the seventh one, T-Bone walked slowly to the center of the room and sat down on top of the large table. It shook a bit under his massive weight. Gabe thought it would have been a funny sight to see, a fat man sitting down on a metal table that was supposed to hold a lot of weight, but instead it crashes to the floor underneath him. But that didn't happen. The table had shaken a bit but stood strong under the knife-wielding bartender.

T-Bone was covered from head to toe in blood and pieces of flesh and guts. It was a macabre sight to behold. Gabe had never seen anything like it, not even in the goriest horror movies he had seen over the years. And that was saying a lot, as Gabe was as big of a horror movie buff as they come. He had loved the stuff ever since he had been a kid. It almost gave Gabe a hard-on watching Jason and Michael carving their way through victim after victim. But the real-life shit was more than Gabe could take. He bent over and vomited onto the dirt floor.

After standing up and wiping his mouth, he promised himself that it would be the last time he would do that tonight. He knew it would be gut-check time soon and he would have to be the referee.

Once the buzzer sounds, it's go time! Gabe screamed to himself.

Gabe looked over at Alan. He still looked to be asleep. His chin was touching his busted-up chest. His eyes were closed. From the thirty or so feet it was between Erin's pillar and his, Gabe couldn't tell if Alan's chest was moving or not. He hoped it was.

If he's dead, Erin would be all yours, Gabe's head told him.

No!

He has to be alive. He just has to. I don't know what I would do if Alan died here tonight. Hell, maybe he's already dead and I don't even know it. Then I could have Erin and do all sorts of...

Stop it!

Gabe turned his head and looked back at Erin. He couldn't be certain she had been thinking the same thing about Alan, whether or not he was alive or dead, but she was *looking* in his general direction. It was always a possibility she was looking at the poor souls that had been slaughtered at the two pillars on the other side of him, but Gabe doubted that was the case. He had trouble watching the last few people being cut up, and even though he hadn't seen whether Erin had still been watching or not, he doubted that she had been. She had started crying soon after the crazy fucker had started his slicin' n' dicin' spree, and Gabe assumed that she had closed her eyes after the first few.

After another few moments, Gabe whispered back to Erin, "I'm sure he's okay, sweetie. We'll get you and him outta here in a few minutes. Okay?" She looked Gabe in the eyes but didn't say anything.

Don't lose it now, girl, Gabe thought. *We still got a long way to go and time is runnin' out to get there. Soon it's gonna come down to just him and us. Hang in there, Erin.*

He wanted to tell her that, but he didn't. He didn't want to scare his friend any more than necessary.

What he really wanted to do, dead Alan or not, was to turn around and take Erin into his arms. To hold her tight and tell her that everything was going to be all right and that he would protect her through anything. That he would put his life on the line to save her…and Alan, if it came down to it. No. He couldn't say the last part. He would have to say that he would save them both and then the three of them, just like they had come into the bar, would walk out together.

Gabe was about to say something along those lines to Erin when the bartender's voice broke through his thoughts. He turned his head and looked at the big blood-covered man.

"So, now you youngins believe me," T-Bone asked.

"Believe you, what?" Gabe replied. Erin didn't say anything. She sniffled a few times and then went silent.

"That everyone is responsible for their own tabs. That you don't just go through life depending on someone else to pay your way. You earn your keep…plain and simple."

"I really don't know how you slaughtering all these people proves your point," Gabe replied.

"No?"

"No. I don't."

"Ah. I see. Well… What if I told you that you will?"

"I will…what?"

"Believe."

Gabe was getting sick of the back and forth bullshit with the bartender.

"What the fuck are you talking about, you crazy motherfucker?!" Gabe screamed.

Without another word, T-Bone stood up from the large metal table, picked out a scalpel from among the various instruments of death, and started walking.

Towards Alan.

Gabe's stomach dropped.

Erin screamed.

Chapter 23

Gabe and Erin watched the bartender's precision work with the scalpel as he sliced and diced his way into Alan's body. Alan didn't move or make a sound throughout the whole ordeal. Gabe was glad about that. Erin didn't make a sound once T-Bone started working on Alan's body.

The first thing he had done was slice across Alan's throat. Gabe could instantly tell that his friend *had* still been alive by the way the blood squirted out onto T-Bone and the dirt floor. The crazed bartender didn't seem to care. He was already covered in blood from his other victims. What was a little more blood at that point Gabe knew that if Alan had already been dead, any blood that would have come out of the gash from his right ear to his left would have just oozed out, not shot out like a stream from the end of a water pistol.

After the arc of blood had died down to a trickle, the bartender really started working on Alan.

First, he sliced off his nose, ears, and lips, and then started working the blade down to his chest. He made circular cuts around each areola and then ripped the entire area off Alan's body by grabbing the nipples and giving them a hard tug. Gabe could hear his friend's skin tearing and watched as the bartender threw the useless pieces of flesh onto the floor.

He lowered the blade even further down Alan's body. Gabe knew what was coming next. He didn't want to watch. He turned his head and looked at Erin. She either must have stopped watching a long time ago or had just closed her eyes. Her head was turned away and resting on her right shoulder. Gabe wanted to tell her that everything was going to be all right, but knew he would be lying. Everything was not all right, not even close. He was standing there watching a crazy fucking bartender cut up his best friend, Erin's boyfriend, and he wasn't doing a thing about it. It wasn't like he was defenseless either. He was still holding the large saw behind his back and could probably do some damage to the crazy fucker if he was quick about it. He could run up as T-Bone sawed away at Alan's stick and berries, and chop right into the back of the bartender's head. It may not kill him outright, but it'd more than likely stun him enough that he would drop to his knees and give Gabe a chance to really go to work on him. Gabe imagined it all in his head, but still didn't do anything. Not a single thing. He was just too damn scared. Scared of the people he had met throughout the night, scared of the bartender, scared of the crazy-ass room they were now in under the bar – he was just plain scared to death.

Gabe turned his head away from Erin and screamed. It was a primordial scream from the bottom of his belly. His soul was letting out all the hurt of a lifetime. His scream encompassed all the times he had been made fun of, for being a band geek in high school and for studying political science in college. Sure, he had a great future lined up for him, and the way things were looking now, a great girl to go through life with, but that didn't take away all the shit he had to go through to get there in the first place. And the real kicker was that he wasn't spending the last night of his junior year getting wasted with his friends. No, he was in the basement of some stupid fucking bar that Alan had picked out so they could experience something new to remember the night by for a long time.

Well, ol' buddy, Gabe thought. *You got what you wanted. We'll never forget this night. Not one single fucking part of it. I'll remember this night till I fucking die. But as for you, you won't remember shit...cause you are the stupid motherfucker, just like all the rest in the past, that thought they were tough shit and always started shit with people like me. Well, now you've done it, Alan-Baby. You're fucked.*

Well...if you can't beat em' I guess you join em'.

Gabe screamed again to get the bartender's attention.

Fuck it. Fuck all this fucking bullshit. I'm done.

The bartender finished lopping off Alan's penis and then turned to face Gabe and Erin. Erin was still looking away. T-Bone was holding one of Alan's testicles in his hand.

He threw the egg-shaped ball. It whizzed past Gabe's head and hit Erin in the face. She flinched, but didn't make a sound. The bartender laughed and then started to speak again.

"So, what do you think, boy?" T-Bone slurred.

"I think you do nice work, actually."

A wide smile stretched across the bartender's grisly face.

"*Really?*"

"Yeah. Really. You may not believe this," Gabe said, "but I've always been a fan of sick shit. I mean, I've never witnessed anything like this before, but I've always loved the old school horror movies, ya know, where there is some crazy...er...cool killer running around torturing people. Hell, I've been tortured my entire life and I'm guessing you have too, or you wouldn't be doing shit, er, stuff like this. Am I right?"

T-Bone started to speak and then stopped himself. Even from the distance between them, Gabe could see tears forming in the bartender's eyes. He had hit a nerve. He continued talking to the once-crazed drink pourer.

"Like I said, I know how you're feeling. I mean, I know you're older than me and shit, but we've probably had to deal with the same stuff over the years. You for a longer time, of course. What I mean is, I bet people made fun of you in school for this or that and it really got on your nerves, but you didn't do anything. Just like me. I've held it in for so long. Everybody but me always seemed to get what they wanted out of life. The kids back in high school would make fun of me for having zits, or living in a small house, or for my parents not having a ton of money to buy me a new car when I turned eighteen, or being in the marching band, or…"

T-Bone cut Gabe off – the bartender's eyes were open very wide.

"What did you just say?" the bartender asked as he started walking towards Gabe. Gabe thought about throwing the saw onto the dirt floor. Instead he clutched it tighter behind his back.

Not just yet.

"What?" Gabe asked.

"Did you just say you were in the marching band in high school and people made fun of you for it?"

"Yeah. Why?"

"Because, man. I was in the marching band too. Class of Marbury High back in 1983. I played the tuba. Wish I had a son that could one day follow in my footsteps and play the same thing. Unfortunately, nobody wants anything to do with a fat slob bartender. They definitely don't want to marry and have a kid with one."

Gabe smiled and then said, "Well, shit, T-Bone. I think you're right…and you know what else?"

"What?" the bartender replied, scrunching up his face.

Gabe said, "I played the tuba too," then slashed T-Bone's throat.

Chapter 24

The warm sun felt wonderful on Gabe's bare chest. He looked down at his golden-colored skin and decided it was a good time to turn over. He stretched his arms over his head and then rolled over onto his back. The sweat on his chest and stomach soaked into the towel underneath him. The sun on his back felt just as wonderful as it did on his front side. He reached behind him and pulled his bathing suit from the crevice between his buttocks.

Life was good.

After fifteen or twenty minutes, the sun got the best of Gabe. He stretched his neck over the side of the lounger and grabbed his Long Island Iced Tea. He put the straw to his lips and sucked. Hard. The cold liquid shot up the straw and into his parched mouth. It tasted wonderful. After a few more swallows, he placed the glass back onto the deck and rested his head down on the towel. Sweat was beginning to roll off his forehead and into his eyes. He reached up and whisked the sweat away with the back of his hand. Then he rolled over onto his back again. He squinted up into the sky – it was clear, not a cloud in sight. The only thing looming above him was the yellow-orange sun.

Life was good.

After lying around on the top-deck a few more hours, Gabe decided it was time to call it a day. He knew he had many preparations to make before tonight and it was time to get a move on. He swung his legs off the lounger. His right foot kicked the empty glass that his alcoholic iced tea had been in. He was able to catch it in time before it tipped over.

Gabe walked to the deck's door and grabbed the handle. He gave it a hard tug. At first it didn't budge. He thought back to the time when he was inside the bar and the door to the men's restroom had given him trouble. He laughed, then gave the sliding glass door another pull. This time it shot open. Gabe had to catch it before it banged against the opposite wall. He stepped into his bedroom and slid the door shut behind him.

As he walked over to the bed, Gabe started to untie the drawstring around his waist. Once he got to the bed, he placed one hand down on top of it and let his shorts fall to the floor. He kicked them out of the way. They sailed through the air a few feet and then landed neatly into the dirty clothes bin.

Swish!

He walked into the bathroom, urinated, brushed his teeth, and started the shower – nice and cold. After a few seconds of letting the water run, he checked the temperature and stepped inside. The cold water splashed down on top of his sweaty hair, face, and beard, running down onto his belly, groin, and legs. Soon after, he shampooed his long hair and beard and then used the suds that were in his hands to do his chest, stomach, groin, and legs. He turned around in tight little circles, letting the cold water rain down upon him. The turning around made him think back to when he had first seen the inside of the large domed room underneath the bar with all the pillars in it. He laughed at how scared he had been the entire night. Gabe found it somewhat fascinating that the soapy bubbles being rinsed off his body were now piling on top of the drain. Soon they started to go down.

After making sure that his skin was all shiny and no more soap remained on it, he reached down and shut off the shower. The nozzle dripped down on his head as he stood back up. He slid open the shower curtain and reached over to his towel rack. With water in his eyes, he felt around for a few seconds and then grabbed his fluffy white towel. He stepped from the shower and dried himself from head to foot. After getting as dry as possible, Gabe stepped over to the mirror. It was fogged over with steam. He reached his hand up and wiped away the water vapor.

A face was staring back at him.

Gabe screamed and leapt back from the face of T-Bone.

Chapter 25

The first night of the new semester had been a good one. There had been plenty of underclassmen and upperclassmen alike that had come in, thanks to Gabe's keen marketing skills.

College be damned.

But, boy, do those college kids like to spend mommy and daddy's money, Gabe thought.

Once the last person was gone, Gabe finished cleaning up and then walked to the door and locked it. He shook the handle for good measure. The door didn't move.

Locked up all nice and tight without a peep getting out at night.

He walked to the far end of the room and started down the hallway. It was dark and he couldn't see very far in front of him, but he didn't worry about bumping into anything or knocking anything over. He knew his surroundings very well now.

It felt natural.

Comforting.

It felt like home.

His home.

He came to a door, reached up, and ran his fingers along the top of the door frame, finding the small key he had put there. He brought it down and unlocked the door, then replaced the key where he had found it. He pushed open the door, stepped through, and locked it behind him.

He trudged down a steep flight of stairs.

It was dark.

Almost too dark.

But it still felt just fine.

At the bottom of the stairs, Gabe turned left and started walking; loose dirt and gravel crunched under his shoes. It was chilly. He was glad that he remembered to bring his long-sleeved flannel this time. The last few times he had forgotten and had to suffer for hours without it. But not this time.

Gabe came to a second doorway and stepped through it. He placed one hand against the wall and shuffled his feet down the steep slope.

As he neared the bottom, he started seeing a familiar glow.

His insides went cold at first, then grew warm.

His penis grew rigid inside his jeans.

At the bottom of the slope, Gabe turned left and started down a short hallway. Reaching the end, he turned right, then continued until it dead-ended.

He turned and faced the solid steel door he had installed just a few months ago.

He drew an old-fashioned skeleton key from his rear pocket and jabbed it into the keyhole.

He pushed the door.

It glided open, and did not hit the wall behind it.

He stepped into the well-lit room and smiled.

Erin, chained to the only inhabited pillar, screamed.

It was music to his ears.

Tones of Home
Thom Erb

Chapter 1
"Till There Was You"

"I'm not so sure about this, Ash," Maurice Ware said as he stared into the snowy night outside the passenger side window of the car. He wrung his hands and could feel his chest tighten. A green sign with white letters appeared out of the night, reading: *Sterling Point - 21 Miles; Geneva - 14 Miles; Arcadia Falls - 10 Miles,* and at the bottom, in faded print: *Miller Falls - 5 Miles.* He felt his pulse quicken, and a lump the size of a tennis ball grew in his throat.

"Ah, come on now, honey. You're not getting cold feet already, are you?" Ashley Vanslycke teased as she squinted out the snow-covered windshield of the late model Hyundai. He could sense she was smiling and always loved the way her blonde hair fell over her right eye, almost hiding it completely.

"No, of course not, babe, it's just... I've never met your parents before, let alone your entire family and your friends," he admitted, and let out a laugh.

"Oh, they're gonna just love you." She leaned over quickly and kissed him. Her tongue darted into his mouth, lost in his dark lips.

"Uh...just keep your eyes on the road, would you?" He gently pushed her away and chuckled.

"Ah, how could they not? Look at that cute little face." She cooed and pinched his ebony cheek and gave him a wink.

"Okay, I hope so."

"Well, I love you, and that's all that matters, right?" She cocked an eyebrow and gave him a smirk. It did little to ease his queasy stomach and sweaty hands. Her almond-shaped brown eyes could usually warm and center him. This time, however, it was a completely different world he was walking into. He wrung his clammy hands tighter.

The drumming of the windshield wipers did little to keep the snow away as they drove along the deserted Route 31. The snow hadn't let up since they left the Interstate and headed north toward the town of Miller Falls. The road had been getting snow-covered and more treacherous, and Maurice wasn't used to the backwoods roads of New York.

"You okay, city boy?" Ashley teased, and blew him a kiss. She reached down and turned up the volume on the CD player and Taylor Swift came pining out of the speakers crying "Our Song." He just shook his head.

"How can you listen to that crap?" he asked with a wry smile.

"It's good music, babe. Sorry if it's not your fancy schmancy Miles Duffiss," she laughed.

"Davis. It's Miles *DAVIS*, you should know that by now," he retorted and laughed, grabbing her thigh and giving it a gentle squeeze. "Can we please play something – *anything* – else?" he pleaded, reaching for the eject button on the CD player. She playfully smacked his hand away.

"I guess so, but you owe me, Mo." Her eyes and facial expression told him exactly the price that would have to be paid. He didn't mind. He never did.

"Ah, excellent! I have just the thing to mellow me out," he said, and grabbed a CD from the sun visor above him.

The lilting opening piano notes and soft bass floated through the car's interior, and the blissful sound raised his spirits immediately. "So What" was always one of his favorite Miles Davis tunes. It took him to a good place. He was happy now. She feigned protest, but he had gotten her into Miles and he always loved the way she danced and moved her beautiful body to the syncopated grooves. Maurice was neck-deep in love with her. He knew it from the first time they met at Nazareth College in Rochester and again during the required child abuse workshop last summer. He was studying to be a music teacher, and she was on her way to becoming an art teacher. He loved her deeply. He'd never felt love so completely and without doubt before. Maybe his mother, but that was different. Ashley was the perfect soulmate. He stared at her and couldn't believe she'd actually said yes. The ring, while small, still caught the bluish light from the dash lights and sparkled, making him smile widely.

They were polar opposites on the surface and in every other way. Her with her long, flowing blonde hair and enrapturing brown eyes that stole his heart and soul the minute he gazed into them. Her alabaster skin was almost like porcelain. It reminded him of the China dolls his grandma Arlene used to have on her shelves in her living room. It was made even brighter when she was next to his almost jet-black skin tone. She was so outgoing and hyperactive. While he preferred to stay in her dorm room and watch old *West Wing* or *NCIS* reruns, she was always the one who would drag him out to the club to dance and drink. He preferred the shadow instead of the multi-colored, throbbing lights of the Rochester club scene. She was the one to dance on top of a table, while he stood hiding his face in the darkness. They were never dark enough for him. But he would do anything for her, and she knew it.

He never thought he would fall in love with a white girl. Not that he didn't find them attractive, it was more of where he came from. The family back in Pittsboro wouldn't approve. Things were different back home. He was already the first in the family to go to college. For him to leave home and come to New York was a slap in his father's face. He needed to put some distance between himself and his father. A sudden icy chill overtook him, causing him to shiver.

"Still not used to these upstate New York winters, huh, Mo?" Ashley chided, and turned up the heat.

"Ah, it is what it is, Ash, but you can keep me warm." He smiled and grabbed her hand and gave it a kiss. He caught her blushing.

They both jumped as the Sugarland's "Baby Girl" ringtone shattered their loving moment.

She snatched the cell phone from the center console and answered. Maurice grew more nervous as the snow pelted the car and the wind sent white drifts in their path.

"Hello, Daddy." Ashley's voice took on a little girl tone, and she shot Maurice a sidelong glance.

He gulped, not knowing which freaked him out more – her talking on the phone while driving through a snowstorm, or the sound of his soon-to-be father-in-law's deep voice on the phone. He couldn't hear specific words, just the low tenor of his speech. That was all he needed to hear.

Growing up in the sticks of North Carolina, he had experienced his share of racism and bigotry. He had heard tales of Wayne County and they came rushing back as they passed a sign that read, *Welcome to Wayne County*. Apparently, rednecks and racist pricks weren't only indigenous to the South. His friend Joe Ward, back at college, warned him of the backwoods mentality some people in Wayne County had towards blacks, and the fact that he was engaged to a pasty white girl didn't help matters any. He knew little about her, or her family. All he knew about the Vanslycke family was that they were potato farmers and had tons of relatives in the area. That aside, he knew he loved Ashley deeply and she was going to be his bride. The thought sent shivers all over his body and a wide smile broke across his face. He'd never been this happy. Every time he looked at her, he fought to catch his breath. This time was no different.

"Mo, you are gonna so love my *FAM*, I guarantee it." Ashley beamed from underneath her knitted cap. The shaggy tan ball bounced against her face as she boogied to the music. She shot him a wink and her eyes grew wide.

"Ah… We're here, babe." She was almost shouting as she pointed toward the large sign offering the only light that could be seen in the shock white of the December snowstorm. Maurice looked out the passenger side window and tried to read the old tow-behind light-up sign: "Monday Night Football wings and drafts 1/2 price. Thursday night dart league. Christmas Eve – Live Music – *Mo 'Whiskey and the Shanty Town Revelers."*

"Oh, this should be just perfect," he muttered.

"What's that, babe?" she asked as she pulled the car slowly off the road and began looking for a parking spot in the packed bar parking lot.

"Oh, uh, that spot over there next to the big Chevy with the humongous tires should be perfect," he quickly quibbled. *Well, it is what it is, Mo. You love her, so suck it up, bro,* he thought. It amazed him, the number of mammoth-sized trucks in the snow-covered lot. He could hear the twangy sounds of country music booming from inside the roadside bar.

A large layer of snow covered the low sloping roof of the one-story building. It looked more like a poor man's ski lodge than a podunk bar. It had a large picture window facing the road; in its center hung a large Genessee Cream Ale neon sign, sending green and red light splintering the quarter-sized snowflakes pelting the outside, burying the patrons' 4x4s. A large, shoddily built deck, obviously made of used wood, jutted out from the side and broke the parking lot in half. A gaggle of rowdy smokers could be seen on the deck. Maurice and Ashley parked and looked about the lot. An old white Chevy van pulled in behind them and headed back down toward the volleyball court. It left deep trenches of tire tracks as it disappeared behind the building into the snowy night.

"There's no way in hell I'd park down back. This time of year, unless you have four-wheel drive, boy, are they screwed." Ashley laughed, turned the car off, gave Maurice a quick smooch, then wrapped her knitted scarf around her face and got out. Maurice wasn't relishing the thought of getting out in the cold storm, but *It is what it is,* he told himself, and pulled the hood up on his jacket and zipped it up to his nose. He forced the door open, fighting against the strong wind blowing in from the north.

The entrance was a simple wooden door with an *Open* sign hung off-kilter, and it offered a slight beacon of welcome. The weather-worn wood had the stains of many years embedded in its deep grains. The tall, roughly poured cement steps that led into the bar lay buried in deep, powdery fluff.

"Huh, no footprints," Maurice said.

"Ha, yeah, I'm sure the boys have been here a long while, babe," Ashley chuckled. She paused in front of the nearly covered step.

"You ready, Mo?" She winked and hugged him, giving him a tight kiss.

"Cut that shit out, or get a goddamn room," a booming voice punched through the howling winds.

Maurice's heart stopped and his breath froze in the freezing night air.

Chapter 2
"Oh Darling"

A wave of snow rushed across the packed parking lot and washed over Maurice and Ashley, leaving them covered in freezing snow. All Maurice heard was Ashley laughing. He didn't even want to look at the source of the comment. His chest squeezed tight.

Before them, beside the open door, was a monster of a man dressed in stained, dark brown, Carhartt bib overalls and wearing what looked like a dead raccoon on his head. His long black beard reached his chest and appeared to be matted with a sticky liquid. His lower lip bulged as he smiled. Chewing tobacco, Maurice surmised, and that would also explain the nasty beard.

"'Bout time you got yur ass here, Ash, we've been waiting and ya know Big Daddy don't like waitin'." The burly man looked down at Maurice and gave him a nod and a wink.

"You must be Mooooorice?" He smiled and a long brown tendril of spit escaped from his broken-toothed smile and slithered down until lost in the tangled mess of his beard. The man-bear looked Maurice up and down and smiled.

"Uh, yes, I am. Nice to meet you, uhm?" Maurice stuck out his hand and the big man ignored it.

"Do you mind if we come inside, Butch?" Ashley asked, still laughing slightly as she pushed him. He laughed and shifted slightly closer to the door, waving his right hand in a gesture of entrance.

"Sure, come on in," Butch bellowed, and watched Maurice squeeze through the small entrance, because the big man took up most of the doorway.

"Come on in, get warm and have a drink. Dad's buying." Butch smiled; more foul-smelling liquid drained from the open spot in his brown and yellow teeth. Maurice felt the man's big belly jut out as he squeezed through and could smell his foul breath as the man laughed. Maurice smiled and held his breath as he finally entered the packed bar. Then he wished he could have his breath back.

If he thought it was white outside, the great snowstorm had nothing on the wall-to-wall, all-white occupants of the Torchlight Inn. It looked like the cast of *Leave it to Beaver* and *The Andy Griffith Show* had a freakish, redneck love child. The bar was filled with laughing, dancing people of all shapes and sizes. All seemed to be fond of either brown Carhartt jackets or random snowmobile winter attire. The air was redolent with cigarette smoke, stale beer, and body odor. *A splendid time is guaranteed for all*, Maurice thought as he forced a wide smile.

Toby Keith's "Should've Been a Cowboy" seemed to come to a screaming halt, along with all conversation and action inside the dimly lit bar. Maurice could almost swear you could hear his sweat splattering on the well-worn wooden floor. All those white, sweaty, flushed faces were all turned toward him. His stomach churned, and he felt bile fight its way up his throat and wash around in the back of his mouth. He continued to force a smile. He knew he looked like a lone raisin in a basket full of flour, but he tried to keep calm. The clinking of glasses and plinking of quarters into the jukebox broke the tension, and Maurice could feel his body leaning toward the door. He slowly stepped back and his movement suddenly stopped.

"Gotta stay for at least one drink, Mooooooorice." Butch's jack-o-lantern smile seemed too wide, and his large body blocked any escape Maurice had hoped to find.

"Merry Christmas, everybody!" Ashley belted, and threw her arms wide open, mimicking an enormous hug to the entire bar. Maurice couldn't help but watch her ass in her tight jeans and Lugz boots. He'd never seen such a beautiful woman, and the thought of being engaged to her made his member swell. Maurice hurried his hands in front of his crotch. He kept smiling. Butch shuffled forward and Maurice felt himself move forward as well. Ashley grabbed him by his shaking arm and made for the bar.

The twangy refrain of Tim McGraw's "Live Like You're Dying" seemed to shake the patrons, and the frivolity resumed. The rowdiness continued and laughter filled the country bar, but Maurice could still feel the steely gaze upon him as they made their way through the thick crowd and to the pool room of the bar. Many smiles, hugs, and kisses welcomed his blonde bride-to-be, but it seemed like he didn't exist as they moved toward the back room.

"Heya, Ash, the usual, kid?" a short, shaggy salt-and-pepper-haired lady asked from behind the bar with a twisty smile.

"You bet yer ass, Bessie… Hook me and my man up." Ashley smiled and pushed on through the glad-handing crowd. The yellowish lights from the Genessee Cream Ale light hanging above the pool table washed out the whiteness even more from the people in the bar as Maurice excused himself, following his fiancée forging her way past them. The stares continued. Maurice could almost feel the crowd closing in. He hoped it was just his paranoia creeping up his spine.

The pool room sat packed and beyond it hung the doors to the smoker's deck outside. A lanky man in a leather vest tossed his pool cue onto the table, sending the balls scattering. He adjusted his long reddish-brown ponytail and smiled as he saw Ashley making her way through the crowd. A short, pudgy patron with a waist-long mullet threw up his fat arms in protest. The tall man ignored him.

"Hey, heaven, you was a long time gone, sexy," he said, and stepped between Ashley and Maurice.

Chapter 3
"Don't Pass Me By"

"Hey, Scooter, what's new?" Ashley feigned interest, her movement halted by the lanky biker blocking her way into the back room.

"Not a thing, baby. Missed ya, though. You never said goodbye when ya ran off last summer. Trying to hurt my feelings or what?" Scooter DeRueter's two missing front teeth made his Ss sound serpentine. Maurice tried to catch up to his fiancée but a tussle over the next quarter on the pool table blocked his passage. The jukebox blared on eleven and Keith Urban crooned about how someone looked good in his shirt. The song, setting, and crowd made his dark skin crawl. He had a bad feeling about this whole "telling the parents" thing. Still, he was here, like it or not. He faked his best polite smile and tried to keep his eye on Ashley, avoiding the glaring eyes of the all-Caucasian crowd.

"Excuse me, please," he said, but his voice was quickly lost amongst the din of the country music and shouting around the pool table. He was losing his composure. Three large good ol' boys shot him a death look and stopped their fighting over the pool table. Maurice wished they hadn't done that.

"I'm thinkin' you owe me at *least* a kiss, Ash." Scooter grabbed her with his long, bony fingers and smiled. His pale, freckled skin seemed ghostly in the light from the bluish beer sign hanging on the wall next to the dartboard. He already looked half-dead, with his almost translucent skin wrapped tightly over his cheekbones. She tried to pull away.

"Now come on, hon, you could at least buy a lady a drink first." She winked and pulled away. It was too late. He held her in his skeletal grasp. He smiled.

She felt bile rise in the back of her throat.

"Well, when you left, Ash, you kinda left things…undone." Scooter's flirtatious smile transformed into a sneer. His bony grip bore into her tender, pale skin. Maurice noticed, tensed, and clinched his fists. He found himself blocked in. On one side, a younger looking man wearing an Arcadia Falls Wrestling t-shirt and backwards New York Yankees ball cap. On the other side of the human blockade was the short, portly pool player. He closed in on Maurice, cocked his head back, and smiled. The flab of his arms oozed through the worse-for-wear, yellow-stained long underwear sleeves. He pushed up his Coke-bottle glasses and spat a brown wad onto the worn linoleum floor. A long, brown trail of spit slowly dripped from his unshaven face.

Maurice's face ran with sweat. It felt like someone had cranked the heat up to eighty. He wasn't sure if it was the mass of bodies in the small bar or his anger brewing inside him as he watched the scarecrow-looking motherfucker molesting his woman. The anger surprised him. He usually had a low boiling point, but this piece of shit redneck was pushing his luck. The lanky bastard dropped his skeletal hand down and grabbed Ashley's ass, and Maurice could feel his temples throb. He lunged forward. The fat pool player with a Jeff Gordon 24 ball cap stopped his efforts.

"What ya doin', bro? Can't ya see we're in the middle of a game here?" His breath stank of onion rings and beer. The leftover spittle lashed out toward Maurice as he spoke. The words seemed to drip with contempt and condescension. Maurice was damn sure this walking dung pile didn't even know what *condescension* meant. He turned his head, took a deep breath, and turned back to his odious obstacle.

"All I see is a drunk, ignorant fuck that's about to get his fat ass handed to him if he doesn't get out of my way," Maurice spat, his gaze slowly breaking from Ashley and finally freezing on the Jeff Gordon fan in front of him. The fat man just smirked. The peach fuzz on his chin jiggled as he shook his head.

"Now see, that's just what I'd expect from a nig–"

"Nah, no worries, boss. Teddy here is shit-faced, don't worry about him, man." The Yankee's fan patted Maurice on the shoulder and offered a pacifying smile. Maurice wasn't buying it or giving a shit. He focused on the scrawny scarecrow feeling up his fiancée's ass and wondered if he truly had a brain.

Chapter 4
"Get Back"

"I'm gonna stomp a mud hole in your already brown ass, boy," the fat pool player grunted. He shoved the Yankee's fan aside and rushed at Maurice. It all happened so fast. Maurice grabbed him by his dirty shirt, sidestepped, and shoved him towards the jukebox. His enormous frame slammed into the jukebox and made Taylor Swift skip a beat. *That's the best she's ever sounded*, Maurice laughed and turned his head on swivel. He had little time to waste. He hated to fight, especially when the nasty-ass rednecks could be his fiancée's family. Hell, they're all probably related anyway. A blur of motion from his right cut his laughter short. He heard Ashley screaming for them to stop. It was no use. He squatted down; a large hairy-knuckled fist nearly took his head clean off. He knew he needed to make this quick and try to get the hell out of there before all the inbred hicks piled on top of him.

He swung his fist upward and stopped his attacker with an uppercut. It caught the drunkard off guard and Maurice saw blood mixed with white and yellow shards exit the staggering man's gaping mouth. He knew this was his chance. He shot a risky look at Ashley; she was crying and being held with her arms across her body. Scooter, the "scarecrow," held her fast and just glared at Maurice with a yellow-and brown-toothed grin. She fought for release, but it was no use. Maurice could hear her protesting and begging them to stop. That wasn't working either. He saw a narrow gap in the crowd from where they came in and the glowing red of the exit sign. This was his last chance to get the hell out of here while he could still walk upright. The entire bar area was hooting and hollering, calling for the crowd to kick his ass, and giving the brawlers tips on the best way to *get 'er done*. He found his first movement was toward the gap. He froze as all the shouting and country music seemed to stop. All sound became isolated – Ashley's begging cries were the only thing inside his head. His next move was to his left, toward the fat pool player and the scarecrow squeezing the daylights out of his woman, his fiancée.

"Whoa, are ya gonna pay for that, bro?!" the fat man yelled, but Maurice couldn't hear him. His focus was on Ashley and the fastest way to get to her. A sharp pain filled the left side of his face and his eye swelled shut. He staggered and caught himself on the edge of the pool table. The roar from the crowd brought him back to his senses and he could feel the big man lumbering for him. Maurice snatched up the pool cue that was lying atop the table and swung it in a wide arc in the fat man's direction. His hands vibrated as the stick made contact and the crowd let out a collective *oooohhhhhhh*, as if the air was let out of a huge tractor tire. Maurice regained his balance and stepped over the knocked-out pool player. He almost tripped on his large, rotund belly, but his Timberland hiker found purchase on the wet tiled floor. He looked around and held the broken pool cue like a sword in front of him. He could feel the heat from the jukebox against his back; his chest rose and fell quickly, and he could feel his pulse pounding in his temples. The neon lights from the multitude of beer signs made his head ache and his eyes burned with pain. He tightened the grip on the shattered pool stick and turned as he heard Ashley screaming.

The crowd returned to its frenzied pitch just as his left eye slowly swelling shut from the fat man's sucker punch.

The jukebox cranked out "Boot Scootin' Boogie." It startled Maurice and he jumped, almost losing grip on the stick. Two of the fat man's friends grit their summer teeth, punched their hands, and slowly approached him. He tensed and brought the stick back like a Louisville Slugger.

"Okay, knock that shit off, *goddammit!*" A loud, deep, booming voice filled the bar and made Maurice cringe; he thought he knew the voice and waited for the piling on to begin.

"Scooter, if ya don't get yur goddamn dickskinners off my daughter, I'm gonna gut you like a fuckin' pig." The booming voice belonged to an even bigger man.

Maurice tensed and turned to face the entrance to the back room. A man far bigger than the ox who greeted them at the door stood staring at the redneck scarecrow manhandling Ashley. He had to duck to avoid rapping his head on the doorway. He didn't look pleased.

"Daddy!" Ashley screamed and broke free from Scooter, who was now trembling. Maurice could have sworn he saw a wet stain beginning to spread on the dirtbag's ragged jeans. He smiled.

Daddy stepped into the room, and somehow it seemed to shrink. The colors washed out, and the lights dimmed. The crowd around the pool table scrambled out and funneled into the main bar area – leaving only Ashley, Scooter, *Jeff Gordon,* and Maurice. This wasn't the way he wanted to meet his future father-in-law. But here he was.

"Daddy, I've missed you so much." Ashley ran to the big man, wearing black Carhartt bib overalls and a red and blue shirt over white long-underwear. He was clean-shaven, save for solid white muttonchops. His big head was shaved as Mr. Clean and looked like he could clean up just about anything he set his mind to. Maurice swallowed hard, took a deep breath, and rubbed his swelling eye.

"Oh, Daddy, I've got someone you have to meet." She looked to Maurice and her big brown eyes seemed to calm his nerves and make him all warm inside. As they always did. The big man released his clinging daughter and slowly walked toward Maurice. Maurice worried about a piss stain appearing on his own pants. Nothing came, and for that he was grateful. He stood straight up and tried to look tough. It didn't work.

"Who the hell are you?" Daddy questioned Maurice, and shoved a gigantic hand into Scooter's chest, sending him tumbling into the popcorn machine. A small round of laughter could be heard from the main bar room. Daddy shot them a look, and all fell silent. He turned his attention back to Maurice and his grimace didn't change. Someone shouted something about kicking his ass, but Maurice tried to ignore it.

"Uh, that's Maurice, Daddy," Ashley said, and ran to put herself between her imposing father and nervous fiancé. "Maurice Ware, yeah, I told you about him, Daddy. He's the guy from North Carolina and he goes to Naz with me. He's a musician." Her voice slathered in a sloppy mix of desperation and hope. Maurice prayed that hope would win out, but he wasn't placing any bets.

"Ah, so you some kinda rapper or sum shit, Moooooorice?" Daddy said as he leaned down and looked deep into Maurice's dark brown eyes. He stood a good foot taller than him and at least two feet wider as well. He used his bulk to his oppressive advantage.

"No, sir, I *hate* rap. I feel it leads to…deeper acceptance of…the ignorant theory that all black men are angry or trying to get something for nothing." Maurice tightened his jaw and stared the big man in the eye as he answered.

"And my momma brought me up thinkin' that every man must make his own path in life and that nobody owes me anything," he finished with a rising, confident tone.

Daddy stood straight up and took a deep breath, and it seemed like an hour passed before he spoke. The jukebox fell silent and the entire bar room seemed to take a collective breath.

"So, Moooooorice, are you…dating my punkin'?" Daddy's bright blue eyes grew wide as he waited for the answer.

"Well sir, I…uh… Yes…me…um…." The crowd, no longer held at bay, swarmed in, their angry faces and muddled comments becoming a roar as they surrounded Maurice. He didn't like where things were headed. He felt his ass tighten and knew that a slight piss stain was about to be the least of his concerns.

The big man leaned close, his nose crooked and bent. Maurice could tell it had been broken many times as said-nose touched his. The big man's breath stunk of beer and cigar smoke. Daddy's harsh eyes squinted and his thick, white, bushy eyebrows furrowed as he gritted his teeth and shoved a large, stubby finger into Maurice's quivering chest. The only sounds in the bar room were that of a few hushed *"Get 'em"* and *"Kick his ass."*

A glass mug shattered the silence as the bartender dropped it on the hard wooden floor.

Daddy grabbed Maurice with his left hand and he noticed it was missing its index finger, leaving only a stub. His grip was still strong, and jolts of pain shot through Maurice's shoulder up into his neck. Daddy pressed in even closer.

Maurice's jaw clenched, and he slowly raised the broken pool cue, ready to fend off the big man. He saw something from the corner of his eye and it slowed his heart back down. Ashley's beautiful, pale face broke into a wide smile. He felt his stomach gurgle and bile raced for the back of his throat. *What the fuck is going on?* he thought as panic filled his mind.

Chapter 5
"Fool on the Hill"

"I hear you want to marry my Ashley-girl, is that true, Mooooooorice?" Daddy inquired, never moving, and maintaining his intense stare.

"Yesss… S…ir… I…do…" Maurice eked out the words.

"You better remember those words, son," Daddy bellowed, and his violent sneer turned into a wide smile that matched his daughter's. He gave Maurice a quick wink and let his tight grip on his shoulder go, pulling him into an engulfing bear hug.

"Welcome to the family, Maurice," Daddy said, and squeezed harder.

"Uh…oh, um… *Thank* you, sir." Maurice stood stunned and felt himself shaking, and his heart beat in a syncopated rhythm that would make Buddy Rich proud. His hands shook and he let the pool cue drop to the floor. Ashley ran over to him, joined in the group hug, and kissed him on the cheek. He recoiled as sharp pains blasted his swollen left eye.

"Oh, babe, I'm so sorry about that," she cooed. She kissed him again, laughing.

Daddy released him. He felt blood rush back into his right arm and the urge to piss and shit himself dissipated, for which he was grateful. He still had no clue what the hell was going on. The thought must have translated into a look on his sweaty face as Daddy let out a bellowing laugh that shook the thick, smoke-treated, exposed beams of the Torchlight Inn.

"Oh, we were just bustin 'yer balls, son." Daddy let loose another volley of belly laughs and the entire bar erupted in matching catcalls and hollers. Maurice just stood there stupefied, with a swollen shut, purple and black left eye and a bloody-knuckled right hand.

"Babe, I called Daddy and told him the day after you asked me to marry you. It was his idea to mess with you." She gently pulled on his slack jaw and forced him to look into her enthralling brown eyes. "It's his way of welcoming you into the family, babe. You thought they were all a bunch of inbred, sister-boffin' rednecks, huh?" She winked and kissed his nose and hugged him close.

"They… *We* are good people, babe." She pulled back, looked up at her Daddy, and smiled.

"He's the one, Daddy."

"I see that, punkin'," Daddy said, and pulled her close and kissed the top of her head.

"I hate to…um, ask, but, if this was all a joke, why did those guys jump me like that?" Maurice asked, lightly touching his sensitive eye.

"Oh…those boys just got carried away. I reckon they was drinkin' too much Genny, nothin' new there. Sorry about that, son." Daddy's bright blue eyes twinkled as he winked and slapped Maurice on the shoulder, almost knocking him to his already weak knees.

"Yeah, him and the other gu–"

"Nice punch. Damn kid could never take a punch." Daddy laughed again, yanked Maurice away from Ashley, and pulled him toward the bar. "Woody, help those poor bastards up. They look like two goddamn turtles on their backs." Daddy's bear-like laugh filled the bar.

"Ya know, Maurice, I know we all look like somethin' that stepped out of *Deliverance* or a Larry the Cable Guy punch line, but we are just hard workin' folks, just like your family probably is, I reckon." He shot him another wink, and for the first time, Maurice's heart and stomach slowed down and stopped flip-flopping. He let a smile slip out, nodded his head, and felt his feet barely touch the floor as his future father-in-law "carried" him to the bar.

Daddy propped Maurice against the bar, offered the old bartender a soft smile, and ordered a round of drinks. Ashley followed quickly and hugged Maurice from behind.

"And hey, Bessie, can you get my future son-in-law here some ice for his shiner?" Daddy gave the short older bartender a flirtatious wink.

"Here ya are, hon. It's gonna be a doozy, too." Bessie nodded her head and handed Maurice a black checkered bar towel full of ice. She gave him a pat on the arm, shot Big Daddy a return wink, and smiled. Her chubby cheeks turned a rosy red, and she walked away down to the other side of the bar. Daddy looked at Ashley as she hopped up on a barstool next to Maurice and smiled.

"You're not mad, are you?" she said. She playfully darted her tongue in and over his ear. He shrugged and took the drink the smiling bartender placed before him, smiling himself.

"Well, meeting your fiancée's parents is a pretty scary event by normal standards. But I didn't expect to get punched in the face," he answered honestly, and surprised himself at his chuckle. Daddy snatched his shot glass full of brown liquid with his huge hand and gave Maurice another wink.

"Son, sorry about that again, but it seems you came out on top of that exchange, and I gotta say, I'm impressed. They must have taught ya well down in Durham." Daddy smiled wide and put the shot glass to his mouth, jerked his large head back and swallowed the burning booze. He slammed it down on the bar and motioned Bessie for another. The big man looked at Maurice and then to his full shot glass and raised a fuzzy gray eyebrow.

"That shot sure as hell ain't gonna drink itself, son." He grinned, and raised the new shot glass to his lips.

Maurice nodded, swallowed the shot, and slammed the glass down, only to be met by another full shot glass. Ashley let out a laugh and quickly snatched the shot from his hand. She swallowed it in one quick motion and let out a deep exhale as she slammed it down on the bar next to her father's empty glass.

I can see where she gets that from. Maurice raised his eyebrow and she grabbed him in a powerful hug and kissed him deeply. He could taste the whiskey burning his gums and tongue as she explored his mouth. She let out a low moan, and they both smiled.

"Cut that shit out, you two lovebirds. This IS a public place, for Christ's sake," Daddy ordered and half-smiled. "Hey, Bessie, dear, could you have Ellen bring us back a couple pitchers of Genny, hon?" He blew her a kiss and tossed a hundred-dollar bill on the bar. "And keep 'em comin', sweetie."

"You got it, honeypie," Bessie answered, and motioned to a short, young brunette at the other end of the bar.

They passed the pool table, where Scooter and another guy in snowmobile overalls were helping hold up the fat pool player, who was shaking his head and wiping blood from his eyes. The other guy, the one Maurice had knocked the fuck out, was still lying on the pool table. His scrawny, scraggly haired girlfriend was trying to wake him up by dumping a beer over his face. It didn't work, and she shot Ashley a death glare. He turned to Ashley, and she just rolled her eyes and flipped the girl off as they passed.

"Come on, kids, the party's out back." Daddy grabbed Maurice by his blue winter jacket and pulled him toward the back room. "Time to meet the rest of the Vanslycke clan. You're gonna need that beer they're bringing out." He threw his head back and another belly laugh escaped from his gigantic frame.

"He's not kidding, babe." Ashley nodded and shrugged her shoulders as she followed them to the back room.

Ah, swell, Maurice thought. He wished for another shot.

Chapter 6
"With a Little Help From My Friends"

Big Daddy escorted Maurice into the back room; he was sandwiched between the big man on his left and Ashley on his right. They both had their arms around him. Making sure he wouldn't make a break for it. He chortled to himself. Once he got a good look inside the dimly lit room, he guessed he was right. The "back room" was an outdoor deck, converted into what could best be explained as a large, three season porch. Sheets of graying plywood made crude walls halfway to the ceiling. The rest of the walls were two-by-fours and blue and black poly tarps held to the wood by screws and twist ties. Benches lined the walls and four large wooden spools acted as tables. In the center was a 50-gallon drum cut in half with a glowing red fire inside of it. There were people of various sizes and sexes huddled around the heat source. Maurice quickly glanced around the room and estimated there were at least fifty people packed in this plastic haven.

He *really* wanted that shot now.

"Well, lookie here who I found at the bar." Daddy's voice was proud, and that made Maurice relax a little. Not a lot, but it was enough.

The sizable crowd let out loud cheers, and shouts of *"Welcome home, Ashley"* rang out. The faces in the crowd were hard to make out for Maurice. The flickering yellow and red flames cast jerky shadows upon the tarps that ebbed and flowed with the powerful winter winds outside. He wasn't sure if the joke was over yet.

"Clear a path, you dumbasses," Daddy shouted, and just like a plaid Carhartt-wearing Moses, the mumbling crowd split in front of them and there, hanging on the makeshift blue and black wall, was a white bedsheet. On it in orange spray paint were huge splashy letters. Ashley hugged him tight as he tried to make out just what it read: *Congratulations Ashley and Moreese!* The thin linen fought against its zip-ties, matching the movement of the tarp billowing behind it. He could feel Ashley tremble and he heard her cry. His eyes watered up too; he felt warm all over, and he was glad that this time it wasn't his fight-or-flight response causing his temperature change. He was happy, and seeing Ashley so happy made his swollen eye feel like such a small price to pay.

"I could really use that drink now," he joked, and the smiling crowd roared with laughter. They threw a myriad of names and greetings at him and he sure hoped he could remember them, but with the combination of the punch upside his head and the shots he drank, he feared it was just wishful thinking.

With perfect timing, Ellen shoved her way into the craziness of *Chateau Vanslycke*, carrying two overflowing pitchers of beer. The deafening cry filled the smoky air inside the tent city of the back room once more.

"Oh, God bless your ever-lovin' soul, Ellen." Daddy smiled and poured four red plastic cups full of beer and handed one to Maurice and Ashley, keeping the pitcher for himself. He raised the frothy over-sized mug on high, loosed a big grin, and swooped around, trying to get each of the partygoers 'attention.

Ellen shot Maurice a flirtatious smile and a wink as she looked him up and down. He turned away, trying to ignore her.

"I have something to say, so all you assholes, shut the hell up." He chuckled and winked at Maurice and Ashley. Maurice was beginning to feel no pain, and that was good. But feared he it was going to talk a lot more alcohol to numb his newly acquired injuries. His left eye was numb from the ice, and from all the tense bullshit from the confrontation, he ached all over. All the time spent in college had softened him, and he feared he'd lost his skills from surviving in the dangerous streets of Durham. He hoped all the "friendly jokes" were over for the night. He looked at Daddy, who climbed on top of a rickety-looking wooden chair and raised the pitcher of beer again. The crowd silenced, all attention turned to the big man.

"Well, it's about time ya'll shut the hell up." Daddy laughed. His barrel chest bounced and Maurice thought the bowing chair was going to splinter into pieces and send the large man sprawling on the worn floor. But it held; it just creaked and flexed in protest. Maurice smiled and Ashley tugged on his arm and brought his attention back to Daddy in the center of the room.

"First, I want to welcome my lil' punkin' home. It's been a long time since she headed off to school in August." Daddy looked down at Ashley and his broad jaw quivered; Maurice could tell the big man was fighting to keep his wide smile from turning into a frown. "It was a long time to leave your old man alone." The flickering light from the fire barrel formed sharp shadows on the man's weather-worn face, and his deep-set blue eyes got misty. He took a big swig from the pitcher and an indistinct murmur came over the crowd.

It was then that Maurice realized Ashley never talked about her mother, and when Daddy spoke of being alone, he wondered where her mother was. One thing he knew for sure was now wasn't the time to ask. He could feel Ashley squeeze his arm tighter and she too began to cry.

"Now, this ain't no time for bein' all maudlin and all that bullshit. *Hell* no. This is a time for celebration. As you all know, my baby girl is getting married." His voice cracked. The crowd went crazy, shouting and throwing their hands up in the air. Beer, whiskey, and lord knows what other liquids flew up into the air as well, and Maurice could feel the worn wooden planks on the floor shake from the cheering family.

"It's been a tough few years since Julia's been gone, and I don't think I could have made it if it weren't for Ashley-girl, here. It's been just her 'n me and I think we did okay, don't you, punkin'?" Daddy looked at Ashley and big teardrops glistened as they fell down his smiling cheeks. It moved Maurice to see that the big man didn't give a shit about crying in front of all these people. They were family, sure, but for the rugged, tough-as-nails man that Daddy seemed to be, it was a pleasant surprise, and he thought maybe he had prejudged these "rednecks" too soon.

All eyes were on Maurice, and he reflexively drained the remainder of his beer and wiped the foam on his jacket sleeve. Someone behind him, in a Buffalo Bills jacket, reached over and refilled his cup from his pitcher. An old man with Coke-bottle glasses and a Santa Claus beard gave him a jack-o-lantern smile and patted him on the back.

"Uh, thanks," Maurice said. He wouldn't have normally drunk from strangers' pitcher, but hell, this night was far from normal and he didn't see it getting that way any time soon. So he toasted his new friend and took a deep drink from it. Daddy jumped down, and the entire room shuttered with the impact. The raucous crowd responded with roars and *yee-haws*. Maurice chuckled, but still worried this jimmy-rigged room was going to crash to the ground.

Daddy held up his hands again and silenced the rowdy ensemble.

"Now everyone, let me introduce y'all to our newest family member." Daddy yanked Maurice from Ashley's tight embrace and pulled him to his side. He thought he felt his ribs crack and his shoulder pop from the powerful man's hug. He smiled and nodded as he looked around at the full room. "This here is Maurice Ware, and he has one helluva uppercut," Daddy said. His wide face grew wider into a smile and he motioned around the tarped room, waved his big hand in a swooping motion, and brought it back to Maurice's chest that was now rising and falling with anxiety. "And he is my soon-to-be son-in-law and a welcome addition to our insanely fucked-up family." The jovial whooping and hollering of the rest of the Vanslycke family once again matched Daddy's raucous laughter. They all gathered in closer and raised their drink of choice. It looked like a scene straight out of a Garth Brooks song. Cowboy hats, NASCAR jackets, and Ski-doo winter coats abounded. To Maurice's surprise, they were all welcoming and embracing him. His color didn't seem to matter. His breath caught in his chest and he, too, began to cry.

Chapter 7
"I'm a Loser"

Cody Reynolds really needed a smoke. The damn laws in New York, just like every other goddamned place in the country, prohibited him from the joys of his precious nicotine. He didn't really want to venture out in the cold. He'd spent the better part of the night working on Patti Pierce, and it had been a long drought for him. Cody *really* needed to get laid. The bar was packed and there was some kinda bullshit party going on in the backroom where the smokers usually went to get their fix on. Not tonight, though. He knew that if he left Patti for two seconds, one of the other douchebags would flock to her hot ass like a deer to a damn salt lick. He would be damned if he was gonna let that happen. His dry period was ending tonight, even if it killed him. He leaned in and kissed Patti on her fake-tanned cheek and she smiled and licked his pug nose and gave it a fake bite. He smiled.

"Hey, darlin', I need to go grab a quick smoke. Why don't ya grab us another round and play some tunes on the jukebox." He winked and threw a twenty on the bar, pulled her close and cradled her wide ass in her tight-fitting Levi's. She let go a soft moan, shoved her wide tongue into his small mouth, grabbed his crotch, and giggled.

"Sure thing, hon. Hurry back though. You don't want me gettin' cold and lonely now, do ya?" She patted his ass as he kicked the barstool back and headed for the door. He knew he shouldn't leave, and he felt his crotch throb; he was determined to get some tonight. The biting Canadian gale pushed him back as he opened the door. The snow felt like a million minuscule needles piercing his exposed skin. He pulled his Mack Tools hoodie over his head, zipped up his leather jacket, and stepped out into the frigid night. Another powerful gust yanked the door from his hands and it slammed shut. Cody abruptly decided he needed to quit smoking or it would be the death of him. Adjusting the bulge in his pants, he squinted through the pelting snow to see where he'd parked his truck. He ran toward the back of the parking lot, by the snow-buried volleyball court. Cody hurried past a late seventies Chevy van covered in at least three inches of snow. He thought he saw movement, but he was too damn cold and needed a smoke too bad to give a shit. He squeezed his way past a Dodge Neon that sat parked extremely close to his truck and opened the door. It creaked open in protest, and he climbed inside and slammed it shut.

His icy hands shook as he dug deep into his jacket for the keys. They found purchase on his Stewie Griffin keychain, and he plucked the key out and shoved it into the ignition. The old engine shuddered, hesitated, then roared to life. Cody prayed for heat. It was slow to come, but it cheered him up remembering he had a bottle of Captain Morgan tucked behind the seat. He felt with his numb fingers and let out a big laugh as he found the cold bottle. He brought it out, twisted the cap off, and took a sip. Satisfied, he fetched a Doral menthol from his jacket pocket and pushed the lighter in on the truck's ashtray. To hold him over, he took another swig and turned the radio on. Tom T. Hall crooned about how he liked beer, and it made Cody chuckle. Cody hiccuped and took another drink. He almost pissed himself as a rapping on his driver side window echoed through the small cab. He pulled a juggling act to make sure he didn't dump the rum bottle out on the passenger seat. It's a good thing he caught it too, because the last thing he needed was to be pulled over and nailed for another DWI. This one would send his happy ass to jail for a long while. He felt a trickle of piss spread across his worn jeans. Fumbling with the bottle, he capped it, then shoved it under the seat, bitching and grumbling all the while. He grabbed a few leftover McDonald's napkins and dabbed at his wet crotch. He really hoped it wasn't the cops and would have given anything for a piece of fucking gum or a breath mint.

The rapping came again, heavier, more insistent this time. He flicked the radio off and cranked the window down halfway, so as not to let all the warm air out. Cody could barely see anything through the near-whiteout conditions.

"Yeah, yeah, gimme a damn second, Jesus fuckin' Christ," Cody shouted over the howling winds. He shoved the cigarette into his mouth and stared impatiently at the lighter in the ashtray. He gave his best fake smile and turned to the window as snow filled the opening. Cody wasn't sure if what he was seeing was real, a trick of the snowstorm, or the result of too much booze, but he could swear the face in his window was that of Paul McCartney. He shook his head and looked again. His mouth dropped open, the cigarette hanging from his bottom lip, dangling down, bouncing against his chin. The figure standing outside his window *was* Paul fucking McCartney.

The strong winds pounded at Cody's small truck, and the flip-flapping trench coat of the Beatle standing outside it cast jagged shadows from the dusk-to-dawn bar lights high above and behind them. The figure blotted out the lights and its features were partially hidden in the blackness of its shadow. Cody chuckled and, seeing it wasn't a cop, reached back behind the seat and pulled out the bottle of rum. The figure laughed and the sound floated off into the wintry mix of snow and ice consuming the entire area. The laughter seemed to be followed by a familiar song. *Damn familiar,* Cody thought as he smiled at the stranger and took a sip from the bottle.

Cody rolled the window down the rest of the way. A biting gust of wind knocked his ball cap off, and it smacked against the passenger side window. He heard a feminine giggle come from the shadowy stranger. The lilting strains of oboes and harpsichords came through the window on the crisp wind. *I know that song,* he thought again.

"What's shakin'?" Cody asked. He nodded and took another sip from the bottle of rum.

"Good evening, sir. Might I bother you for a fag?" a soft but curt voice asked, and leaned into the window, exposing its face.

"You *are* fuckin' Paul McCartney," Cody exclaimed with a raspy laugh and kept nodding his head in justification.

"Well, not quite, love, but for tonight, it will do." The feminine voice grew louder to compete with the raging storm. The pale white of the Paul mask seemed to glow inside the cab. The figure reached in with a slender, leather-sleeved arm, caressed Cody's face and let loose a giggle. Cody felt his member stiffen inside his jeans.

"I was hoping you would share some of that bottle with me, love," she said, and traced her leather-gloved hand from his cheek, down his arm, onto his stomach and then his bulging pants. *Paul* looked at Cody, laughed again, and traced her finger back up the half-empty bottle.

"Uh, yeah, sure, plenty here to go around, sweetie." Cody's voice shook, and the figure snatched the bottle from his quivering hand. The all-too familiar tune finally came to mind, and he smiled as a gloved hand caressed his hard package.

"Helter Skelter!" Cody's mind raced and he smiled with final recognition.

He suddenly became colder, and he couldn't feel his hand as it flopped down onto the leather seat. The familiar song grew louder as the inside of the windshield gushed with a red substance, like someone had taken a paint bucket and tossed its contents all over it. A warm sensation came back to his body, along with a ringing laughter. The color of the windshield was red...*blood* red. Cody's breath caught in his throat and his heartbeat waned. It was *his* blood.

"What's wrong, love? Feeling a little...low?" *Paul's* voice grew as cold and numb as the harsh winter air filling the cab. Blood rained from the large gash in Cody's throat. The leather-clad hand held a long, crimson blade, and it bobbed up and down to the final chorus of the Beatles' "Helter Skelter."

Cody felt numb all over; his limp head dropped against his chest, and he watched as *Paul McCartney* opened the door, unzipped his blood-soaked jeans, and yanked out his limp penis. The chalky-white mask looked up at his blinking, fading eyes, sliced through the loose skin of his scrotum and penis, and yanked it from his limp body. His senses were fading, but he heard the opening lines of "Hello, Goodbye" as the bloody and mangled pieces of his manhood dangled before him. Then all things went dark.

Chapter 8
"I Don't Want to Spoil the Party"

The doors slammed shut and the deeply piled snow glistened as it flitted in the florescent lights of the Torchlight Inn's parking lot. Only two sounds filled the snowy night: the thumping bass line of "John Deere Green" filtering out of the bar, and the chambering of shotguns. Somewhere off in the wintry distance, a lone dog barked. It sounded hollow and melancholy.

The man in the lead pulled his mask down over his large face and stopped before the almost snowed-in entrance to the bar. The odd shape created an even odder shadow on the step before him.

"Check your gear, mates." His tone was as cold as the whipping Lake Ontario wind that lapped at the four figures dressed in black fur and ankle-length leather jackets. The quartet examined their weapons. Shotguns, extra shells, nylon rope, and machetes were all in their proper places. Then they pulled down their masks and loud, collective laughter joined the crying canine, lost in the raging snowstorm racing in from the lake.

Hard-packed snow crunched underneath their sleek black boots as they approached the pulsating bar. Large, dime-sized snowflakes fell from the black sky and cut visibility close to zero, creating a white curtain in front of them. The red and blue neon beer signs acted like beacons and targets in the brisk night.

The four figures stood at attention in front of the white van, and the lead figure began examining them from head to toe. He adjusted his John Lennon mask and gave an approving nod.

He looked them over. An enormous man, nearly reaching the top of the van, stood with his broad chest pushed outward. *John* surveyed the big man and patted him on the chest. The man-mountain nodded; his Ringo Starr mask and his barrel chest seemed to protrude even more into the night's frigid air.

John continued down the line to a small but lithe frame. He took his time observing the curvaceous figure donning the Paul McCartney mask. She was well equipped for brutality and covered in fresh blood. She held a glob of flesh in her gloved right hand.

He was happy and moved on.

A very athletic figure finished *John's* examination. *George Harrison* stood tall, erect, and ready for action. He was happy.

John turned and walked to the door of the Torchlight Inn. He faced his compatriots. His long black fur jacket flowed in the harsh wind, exposing the multi-colored pants beneath. He pumped the shotgun, reached into his jacket, and fetched out a white object. He turned the iPod on, and the beginning traffic noises of "Sgt. Pepper's Lonely Hearts Club Band" filled his wireless ear buds. The three followed suit and placed their earpieces in.

"You all look fabulous. Let's knock 'em dead, mates." His voice was as cold as the northeast gusts assailing the bar. Finished, he nodded, turned, grabbed the metal handle of the door, and yanked it open.

No one heard the little bells jingle-jangle as the *Frightful Four* entered the loud, packed bar.

Chapter 9
"Come Together"

"Babe, I told you they were awesome," Ashley gushed, and downed another shot. She was shit-faced, and he knew it. However, this was a night of celebration and far be it from him to put an end to it. He was just so happy it didn't end up with him getting his ass kicked, or worse. It troubled him thinking that way, and he had fought those thoughts and feelings from day one of their relationship. But they were there, whether he liked it or not. He figured he would have to wrestle with those emotions and suck them up. He loved Ashley and would do anything to make her happy. Daddy shoved another shot in front of him and winked. Maurice, of course, obliged.

"They are great, kiddo," Maurice said, and gave Ashley a kiss on the cheek. She yanked him in close, digging her bright pink fingernails into the back of his neck. Her perky nipples poked through the Nazareth College long-sleeve t-shirt. She cooed and kissed him hard. A rowdy call filled the makeshift backroom, followed by laughter and dirty catcalls. Daddy laughed loudly and patted Maurice on the shoulder, interrupting their private moment.

"Heads up, son, you got eyes on ya." Daddy leaned in and pointed back toward the pool table area. Scooter stood leaning against the pool table, his arms crossed. He was drinking a Budweiser. His deep-set eyes were fixed on the entwined lovers. The fat pool dude leaned in to his ear and whispered something while dabbing a red-stained bar towel on his head. Maurice knew the night was far from over. He didn't give a rat's ass. He wasn't gonna let a couple of drunken idiots ruin his fiancée's night.

"Let's get another round, Ash." He turned to her and smiled. Even three sheets to the wind, she was still the most beautiful woman he'd ever seen. Her long blonde hair tussled to one side as she shot him a wide smile and bit her lower lip. She knew that drove him crazy. She *always* drove him crazy. He laughed and, for the first time that night, didn't feel self-conscious. *Screw Scooter and his lard-ass pal*, he thought, and motioned toward the bar. He grabbed her by the hand and they made their way to the pool room. Van Morrison's "Tupelo Honey" began playing on the jukebox, and Maurice nodded with approval. Ashley was as sweet as Tupelo honey, and he felt deep warmth grow inside his stomach and spread all over. He was happy and buzzed. He laughed. Ashley joined him, in perfect timing, as they squeezed past Scooter and his portly pal. Scooter's deep-set eyes never left Maurice. That made him chuckle as he continued toward the bar.

"Howdy, fellas." Maurice nodded at Scooter and the pool guy and smiled. Ashley shot him a wink and grinned. Scooter's face flushed red and his bright blue eyes bulged with anger. The bloody pool guy continued whispering in his ear. The minute the words came out of his mouth, Maurice knew it was stupid. And knew he should try to keep things smooth, not be a smart-ass. He knew better. He spotted an opening at the bar, handed Ashley a twenty-dollar bill, and pointed at the lucky opening.

"Hey, Ash, that was a douchebag move I made back there. Why don't you grab a couple beers for your friends there. I'm going to talk to them."

"Are you sure you want to do that, babe?" Ashley cocked her head to one side, her blonde locks falling playfully across her right eye. *Again with the biting of the lip*, he thought.

"Yeah, I should at least give it a try." He slapped her on the ass and she hopped, then ran for the open slot with her arm raised high, flashing the money to Bessie for service.

Maurice turned on his heel and walked back to Scooter and Pool-Guy. He stuck his hand out to Scooter, whose eyes still had a bead on him.

"Hey, guys, just wanted to say sorry about all…*that.*" He motioned to Pool-Guy's bloody scalp and offered them a slight smile. Maurice kept his hand out in front of Scooter, waiting for reciprocation.

"Hear that, Sacks. Moooooorice here is sorry." Scooter's gaze stayed fixed on Maurice. He spit a gob of brown goo onto the floor, nearly hitting Maurice's shoe, and smiled back at him. He finished his beer and set it down on the green felt of the pool table, interrupting a game between two local under-aged high school kids. They just raised their shoulders in a *what the hell?* gesture, then tossed their cues on the table, grabbed their beers, and walked out into the back room.

"Now, I'm not trying to be a jerk, guys. I get it was all a joke, and we all got carried away." Maurice moved his hand and made a wide-open gesture. "I know y'all been friends with Ashley forever and I just want to be cool with the people who mean a lot to her, know what I'm saying?" he said, and tried to hide his indignation at the rebuffing of his handshake offer.

Scooter stood up, put his thin hands on his hips, and smiled widely. He loomed a good half-foot taller than Maurice and took a step closer.

"*Friends*, huh? Is that what she told you we were?" He leaned down, tilted his thin head to the side, holding a crooked smirk on his face. Maurice could smell the cheap beer and ass-stench of chewing tobacco on his breath. "Me and Ash, yeah, we were much more than *that*, Moooooorice," he snapped, and sent an umber-colored wad onto the floor next to Maurice's foot.

"Ya don't say?" Maurice took a deep breath and tried hard not to show that Scooter had gotten his *goat,* as his mother always said. He held his breath, trying not to inhale the foul stench of Scooter's mouth. "Well, that was then, and this is now, Scooter. I'm just here to offer a handshake and a drink."

"Here we go boys, drink up." Ashley couldn't have had better timing, Maurice thought; a smile broke through his anger and he helped her with the drinks she was carrying. He grabbed two cold bottles of Bud, offered them to Scooter and Pool-Guy. He stared straight in their eyes and grinned.

"As I was saying, a peace offering, guys." He held out the dripping beer bottles and offered his best *come on* grin. Ashley leaned into him, flashed her long eyelashes, and threw out her best pouting lips.

The sound of the harmonic slide guitar of the Allman Brothers' "Old Friend" broke the tension. Scooter's hard exterior broke, and he dropped his shoulders, grinned, and gave a wink to Ashley. He reached out, snagged the beer from Maurice, and patted him on the shoulder.

"Just fuckin' with ya, bro. No hard feelings," Scooter slurred and looked at his pouting, pudgy friend. "Well, 'cept maybe *his* sorry ass." He laughed and gripped tightly onto Maurice's shoulder, leaning into him.

The battered Pool-Guy reluctantly took the beer from Maurice and quickly stepped back against the comfort of the pool table. Maurice and Scooter chuckled.

"Ah, come on, Sacks, Whaddya want the guy to do? You charged him like a goddamn bull-moose, for fuck's sake." Scooter held onto Maurice while reaching out with his left arm and snatching Sacks by the scruff of his neck and pulling him closer, laughing all the while.

"Heya, fellas, drink up. This *is* a party after all... MY PARTY!" Ashley whooped, hollered, and fell into the three interlocked drinkers. They all collapsed into each other in a buzzed, laughing, weaving unit.

"That it is, darlin', and here's to you and your man Maurice here." Scooter let Maurice and Sacks loose and helped Ashley regain her balance. He picked up his beer from the pool table, raised it high, and lifted his sharp-angled chin with it.

"I hope you guys are happy. And Maurice, you better take damn good care of my gal here. She's the best thing that ever came outta this shithole town." His words caught in his throat and Maurice could tell he was fighting back tears.

"Oh, I will, Scooter, trust me. I'm not letting her go." He clunked his bottle against Scooter's and Sacks reluctantly joined in. Ashley began shaking her hips to Kid Rock's "All Summer Long." She looked at her *boys* and smiled, stood on her tiptoes, and clanked her bottle with theirs.

"Well, if I'm not the luckiest girl in the entire world." She kept seductively swaying her hips to the thumping sampled music of Lynyrd Skynyrd and Warren Zevon. She bumped her hips into Maurice and it sent him bashing into Scooter as they were both drinking their beers. A spray of golden liquid splashed over them. They laughed even harder, and they staggered and fought to catch their balance.

Scooter pulled Maurice into him and his fuzzy eyes fought to find purchase on him.

"I gotta tell ya something'." He looked around, looked at Ashley, then back to Maurice. "The kick in the nuts is, Mo; I bet you were thinkin' Ash and I were an item or somethin', huh?" He tilted the beer bottle back and smirked, then swallowed.

"Uh, well, yeah, I did," Maurice answered, and raised an eyebrow. He looked at Ashley, who swayed contently, lost in a world of booze and grinding to the music. He didn't know whether to bust Scooter in the mouth in a jealous rage or throw her down on the pool table and make love to her right there.. Maurice laughed to himself, as he had always known he was a lover, not a fighter. He turned his attention back to Scooter, who was enjoying the tension-filled, pregnant pause.

"Go on…" Maurice stressed his impatience with a smile and a big swig from his beer, draining it.

"Haaaaaaaaa, I like you, Maurice. You're all right, bro." Scooter slapped Maurice on the back and the force made him stagger forward into Ashley, who was eyeing the table next to them. He grabbed onto her and they both let out a wild, drunken laugh.

"Nah, nah, come here, I gotta tell ya." Scooter pulled Maurice away from Ashley and they slammed into each other.

"Okay, okay. What the hell *is* it? Were you guys engaged or something?" Maurice really wanted another beer and wanted his new redneck friend to get to the damn point even more.

"No, bro… That's the fuckin' joke!" Scooter covered his smiling face, leaned into Maurice, and let out a hissing laugh.

"As fuckin' ironic as it sounds, bro, she's my sister." He leaned back and howled until his hat fell off his balding head.

Maurice just stood there dumbfounded, his mouth hanging open. Sacks belted out a laugh as well, not even having a damn clue why.

"We just really wanted to mess with you, bro." Scooter kept laughing, pulled at his long ponytail and motioned with his eyes toward his ball cap on the floor. Sacks swallowed his beer, bent down and grunted as he picked up the hat and handed it to Scooter.

"It's okay. Y'all had me for sure, Scooter, and I think we need another round, don't you?" Maurice was trying to be a good sport, but he needed another social lubricant. He didn't give Scooter a chance to respond and headed for the bar. He caught Ashley standing on top of the table next to the ladies' room, grinding and swaying to some generic country song. They all sounded the same to him. She was having fun, and he needed a drink…fast. He slithered his way through the packed bar and his hands found purchase on the faux-leather railing. The entire place was in a frenzy. He never thought that when he saw the poorly lit sign – "The Torchlight Inn" – from the road, it would be filled with such a crazy crowd. As he waited for one of the two overworked bartenders to get to him, he looked about the small but hectic bar and continued to be amazed and bewildered at the way the evening had transpired. Despite being slugged in the jaw, which was no big deal where he came from, he couldn't have hoped it would have turned out so well. Although as he looked around, it looked like a Ku Klux Klan meeting in blue jeans and winter jackets. These people seemed to be just like the folks back home in North Carolina. They were just honest, hardworking people. As buzzed as he was, Maurice still felt ashamed that he had judged them without giving them a chance. He really needed a drink. He waved the twenty-dollar bill out, trying hard to get Bessie's attention. Ellen appeared out of the cooler, looking angry and frustrated.

"Ellen!" Maurice shouted, impressed that he even remembered her name. He leaned over the bar, trying to get her attention.

She caught him and looked pissed off, but seeing it was Maurice, she transformed her grimace into a smile. She came to him and leaned in, turning her ear to hear him over the twangy Rascal Flatts song blasting through the bar.

"What do you need, honey?" she said. He could hear the aggravation in her voice and noticed Bessie was knee deep with the flailing wall of arms, hands, and dollar bills.

"What's wrong?" he leaned in and yelled.

"Ah, the damn Golden Anniversary keg is kicked and I can't lift the new one, and all these assholes want more beer." She forced a smile and motioned toward the cooler behind her.

He looked at the throng of thirsty patrons and the overwhelmed old lady trying to placate them. He turned back to Ashley; she was busting a move to the crappy music. Scooter caught him looking, held two fingers up, and smiled. She was safe, he thought, and turned back to Ellen as she placed a cold Bud in front of him. He smiled and leaned back in toward her.

"You want me to give you a hand with the keg?" he shouted, and took a quick sip of the beer. It tasted good, and the coolness felt soothing against his throat.

He could see the relief flush over her pale, freckled face and she smiled, nodded in acceptance.

She brought her hands up in a *thank you* prayer gesture.

"Oh, thanks so much, that would be so great!" she yelled over the twangy music and smiled.

He hopped over the bar, grabbed his beer, and followed Ellen into the cooler. The large silver door slowly closed behind them.

Chapter 10
"Hello, Goodbye"

Paul held fast onto the limp, blood-dripping penis as the door to the bar shut behind her. She could still feel the heat from the flaccid member in her gloved hand. As she eyed the throbbing crowd inside the Torchlight Inn, she salivated at the brutally savage possibilities before her. She smiled up at *John* as she felt a warm wetness grow in her groin. *John* sniffed the air, peered down, and shook his masked head. She giggled and shoved the flaccid, bloody member into her breast pocket; small, wriggly red veins and nerves jutted out, hung loosely over the black pocket, and bounced as she stepped into the bar. A few of the drunken patrons in front of the door laughed and pointed and slapped one another on the backs as the odd sight as the four lads from Liverpool entered.

John put his hands on his black-clad hips, surveyed their new surroundings, and sucked in a deep breath. The other three fanned out behind him. The staggering, laughing crowd parted and welcomed them in with smiles and raised glasses. *John* raised his right arm and pointed at the door. *Ringo* nodded and locked it. *George* gave him a hand, and with a huge grunt they hefted the large wooden shuffleboard table and jammed it in front of the exit. *John*'s gaze went from one end of the bar to the other, checking for other points of entry or exit. He snapped his fingers and *Paul* shot a look, followed her boss's pointed finger, and went straight to the jukebox.

The four walked onto the small dance floor, its worse-for-wear wooden underlay peeking through some cracked and missing tiles. The rest of the aging tiles were pock-marked with holes and black boot smudges. The dark, wood-planked walls of the bar made it seem to shrink as the last refrains of Big and Rich's "Save a Horse, Ride a Cowboy" came to a halt. The rowdy crowd groaned and collectively bitched at the sudden stoppage of shit-kicking party music, and turned its attention toward the cleared dance floor.

John snatched a small table and hopped up on it. His black, thick-heeled, pointed boots slid slightly as he landed. He pinwheeled his arms as he gained his balance, his Lennon mask held frozen in a stoic grin. The restless crowd let out a loud laugh as he held his arms out wide in a *ta-da* gesture. It was met with another round of cheering and laughs. No one seemed to notice the barricaded door or even care about the lack of musical entertainment for a second. *John* just smiled beneath his mask.

"Who the hell are you?" some drunk wearing a Miller Falls Volunteer Fire Department t-shirt and sweat-stained DeRueter Brothers' Farm cap shouted. A few of his drunken buddies chimed in, laughing, and punched each other in response.

"Well, my good man, that is a mighty fine question indeed," *John* shouted, and gave the smiling fireman a nod. He stood straight up, put his hands back on his hips, and tilted his head to the side. He threw out his hand toward *Paul*. She frantically fussed with the digital jukebox and the small device she had sitting on a table. A few crackling noises burst through the bar's speakers. *John* shot her a quick glance and just as quickly turned his attention back to the anxious crowd.

"It's too fuckin' late for a band. What are you guys, some kind of comedy act or some shit?" a different drunk cried out, followed by a hoot of laughter and applause.

"Well, it's funny that you should mention that, luv." *John* bowed down, his masked nose almost touching his knee, and swiftly stood back up.

"Say, we didn't hire any entertainment tonight, mister," Bessie shouted, and leaned against the wet bar. She was getting too old for this and just didn't have the energy anymore. She still had to keep things on the up and up for Jack, the owner. She wanted no more trouble; she needed this job. When Elmer passed away last winter, it left her with little money, and she needed all she could just to pay the lot rent at Happy Pines trailer park. So here she was, at almost midnight, serving all these annoying drunks, and now these whacked-out strangers, whether she wanted to or not.

"Oh, have no fear, my dear; we are strictly volunteer." *John* chuckled at the unplanned rhyme and waved a wide, sweeping arm toward the stout, elderly bartender. "And we won't leave your sweet patrons disappointed." The beginning thumping bass lines of "Ob-La-Di, Ob-La-Da" pounded out through the bar's cheap speakers. *John* gave *Paul* an approving nod and turned back to the awaiting crowd.

They began cheering, dancing and swaying to the pounding beat. *John* crossed his arms and nodded along with the bass. The drunken mass of bodies merged into one enormous sea of smiles and flesh as "Twist and Shout" came roaring through the speakers. It only enhanced the craziness of the party inside the Torchlight Inn. *John* and the rest of the Fab Four just nodded in anticipation.

As the song ended and the beginning notes of "The Magical Mystery Tour" played, *John* held his leather-clad arms wide in a welcoming gesture and lip-synced the song to the excited, swaying crowd.

"Roll up, roll up for the mystery tour, step right this way."

He sang along as he swiftly flung his trench coat back and brandished the shotgun. The others followed in concert. The crowd froze in confusion and shock.

"The magical mystery tour is dying to take you away."

They all sang and let loose a volley of shots into the drunken, oblivious mass of bodies.

"Take you today." More shots rang out and the smell of iron and cordite filled the bar. Crimson rain filled the air and met the straining tones of "I Am the Walrus." *John* stepped toward the crowd of panicked customers and spotted a young girl, barely drinking age, hunched underneath the padded bar rail. He paused, jerked his gaze onto her, and lowered the shotgun. He offered her his gloved hand. She stared wide-eyed, her pale skin lay speckled in bloody spots. She looked like she had chickenpox, *John* mused, and tilted his head. He shook his hand at her again and nodded for her to take it. She reached out a trembling, thin hand and wept uncontrollably. He took it gently and helped her up on her wobbly knees. She stared at him in disbelief and shock, and he leaned into her and snatched her by the waist. Her tight jeans and white sweater were a sanguine mess, painted red like a Rorschach test. He whispered in her shaking ear.

"You say hello... I say...goodbye!" The young girl's head exploded with a loud splash, turned to a red and fleshy mush, and splattered the Bud Light sign behind the bar. He let her limp body go, and it landed with a wet and sickly slap. He stared down at the headless corpse and shrugged his shoulders. The bar echoed with gunshots and screams of terror. He felt his member growing in his tight, rainbow-colored bell-bottoms as he jumped up onto the bar.

Below, the entire room was in chaos. His three bandmates were busy blowing heads and limbs off or slicing gaping holes into the stunned patrons. The floor was slowly being swallowed up by the gallons of blood being spilled from the panicking people of the Torchlight Inn. He smiled beneath his mask and reached full erection. He needed to find her. *But which one was she?* he wondered, surveying the carnage before him.

George had the redneck wearing the DeRueter cap deep-throating the Ithaca Deerslayer's barrel as he mockingly thrust his hips at the sobbing farmer. The tears halted as the rifle barrel jerked and vomited the hat and a mass of gristle, bone, and blood in a wide pattern into the scrambling crowd behind it. *George* let the glistening shotgun drop to his side and leaned backwards, his face looking up to the white dry-walled ceiling. He let out a bellow of laughter.

Ringo was fighting off three drunks, obviously under-aged drinkers. A lanky fellow punched him in the jaw, shifting his mask to the side, but he paid no heed and buried his machete into the young man's chest. He buried it so deep, it came poking out the back of his darkly stained Lil' Wayne t-shirt. The other juvenile assailant was short and stocky, with a yellow and black rugby shirt and a backwards ball cap. *Ringo* grasped the punk's throat. He was doing a mighty fine Darth Vader impression, *John* thought, and chuckled. The youth punched and kicked at him. They met frantic cacophonous cries for mercy with cold indifference and mocking laughter. All around them was wild, filled with screams and cries of death and pain. *Ringo* stomped his big booted foot onto the chest of the limp Lil' Wayne fan and yanked the machete free, pulling with it a long, stringy, bloody cobweb of flesh and yellow fat. He wiped the thin blade on the limp body of the scrawny drunk and brought his attention back to the flailing teen in his tight grasp.

The young drunk scratched and clawed at *Ringo's* leather sleeve and desperately kicked at his ribs. Unfortunately for the dangling teen, he was much too short. *John* found that hilarious, letting out a howl. He brought his hands to his hips again and watched on as *Ringo* brought the machete's tip to the spazzing kid's face. His wide blue eyes seemed to want to burst from their sockets as the tip of the blade slightly pricked into the soft skin between them. His mouth gaped open wide in a silent plea, but he didn't utter a word as *Ringo's* forearm muscles tensed, bulged. He thrust the wide blade through the drunken teen's skull. It sank deep, gracefully, as if the flesh and bone were merely Cool Whip. Blood came rushing from the fresh wound and painted *Ringo* in a warm hue of red. He seemed to relish in its warmth. *That is one disturbed individual, John* thought, and his groin called out to him once again. He grabbed it and tried to make it obey; it fought against its tight polyester constraints and refused to go away. *Now is not the damn time, blast it*, he whispered through gritted teeth, and pushed the carnal urge out of his mind. Finding the *One* was the mission, and he must stay on task. He needed to finish assessing the situation before engaging in the urge. A shrill shriek blasted off near the dartboards. He jerked his head to find the source. When he found it, his erection grew harder, and he smiled wide in satisfaction.

Paul stared at the limp body of a woman…a headless woman. In her left hand, she held tightly onto the blood-drenched machete. Long veins of blood and flesh hung from the blade and stretched to the floor, where it spilled out and turned the black and white checkers into one solid color – blood red. That wasn't the sight that made *John* smile with pride and made his groin swell in ecstasy. It was the fixed, blank stare of the dead woman's severed head in *Paul's* right hand that made him shiver with glee. The red and green

Christmas lights caught the glistening, slimy veins as they twitched and splashed in jerky motions from the woman's crudely hewn head. Her mouth hung down, caught in a panicked death scream. *Paul* swung the head back and forth gently like a pendulum. Her laughter grew louder and more intense with every swing of the dead woman's head, as it created an arcing swathe of congealing blood and gristle above the blood-soaked corpse.

"Oh, luv, Edvard Munch would have been oh so proud," *John* shouted over the loud distorted guitar of "Helter Skelter."

The chaos reigned about him. *John* smiled and nodded in satisfaction. However, his hard prick called for attention. He reached down, gave it a tug, and adjusted his package. He must find her – the *One*. His heart stopped as a crowd of burly men came crashing into the bar from behind the pool table, brandishing pistols. However, this wasn't what made *John*'s heart pound or his member salute even higher... No, not at all. It was the ravishing blonde, huddled against the video game. She reminded him of Botticelli's *Birth of Venus*.

"Ah, there she is." He smiled, grabbing both of his guns as he walked down the bar towards the fray. As he looked closer at the hysterical girl, he stopped mid-stride. It *was* her, the one they were there for, he realized, and suddenly the blood returned to his brain and he smiled wide beneath the latex mask.

Chapter 11
"Everybody's Trying to Be My Baby"

"What the hell was that?" Maurice froze as he lifted a case of Coors Light and turned his head toward the cooler door. His breath sent puffs of white vapor into the cooler's soft yellow glow.

"What? I don't hear anything." Ellen lugged a case of frozen chicken wings from the floor and dropped it on top of a stack of Bud Light cases. She wiped her moist forehead and brushed her raven black hair away from her deep green eyes as she grinned wide, exposing a perfectly white smile and mile-deep dimples on her apple cheeks. Maurice couldn't help looking at her large, hard nipples poking through her t-shirt. He tried to ignore them, but he found himself staring. He blushed. She batted her long eyelashes at him and grabbed ahold of the case of beer he was holding. Their hands touched. They were ice cold, but Maurice felt himself sweating. Ellen yanked the case of beer towards her hips and leaned into him, smiling as she kept her hypnotizing gaze locked. He swallowed hard and felt his penis press against his Dockers.

This is bad, man. Get your ass outta here, Mo. NOW!

His conscience spoke loud and clear, but his groin didn't agree and struggled even harder to be free. Ellen yanked the case of beer from his icy grip; it crashed to the concrete floor, and beer began to spread out under their shoes.

"Come on, baby, I've had my eye on you all night. You're wasting your time with that psycho bitch Ashley. She's not all there, honey." Ellen's bright eyes sparkled in the glow and her inviting smile drew his attention.

"Me? Well, babe, I just wanna *fuck* you." Her hand sprang forward and found his swollen crotch. His breath caught in his taut throat. Before he could react, she lunged at him and sunk her moist pink tongue into his surprised mouth as he fell backwards into the stacks of full kegs.

"Hey, what the hell are you doing?" Maurice protested, shoving Ellen away, but she stood fast and her hand didn't let go of his growing member. She lunged at him and tried to unzip his pants. He pulled back and pushed her away. She let go of her grip on his groin and smiled.

"Come on now, you have to know just who your fiancée is, don't you?" Ellen asked as she gained her balance, rubbing her already hard nipples. He forced himself to ignore them and focus on what was going on.

"What the hell are you talkin 'about?" he asked, and stepped back toward the cooler's door.

Then the cooler echoed with the sounds of screams and gunshots.

Chapter 12
"Helter Skelter"

The entire bar room was hell on earth. It was a slaughterhouse with a Liverpool soundtrack. *John* watched on with an aroused smile, compulsively rubbing the protruding bulge in his pants. His target was the thin blonde cowering behind the electronic dartboard. The fear fed his sexual urge. A long drip of drool fell from his gaping mouth and onto his chest. He wiped the spittle from his lips and zeroed in on his prey, his hand never leaving his throbbing package.

"Oh, there she is, there she is," *John* continued cooing as he swung the razor-sharp machete down on top of a man's head. The blade split the Buffalo Bills ball cap in half. The hat stuck to the blade as *John* kicked the rest of the man's body free. A wide-arcing sanguine path followed the limp body as it slid into the screaming crowd that was fighting to find an exit from the nightmare. Blood and grey matter showered them, and their luck was about to take a turn for the worse.

"Where you lil' rabbits runnin' off to?" *Ringo's* deep voice caught three young men and two girls as they smashed a window with a chair, trying desperately to make their escape. They froze in their tracks and all trembled with fear, bubbling large tears. *Ringo* tilted his head as a dog would, finding their fear-filled tears fascinating.

The young kid with one leg halfway out the window stopped and grabbed ahold of a short redheaded girl in front of him. His voice cracked as long streams of tears fell from his wide eyes.

"Hey, dude, I don't know what the hell you guys want but, hey... I... Uh..." His entire body shook and his head darted back and forth between the behemoth holding the gore-covered machete and the trembling girl in front of him. He was struggling with something, *Ringo* could tell, and he felt his malformed lips separate into a surreal smile as the twitchy youngster shoved the frightened girl toward him. *Ringo* laughed as he raised the shotgun, and laughed even more as the slug shattered the escaping lad's chest. The rest of them cried and begged for mercy. *Ringo* was having none of it. He shoved the shotgun back into the side holster.

"Come here, rabbit." He grabbed the redheaded girl in a headlock and pulled her in to his large body. She just collapsed. He saw a wet spot spreading through her jeans and a pool of yellow piss gathering underneath her. He chuckled and gave her a gentle squeeze.

"Silly rabbit." Large muscles in his arm flexed, almost tore his sleeve; the slack girl's eyes seemed to pop out of their sockets just as there was a loud crack. A shard of white vertebrae jabbed out from her neck, followed by warm, bright red blood and a dark brown liquid. It soaked through *Ringo's* jacket and he shook his head in disappointment.

"Stupid rabbit." He threw her limp body down, and it slumped to the wet floor. The other kids stared at their dead friend in horror and disbelief of what was happening all around them. Their bodies refused to move. That pleased *Ringo* and brought a smile back to his distorted face. Suddenly a loud shotgun blast exploded near his left ear and he fell to one knee in agonizing pain as he felt warm blood shoot from his ruptured eardrum. He watched as the other girl, wearing a Lady Gaga shirt, lost her guts. Her entire abdomen just disappeared in a burst of blood and ragged flesh.

"Stop toying with them. They aren't your wee pets, you tosser!" *Paul* looked down at the large man and shook her head. He grumbled and stood up, a bit woozy, and fought to keep his balance. Once the cute tweeting birds stopped their singing, he looked about for his next rabbit. He didn't have to look too long, as several staggering bar patrons shook with fear and tried to make their way out through the broken window. With a few flashes of the machete's blade, the shards of broken glass were pasted with blood and hanging flesh.

The smell of burnt meat filled the room. Grainy smoke billowed out from behind the bar, from the kitchen area. The food attendant lay dead in the doorway between the kitchen and the back bar. Bessie, the old woman, had a broken Jameson bottle jammed into her throat and her life's blood was congealing on the yellowing tiled floor underneath the rubber bar mat. *George* stepped onto the rotund woman's stomach, headed back to the smoky kitchen area, and chuckled as he grabbed a spatula and threw the burning hamburgers into the steel sink next to the large cooler. His pink tongue darted out from the mask and licked the hot fat from the spatula. It burned, but he paid it no mind and turned the corner, heading back around the bar towards the cooler door. Dying to get back into the action.

Chapter 13
"What You're Doing"

"Ah, come here, my precious." *John* hopped down from the bar and approached the terrified blonde who was hiding behind the pool table. She slipped behind the gigantic machine. A flood of bodies rushed between them, including Scooter, who saw the tall, masked man making his way toward the dartboard. He then glimpsed Ashley's long blonde hair. *No fuckin' way*, he thought, then pulled out his Buck knife and shoved Sacks out of the way. He forced his way through the panicked crowd.

A flurry of blows sent many frantic bar-goers tumbling and stumbling as *John* shot and disemboweled them along the path to his target. His treadless boots slipped on the blood and urine as he made his way toward the blonde. He was focused and didn't even notice the lanky form rushing toward him from his right. He lost his breath as he was smashed into the Svedka vodka sign hanging from the opposite wall. The neon sign exploded, sending shards of glass and metal flying. *John* felt the jagged glass penetrate the left side of his mask and puncture his skin. One piece barely missed slicing into his eye and blinding him. He fought to regain his balance and the lanky man brought the knife down toward his chest.

John sidestepped the blade, and it continued, lodging inside the dark wooden wall. He jammed the heel of his boot into the side of the tall man's knee and it made a sickly crunch, then gave way. Scooter crashed to the floor, grasping his knee in agony.

"Motherfucker, I'm gonna gut you like a–"

"Tsk, tsk, my good man." *John* knelt down and grabbed Scooter's scruffy chin. "Don't be a big blue meanie, for it will be I who will be doing the gutting this fine evening." He smiled and brought the dripping machete up to Scooter's throat in a slow, mocking motion.

The overly dramatic gesture gave Ashley the opportunity to make a break for it. She slowly, cautiously, stood up from behind the dartboard and ran for the deck that was still full of screaming people and total chaos. She almost made it to the corner of the pool table when *Paul's* small but lithe frame jumped in her way, blocking her escape.

"Where might you be scurrying off to, my sweet?" *Paul* quizzed, with one hand on her hip and the other shoving the shotgun in her face.

"I... Uh... Please, don't..." Ashley cried, and held her shaking hands to her face.

"Is this the one?" *Paul* called to *John*, who was busy toying with Scooter's busted-up knee. She didn't look away. She held the sawed-off shotgun perfectly motionless, a dead bead on Ashley's quivering head.

"Aye, she be the one," *John* said. His tone was filled with hate, laughter, and lust, all rolled up in a tight, five-word response. *Paul* always loved it when he spoke to her like that.

"She matches the photo, and the paperwork checks out," he finished as he stood up.

"Get the fuck away from her, you bitch!" Scooter screamed through the pain that was ravaging his shattered knee.

"Well, well, well. Look at the spunk in you, mate." *John's* voice rose, and he shook his head in approval. He dropped the slimy blade to his side and lifted the shotgun to Scooter's anguished face. He pulled the trigger. Scooter's entire head disappeared. Large pieces of ripped flesh, shattered bone, and grey matter splattered the Miller Lite 2010 NASCAR schedule poster on the wall behind him. The smell of cordite and blood made his erection harder.

"I hate spunk."

He sheathed the machete as the din of death and chaos reigned throughout the rest of the bar. *Ringo* and *George* were doing their pre-set tasks and laying waste to the entire crowd of the Torchlight Inn. The dreadful cries and pleas for mercy were being answered with the loud clamoring of shotgun blasts and the sick slap of steel on flesh. Those heavenly sounds made *John* a very, very happy man. The meat inside his trousers twitched with compiling excitement.

Chapter 14
"Help"

"Get down," Maurice whispered, and pointed toward the old floor of the cooler. The red and green Christmas lights broke the dim light of the cooler; with it came the sounds of gunfire. It seemed to him like a slaughterhouse out in the bar room. The cries of fear and the baying of the dying filled the small room. Maurice's hair stood up on the back of his neck and forearms. He knew that sound all too well and could feel the adrenaline and endorphins kicking in and coursing their way through his entire body.

Maurice shoved Ellen down onto the floor and followed her. He didn't have a clue what was going on out there, but he knew the gruesome sound and smell of death that was filling the cooler. He scanned the area for anything useful, and let out a small, disappointed breath when he couldn't find anything. Ellen just looked up at him with her wide, green doe-eyes that just cried out for help. He took a deep breath and gently opened up a case of beer, then slowly took out a bottle and held it like a knife. He crouched down and waited.

They stared in confusion as the metallic clunk of the cooler door's latch broke the heavy silence.

The heavy door closed slowly, and the din from hell went with it. Maurice could hear the padding of heavy feet and heavy breathing growing closer. He held the bottle, ready to strike. He could feel his sweat freezing as it rolled down his face and body. His muscles tensed as the form came around the rack full of cases of beer. He brought the bottle down onto the head of the figure as they rounded the corner. They let out a shrill, girlish cry as the bottle smashed. Whoever it was, they staggered backwards, grabbing their head.

"What the *fuc…*" Sackett – *Sacks* – belted as he fell to his knees amidst brown shards of broken glass and beer foam.

Maurice grabbed the large man and pulled him behind the safety of the large stacks of beer. He tried to brush away the broken bottle pieces.

"Man, I'm sorry… What the hell is going *on* out there?" he asked. He tried to hide his fear and thought for sure it didn't work.

"Ah, shit… Ya busted my goddamn noggin', man," Sackett whimpered and rubbed his head. He took his soaked ball cap off and shook it. He leaned against the wall of beer cases and tried to catch his breath.

"Sorry, sorry. Calm down and tell me what's going on." Maurice grabbed him by his shoulders and shook him.

"I…dunno, man… These crazy fuckers came in 'n started playin' some weird 60s music and shit, 'n then started shooting and cutting shit up." Sackett began to cry.

"For no reason?" Ellen chimed in. She leaned closer and wiped the beer and glass shards from Sackett's trembling head.

"I just told you… I don't know what the hell they want." Sackett's tears came down faster and stronger. He cupped his chubby cheeks in his hands and his entire body shook. Maurice knew the man was in shock and knew that he would not get any more useful information from him. He looked about frantically, but didn't know what for. Any brilliant answer wasn't forthcoming, and he knew it.

Ellen cleaned the glass out of Sackett's hair and tried to dry him off with the bar towel she kept tucked into her tight jeans.

"Okay…okay… Do you have any weapons on you?" Maurice asked.

"I, uh, um… I…" Sackett fumbled and looked about, confused.

"Ya know…a gun or a goddamn knife?" Maurice grabbed Sackett's jiggling face and forced his gaze onto him. His fat cheeks pinched and he made an exaggerated fish-lips face. His eyes were wide, and his pupils were dilated.

"Uh…yeah, I…think so." He fumbled around his waist and let out a giggle as he pulled out the biggest knife Maurice had ever seen. And he had seen many blades in his short life.

"Nice." Maurice took the Bowie knife from Sackett's beer- and sweat-covered face and gently patted him on the cheeks. "Now we have something."

"What are we going to do?" Ellen yanked on Maurice's shoulder, nearly knocking him over.

He caught his balance and shot her a sharp look. "We don't know what's going on out there, and *his* drunken ass isn't going to help us at all," he said, pointing to Sackett.

"A bunch of crazy, fuck…" Sackett's words flitted off into the cold air of the cooler. The yellow light flickered and the muffled shouts and screams still penetrated their icy prison. Maurice knew he needed to do something, and fast. It was damn cold and his muscles had tightened up. He stared at the large blade and it caught the flickering light in its reflection. He could see his own panicked eyes staring back at him.

He put his ear against the cold door and didn't have to strain to hear the carnage raging beyond it.

Chapter 15
"Do You Want to Know a Secret?"

"Well hello, love," *John* said, and swaggered toward Ashley.

"Wh-ooo…*are* y-ooou?" she squeaked, struggling against *Paul's* powerful grip on her hair. Her wide brown eyes flickered with tears and refracted the myriad Christmas lights strung haphazardly about the bar's ceiling and walls.

"Oh, no, no, no. The more important question for this fine wintry evening is…" He jumped in close to her face, gently lifted a long strand of her blonde hair and sniffed it, then let it fly freely back down to her quivering shoulder. *Paul* released her and stepped back, letting her leader take control.

"Who are YOU?" *John* suddenly snatched the tumbling golden hair and yanked her head into his chest. Staring deep into her crying eyes, he laughed.

"You have two seconds to let her go, boy, or I'm gonna wipe the goddamned floor with all your sorry asses." Daddy's booming voice startled *John,* and he jumped back, but kept a forceful grip on the screaming girl's golden locks.

Behind Daddy came five or six large men, all wielding pistols of various sizes and calibers. Their intent was obvious, and *John*'s erection returned, twitched, and looked forward to finally having a challenge. He yanked Ashley in front of him, hiding behind her. He stepped backward toward the bar. And he was happy.

"Well, well, welcome to the show, gentlemen," *John* mocked and pulled Ashley closer to him. He jammed the barrel of the shotgun into her quivering mouth, shattering teeth and slicing her pink gums wide open. Blood poured out of her mouth, ran down the barrel, and covered her chin and the front of her shirt. She cried out in pain.

He smiled. "Step right this way."

"Oh, I'll be doin' some steppin' all right, you peckerhead sumbitch. I'll be steppin' a mudhole in your scrawny freak ass!" Daddy screamed, and began to run toward *John*. One of the large men behind him grabbed his tensed arm and yanked him back as *John* shoved the barrel of the sawed-off shotgun deeper into Ashley's bloody mouth. Her muffled scream and the man's forceful grip caused the old farmer to halt in his tracks.

A blast of gunfire took out the pool table light and sent sparks, metallic shrapnel, and plastic flying. *George* stood against the wall next to the pool table, his shotgun smoking from the blast. The rest of the men scrambled backward towards the double doors of the outdoor deck. Splinters of wood filled the air as they took cover.

"Boy, *George*, what a bloody excellent shot," *John* said, and yanked Ashley backward, rubbing her breast against his raging hard-on.

"Why thank you, good sir." *George* nodded and cocked the shotgun, sending the empty shell casing bouncing off the wall and onto the slick, gore-covered floor.

"And for my next trick…" *George* teased, and fired three rounds into the wall next to the door of the deck. A loud groan blasted back, answering the call of the shotgun blast. A short, scrawny man stumbled into the doorway, holding his stomach. A large red stain appeared, rapidly spreading like a napkin soaking up a wonderful red wine. The gaunt man's face turned pale and he fell to his knees in the center of the double doors. *George* took aim and made sure the dying man didn't suffer. It looked as though a crimson watermelon erupted in one burst. The man's face and head disappeared into the darkness of the makeshift room. Screams of horror and anger made the shredded body, collapsing onto the floor, inaudible. *George* chuckled and reloaded.

"What's the matter, lads? Don't have enough stones to come out and play?" *John* teased, gyrating his polyester-covered hips against Ashley's shaking rear end. She tried to scream but the high-pitched cry for help got lost amongst the din of all the dying, gunshots, and the haunting sounds of "With a Little Help From My Friends."

"I'm gonna fuck your world up, you piece of shit," Daddy screamed. His voice, full of rage, boomed over the chaos and music. *John* just let out a belly laugh and motioned with his head toward *Ringo*.

"Some cover would be lovely, if you please." He looked at the overturned table behind *Ringo*. The big man yanked his machete free from a struggling grizzled farmer and the old man's slimy intestines came with it. He flicked the blade, trying to free it from the sausage-like mass, but it clung to it as if glued. He repeatedly shook the blade, but the bloody tube just kept coming out of the dying man, like some horrific magic trick gone wrong.

"'Allo. Would you mind stopping all that shite and get that bloody table over here." *John*'s voice held no humor or appreciation for the comical scene the big lummox was displaying in front of him.

"Right." *Ringo* hung his head and his broad shoulders slumped as he yanked the machete free from the remaining bloody intestines and sheathed it in place on his wide leather belt. He then hurriedly snatched the table up and ran to where *John* stood, tapping his foot. He set the table down and knelt behind it. His colossal frame barely fit behind the large bar table. *John* shook his head and yanked the flailing girl to the bar's sticky floor.

"Stay here, crumpet," *John* said. He took a black plastic zip-tie, yanked her hands to the tarnished brass foot railing of the bar, and secured her. She cried out as the plastic sliced deep into her thin wrists, and blood ran down and joined the thick layer of crimson already covering the floor. *John* ignored her, picked up the shotgun from the gore on the floor, and wiped it on Ashley's heaving back as she retched. He kicked her in the ribs, and she let loose a large *woof* of air and then collapsed, landing with a splash on the wet floor.

"All right, fellows, let's give these buggers an early Happy Christmas gift." *John* aimed from his squat position behind the table and fired into the doorway of the deck. The others followed suit.

The small bar once again filled with smoke and the smell of cordite, sweat, and panic. The Fearsome Four all let out a collective laugh. It echoed all the way into the cooler. Somehow, the chilling laughter was much colder this time.

Chapter 16
"I'll Get You"

"You motherfuckers are done," Daddy said through gritted, chew-stained teeth. "I swear to Christ, I will skull-fuck you *all*." He double checked the bullets in his nickel-plated Smith & Wesson .29 and slammed the cylinder shut with satisfaction, then spat a wad of brackish chunks on the red-soaked floor. Looking across the doorway at the remaining partygoers, Daddy tried to assess the situation. He counted four armed freaks around the bar, but wasn't sure if there were more somewhere else killing his friends and family. Surely all the tough as nails farmers and jocks would have stormed them if there were only two. Or so he'd hoped. Who *knew* anymore, with the pussified world they all lived in? He grumbled and stared down at the bloody mess that was once Butch VanLaken. His body still twitched and nerves kicked his leg out like it was starting his old Harley. Daddy's grasp grew tighter on the walnut grip of his monster pistol. He had two men behind him: Ronnie Cauwels and Sammy Sizemore. Both worked on his farm and were damn hard-working men. Daddy wasn't so sure how they were about fighting with guns and killing, but he didn't have time to worry about that shit. He looked at them and Ronnie was looking pissed and ready for bear. Sammy, on the other hand, looked like he was just nailed in the ass by his prize-winning bull. Daddy then noticed the puddle growing under the chubby man's feet. He shook his head in disgust and focused on Ronnie, whose large brown eyes seemed to want to burst. A huge blue vein popped out of his forehead and throbbed at his temple. His thin upper lip twitched. Daddy smiled at that. He knew the scrawny scrapper would have his back. He held up his pistol and pointed at the cylinder.

"Double-check your ammo, boys," he whispered, and turned back toward the fidgeting figures across the doorway. The smell of gunpowder filled the room. He made the same motion to the four men fighting for hiding space alongside the other wall.

They fiddled about with their pistols, and he hoped they understood what he meant. His friends were good folks, but some of them were dumber than Bachman's bitch, who swam across the river to get a drink of water. His daughter was in deep shit, and he didn't have time to deal with or worry about them. He took a deep breath, held up three fingers to the other group, and brought them down as he mouthed the countdown.

Two... Three...

"Die, you sick *fuck*!" Daddy bellowed as he turned the corner and let loose a volley of shots from his hand-cannon. The others followed behind the big man, guns blazing.

Chapter 17
"Wait"

"Sounds like the damn streets of Durham out there. What the hell is going on?" Maurice said, with his ear pressed against the frost-covered metal door of the cooler. He turned back toward Ellen and Sackett, who was dabbing his wounded head.

"All right, I'm going out there. You guys can do whatever you want. But my fiancée is in the middle of all that shit and she needs me." Maurice forced the words out and took a deep breath.

"I don't think that's such a good idea," Ellen said, clutching his arm and trying to pull him away from the door. He resisted and broke free.

"Screw that, she needs me, goddammit." He glared at her and she backed away, hitting the large stacks.

"I'm goin' with ya." Sackett looked up, tossed the bloody rag to the floor, and reached behind his back. He pulled out a Glock .45 and held it up, smiling.

"Where the hell did you get that?" Maurice stared at him in disbelief.

"Ya didn't think I was gonna give this baby to you, did ya? I may be dumb, but I ain't *stupid*." He laughed with a snort and kissed the flat black barrel.

"Well…just don't shoot me in the back, okay?" Maurice ordered, shaking his head.

"You got it, chief." Sackett winked, gripped the pistol with both hands, and readied himself behind Maurice. He could see Sackett trembling and still sweating inside the 38-degree cooler.

"Ellen, you stay here and keep trying to get a signal, and if you get one, fucking call 911, got it?" Maurice nodded at her, then turned and gripped the cold metal door handle.

"Yeah, but I don't think it's gonna work in here." Her voice was soft, almost a whisper. Maurice didn't even notice or care. The love of his life was out there in the slaughterhouse, and she needed him. He took a deep breath, pulled the long handle toward him, and shoved the heavy door open.

Chapter 18
"Twist and Shout"

Daddy's first shot from the long-barreled pistol caught *George* in the hand and it turned every finger into a bloody mush; his shotgun fell to the floor. Daddy smiled and let loose another shot. It splintered the wall next to *George*'s stunned head. Sharp splinters of wood sprayed into the air and *George* ducked for cover behind the corner. Daddy smiled again, then jumped behind the pool table.

"Come get some, motherfuckers!" Daddy shouted, and peeked over the felt top of the pool table. He could see one form behind an upturned table and the blood splatter on the wall where his first shot had found a home. The big man liked the sight of blood and the smell of gunpowder. He waited to see what other dumb bastard would rear his ugly head so he could blow it off. His little baby lay hurt, and he wasn't about to let anything more happen to the last precious thing he had on this planet. He breathed deep; he could feel his heart race.

"Die!" Ronnie yelled, and let loose with random shots that tore into the bar and shattered several bottles of vodka and whiskey. All three shots missed their mark and left him exposed in the middle of the pool room. *John* chuckled as he pulled the trigger. A bright muzzle flash filled the small room and a pixilated red mist exited Ronnie's back; his bulging eyes just stared forward, not focusing on anything as he dropped to his knees in a heap. Part of his lung hung out through the back of his leather vest, and Daddy did all he could to keep from puking up the night's consumption of beer and whiskey. It didn't work; he let loose a stream of brown and yellow vomit that splattered against the dark walls. He wiped his mouth and watched his friend's lifeblood slowly spread across the white and black checkerboard floor. He tightened his grip on the Smith & Wesson and spat on the floor. The dark brown spittle mixed with the deep red of Ronnie's blood and turned to a brackish clump. Daddy felt bile rise in his burning throat and held back the next round of puke.

"That's one down, mate. Who's next?" *John* laughed as Ronnie let out a death rattle and slid to the floor, his wide eyes fixed on Daddy, who swallowed hard and prayed for the first time in years.

"Get in here, you goddamn pussies!" Daddy bellowed to the men hiding in the shadows of the deck. He heard low whimpers and sobbing. That was the only noise coming from the dark room. He prayed harder.

"I'm guessing you want this precious naughty bit of crumpet I have. Is that correct, mate?" *John* taunted, and winked back at Ashley's unmoving form on the bar floor.

"You piece of shit. I will *kill* you if you harm one hair on her head." Daddy scowled and looked over the top of the pool table.

"Oh, bother, I've already done more than harm her hair, lad. She may need some major dental work, but trust me, she will have bigger concerns than her pearly whites by the time this night is over." *John's* jovial tone dropped and became somber. He looked back at Ashley's limp form and ejected the spent shell. It ricocheted off the table and landed on the slick floor.

Daddy's chest felt like it was being crushed between two eighteen-wheelers and his left arm tingled. His breath left him and sweat oozed from every pore and soaked through his already wet clothes. He was all too familiar with these symptoms. It wasn't his first ride on this bull. His shaky hand fought with the flap of his shirt pocket and he yanked it off in frustration and desperation. Daddy shoved his sweat-covered hand inside, pulled out a handful of small white pills, and jammed them into his mouth. He swallowed hard, took a deep breath and let it out. Springing up fast, he brought the large pistol with him, and aimed toward the sound of the Brit's voice.

As he reached his full height and brought the handgun down, he jumped back as the far end of the pool table quickly rose up and rushed toward him. He back-pedaled and smashed into the wall behind him. The large table came down on him in a flash. The small room filled with grunting and laughter as Daddy found himself pinned against the wall, and he couldn't move. He knew he was screwed.

"Shall I make a pancake out of 'um, *John*?" *Ringo* huffed, his muscles flexed as he shoved the heavy pool table against the wall. "I want to see his squishes come out, like that last mission in Memphis." *Ringo* giggled and looked at *John* for approval.

"Certainly, lad, let's see what comes out of him if you squeeze really hard," *John* said. "But go much slower this time."

"Aye, Mr. *John*." *Ringo* flexed his enormous arms and slowly pushed the pool table. Loud screeching sounds ushered forth as the metal from the sides of the table dug into the linoleum floor. Daddy realized the trouble he had breathing a few moments ago was nothing compared to what was coming.

Chapter 19
"Happiness is a Warm Gun"

Maurice Ware had been witness to many horrifying things in his young life. But growing up in the violent, gang-ridden streets of Durham paled in comparison to what lay before him as he slowly cracked open the cooler door. What he saw caused his mind and soul to pause with fear and disbelief. He felt the heavy body of Sackett behind him and shoved the large redneck backward.

"What the hell's goin' on, man?" Sackett asked, and hopped up and down, trying to see anything through the small opening.

"Shut up," Maurice ordered, shoving the big man backwards. He turned his attention back toward the smoky haze of the dimly lit bar room. Sackett staggered back into Ellen, knocking her to the icy floor.

"Watch it, lard ass." She shot him a look and staggered back to her feet.

"Sorry, Ell, I... I didn't mean..." Sackett's round cheeks flushed, and he stared at the floor.

"Knock that shit off, both of you," Maurice hissed, never taking his eyes off the gore on the other side of the door. "There's some seriously messed up shit going on out there..." His words trailed off and he fought to inhale. The time to act was *now*. He looked back at Ellen and Sackett and reached out his shaking hand.

"Give me the gun, Sackett. I don't trust your dumb ass." His face illustrated to Sackett that it wasn't really a question.

"Fuck that noise, boss." Sackett shook his head. His jowls jiggled and trailed behind the rest of his rotund head. "This is my baby, and you ain't gonna have it. No way." He shuffled his large, booted feet in defiance and pulled the gun away from Maurice, still shaking his head no.

"Ah, the hell with this shit," Maurice said. He gripped the handle tighter and did the same with the large knife in his other hand. "Let's go." He shoved the large door open slowly and kept low. He motioned for Sackett to follow him. The chubby guy did as ordered and, with a smug grin on his face, held the pistol out in front of him, parallel to the ground, just like they do in the movies. Maurice shook his head in frustration.

The cooler door only opened up a couple feet when something blocked it. He tried to push it open, and when he did, a gigantic form fell down in front of him, blocking the entrance. A rusty, bitter smell assaulted his nostrils as he squatted down to examine the body. His eyes darted to the motion beyond the door, and the sounds of metal screeching and digging into something metallic and shrill made him cringe. Maurice hoped no one noticed and nervously turned his attention to the body blocking the doorway.

He grabbed what he thought was the shoulder of a male and felt the body soaked in a sticky liquid. It was warm and slimy, like the skin that formed on top of the warm pudding his mother used to make for him when he wasn't feeling well. The rubbery substance stuck to his hand, and with it came the putrid smell of feces and second-time whiskey. He felt bile rush up into his mouth and he forced himself to swallow.

"Come on, boss, let's go kick some freak ass." Sackett's clumsy attempt at whispering made Maurice shudder.

"Shut the fuck up, you idiot." Maurice let go of the slimy body and tried to flick the goo from his hand. It refused to let go. He fought back more bile and stood up. He looked out into the bar, but could only see the pool table up at one end. A gigantic monster of a man in a long leather trench coat leaned heavily on the table, shoving forward. A slick, shiny film of what Maurice thought looked like blood was splattered on the coat. More vomit roiled in his throat.

"What the hell we waitin' for, boss?" Sackett's shaky voice broke Maurice's gaze at the blood-slathered man and he turned to face him.

"It's worse than I thought. You really need to give me that gun, and I'm fixin' to knock your podunk ass out to get it." Maurice snatched the gun from Sackett's sweaty hands. "There are some bad mothers out there, man. This isn't some damn turkey shoot." He wiped his goo-slathered hand on Sackett's t-shirt and turned his attention back to the scene outside the cooler. "No turkey shoot at all." He stepped over the bloody corpse and ducked behind the bar, not really knowing what to do next.

Chapter 20
"Ask Me Why"

"Feeling a bit cramped, are ya, tough guy?" *John* quipped as he left the safe confines of the upturned table.

"*Paul, George*, finish up with them and take care of the wankers tossing off out there," *John* shouted, and pointed his shotgun at the opening to the outdoor deck. He hoped some fool would pop their head around the corner. He could hear the big redneck fighting to breathe under the pressure of the pool table and the crushing strength of *Ringo*. It made him smile. It was a good night for smiling.

"Fuck off and die, asshole," Daddy threatened as best he could between the wall and pool table.

"Now, now, good sir. One should threaten no one in your, um…position," *John* chortled through the mask, tasting the anger in the trapped man's eyes. It permeated the death-filled air, and it gave him stirrings. Again, he smiled.

"I don't give a flyin' fuck in a rollin' donut, asshole, if you hurt my daughter, I'll *KILL YOU!*" Blood flew from his smothered mouth and his words rang funny, like a little child whose cheeks were being squeezed by an annoying aunt.

George and *Paul* rushed to *John*'s side, raised their shotguns, and slowly approached the darkened outdoor deck. *George* wrapped a bar towel around his mangled hand. Bright red blood immediately soaked through it. He still favored the flesh mound of a hand and, resting the shotgun in the crook of his elbow, he followed *Paul*.

"Make it quick, we have business to tend to, if you please." *John*'s tone was playful, yet focused. He was more than pleased when the blue-tarped room lit up with a flurry of muzzle flashes and cries for mercy and pain. It was like a visceral and auditory Viagra for him. He relished in it.

"Why the hell are you doin' this, you piece of shit?" Daddy forced the words out and more blood trickled from the corner of his mashed face.

"*Why*, you ask?" *John* stepped close and leaned into the big man's flushed, purple and pink face. "That's a fair question." He leaned against the wall and put his hand on the man's shoulder. "It is your daughter. She is the reason you all have to die tonight," *John* whispered into Daddy's ear. A small droplet of deep red blood ran from his inner ear and fell onto his bib overalls.

"My…*daughter*? Ashley-Girl? Wh… *Why*?" Daddy's body went slack and a lone tear glistened in his eye and rolled down his bruised cheek, mixing with the blood running from his ear. The pool table was slowly crushing and cracking each rib. He let out a small whimper. *Ringo* didn't let up the pressure.

"She… What did she…*do*?" Daddy's words came out in a low hush and his head bobbed back and forth. *John* could tell he was about to lose consciousness. "You leave her…alone… I gonna…kill…" His words grew softer and his body went slack.

"Stop." *John* held his hand up to *Ringo* and the big man did as he was told.

"Oh dear, dear Big Daddy." *John* shook his head and patted the waning man's red cheek. "You see, your precious *Ashley-Girl* isn't so innocent." He reached inside his leather trench coat and pulled out a folded sheet of paper; he leaned the shotgun against the blood-soaked wall.

"Wha…ar…yo…talkin'–"

"You and I both know that your sweet little lass isn't *yours*, don't we?" *John*'s mask touched the side of Daddy's swollen and bloodied face. He unfolded the paper and shoved it into the wavering man's face. He mumbled incoherently.

"No, she is not a Vanslycke at all, is she?" *John* said, pointing to the paper. "You *can* read, can't you, Daddy?" *John* teased. "Well then, you can see that this is a birth certificate, correct?" *John* pressed the paper into Daddy's slack face. "Well, this is proof that your *oh so darling* girl, lying over there in a bloody pile, isn't your flesh and blood, and this other document is her adoption papers." He pulled the man's head up with a yank of his hair. "And on this document, it says where she came from and her *REAL* last name," *John* said. "You remember who she was, don't you? You do *remember* her real last name, Big Daddy?" His voice rose in timbre and volume. *Paul* and *George* returned, covered head to toe in blood. The deck behind them lay in a haunting silence.

"It's that minor fact that led us here tonight, my dying friend," *John* continued. "You see, we have a mission, well, a campaign really." He looked back at the others and waved his hand in a sweeping motion toward them. "And you and her, well, and the rest of you backwater sods, have to pay the price."

"Do you know what date it is today? Hmmm?" *John* said. He feigned waiting for a response that he knew wouldn't be forthcoming. "I didn't think so, but considering the bloodline of your beaten sweetness over there, you would think you'd be aware of what a significant day today is." He leaned in and dropped the papers to the floor, where they stuck to the mucky surface, and red splotches slowly appeared through them.

"Today is December 8th, my good man... And do you know what happened on that date, and why your little precious is going to be slaughtered tonight?" *John* straightened and snatched up his shotgun. "Still not ringing any bells?" he said, and sauntered back toward Ashley's prone body. "The brilliance of John Lennon was snuffed out of existence on this date, Big Daddy, and in case the lack of oxygen to that already small brain of yours still isn't making the connection, let me make it easy for you." He lowered the shotgun into Ashley's slowly rising belly and turned his gaze back to Daddy, who slowly raised his head in protest. "On the bloody document, her name wasn't Ashley Vanslycke. It was Julia. Julia *Chapman*." He shoved the barrel deep into the girl's limp body until blood bubbled up and pooled around the steel. "She was next on the list of Mark David Chapman's family members. And I applaud their efforts, and yours, of course, in trying to hide and bury that dark fact. It took many hours of research, and we've left a pretty long, bloody trail on our way to find her." He looked back up at Daddy, whose burning stare could cut *John* into pieces.

"But, alas, the Chapman line ends here... It ends tonight."

The shotgun blast obliterated the tense air and disintegrated the girl's abdomen. Large chunks of bloody flesh, yellow fat, and pieces of intestines, liver, and lungs filled the air and splattered against the old oak bar. What seemed like an ocean of blood poured out from her gaping wound and set to covering the small pool room floor.

"*Ringo*, finish him," *John* ordered, and shoved the shotgun into the holster on his back. He reached inside his jacket and pulled out the machete.

"We have work to do, gents."

Chapter 21
"You're Gonna Lose That Girl"

"NO!" Maurice fell to the floor behind the bar as the shotgun went off. His ears rang and he saw white flashes as pain filled his head. Shaking his head to clear the concussive stun, he didn't know what it was, but his gut told him something bad just happened. He looked around as he lay there, right next to the bloody remains of the old lady bartender. Her vacant eyes peered right into his. Caked blood covered her entire face, and he realized he was lying in the rest of her blood; the slick liquid seeped into his clothes. It was then that his breath left him. Sackett fell on top of him, nearly crushing his ribs.

"Get the hell off me," he whispered and wheezed. He shoved the big man off and slowly crouched.

"Sorry, boss. Sorry." Sackett rolled to one side and rose to a knee next to him. He looked at the old dead woman, and Maurice thought the fat kid was going to cry or puke, maybe both. He looked around for something, anything, to help him. He thought he heard sawing or cutting. Like something he used to hear at the local butchers' shop his uncle ran back in Durham. His stomach turned again and something inside him knew it wasn't good. He didn't think, he didn't fear; he just sprang up, holding the pistol in front of him with two hands and prepared to fire at anything that moved.

When he stood, he saw the carnage, and it made his soul weep. He prayed to God and hoped He was listening, but something told him all the dead and dying souls inside this small bar already had Him busy. He saw a big muscle-bound man in black leather, pushing an upturned pool table into the wall. His heart skipped as he realized it was Daddy being crushed between the table and the wall. Blood covered the floor, and the Christmas lights created ghastly reflections in the sanguine pool. Two other leather-clad figures stood in the yellow light of the bar. He had little time to analyze, but he could swear that they wear wearing Beatles masks – they *were George, Paul,* and *Ringo.* It was *them.* However, if they were there, where was *John?* he wondered as his hands trembled at the surreal scene playing out before him.

"Drop your fucking guns!" Maurice shouted. He saw *George* drop to one knee and raise a shotgun at him. Maurice pulled the trigger. The gun roared in his hands, and the bullet found a home in the figure wearing the George mask's mouth. Blood and skull fragments exploded out the back of his head. The shotgun dropped to the floor and the limp body quickly followed. Maurice pivoted and saw the diminutive figure donned in the Paul McCartney mask raise a shotgun and fire. He ducked down behind the bar in time, but Sackett wasn't so lucky. The slug tore into his barrel chest and sent his heart and lungs splashing against the top-shelf liquor behind him. His eyes bulged, and he dropped the big knife to the floor, then collapsed in a heap next to Maurice.

"Oh, it looks like we have a *live* one, mates," a lilting voice said from the other side of the bar. Maurice leaned over, snagged the knife, and shoved it into his belt. He stared up at the top of the bar, just waiting.

He couldn't believe what was happening. This was supposed to be a wonderful trip. A time to celebrate his engagement to the most amazing woman he'd ever met. Yet here he was, lying in a pool of blood, surrounded by dead people with some kind of psychotic Beatles tribute-band brandishing shotguns like machetes. *What the fuck?* kept repeating in his flurrying mind. Then the image of Ashley came rushing back to him and his heart about shattered into a million pieces. Where was she? Was she okay? The possible answers to those questions filled him with fear.

"Come on out and play. You have one of ours and we took one of yours," the voice called, and it sounded close...*very* close. "You see, hero. No one here gets out of here alive."

Maurice got to his knees and made his way to the swinging bar top. Looking up, he saw the reflection of the freaks in the Labatt's Blue mirror on the wall above the taps. He needed to do this just right. He tried to force the image of Ashley, lying dead amongst all the other slaughtered patrons of the Torchlight Inn, out of his mind, but the pain in his chest was far worse than any bullet or machete could inflict. He would take out as many of those sorry-ass freaks as he could before they got him. He thought he had left the violent "thug" life behind on the dirty streets of North Carolina. He was wrong. Maurice squeezed the grip on the Glock. He checked Sackett's pockets for ammunition. He felt sadness engulf him as he rifled through the dead fat man's pockets. Tears filled his eyes as he found two full clips tucked inside the man's back pocket.

"Thanks, buddy," he whispered, shoving the clips into his front pants pocket.

"You might as well make it easy, sport, and surrender. You're as good as dead anyway, so let's cut to the chase, pardon the pun." The voice chortled, and the remaining *Beatles* joined in. The sound of sawing and cutting continued. Maurice's stomach ached and wanted to expel the night's consumption. He fought it back down and acted.

When he flipped the heavy bar top open, dove into the pool table room, and crashed into the pinball machine, Maurice couldn't believe his eyes. He slid on the slick, blood-covered floor. Before him knelt a slim figure in a long leather trench coat with a machete in one hand and a blue jean-clad leg in the other. Ragged flesh and nerves dangled from it and blood poured out, adding to the quarts already covering the entire room.

John turned toward Maurice, chucked the dismembered limb at him, and sprang up. The bloody stump caught Maurice in the shoulder and he spun backwards. He tried to right himself, but *John* was upon him. Maurice fired the gun, and it tore into the charging Beatle, who pinwheeled backward.

Maurice fought to get to his feet and took cover behind the pinball machine.

"A load of bollocks you are, lad. Excellent shot." The wounded *John* dabbed his shoulder and nodded in approval.

"Stay back, you sick fuck!" Maurice shouted, and aimed the pistol at the wounded Beatle.

"Let me at 'em, Mr. *John*," Ringo said. The large mammoth of a man growled and stepped forward. The wounded *Lennon* held his hand up, stopping the oaf in his tracks.

"No... He's *mine*," he said, and jerked the blood and sinew from the blade of his machete as he slowly approached Maurice.

"Come get some, bitch," Maurice said, and aimed the pistol at *John*'s chest. He looked down where *John* was standing. Something caught his attention, something familiar. The body on the floor, the one the sick fuck was dismembering, was wearing clothes he recognized. He glimpsed something shining in the light. It was a ring. It was Ash's. It hit him like a Mack truck.

"Ashley..." A searing pain awoke him from his momentary paralysis, and he reached for his side. *John* stood before him with bright red blood dripping from his blade. Maurice looked down and saw his side was sliced clean open and fresh blood spilled down his leg and onto the floor. He could see the raw meat and yellow-colored fat hanging loose. Once again, white flashes ruled his vision. He staggered backward and grabbed at the wound. His left side flashed with pain, and the pistol clunked to the floor. His eyes flashed with white and sharp pinpricks of pain punctured his side. He staggered backward into the *Lord of the Rings* pinball machine. It dinged and some ominous voice spoke from it. Maurice's hearing became muddled.

"Was that Chapman bitch yours?" *John* said, and slowly approached Maurice. He twirled the long blade like a baton and tilted his masked head as he closed in.

"*Chapman*... Wha...what? I don't know what the hell you're *talkin'* about," Maurice shouted, and forced himself to stand up straight.

"It's no matter. They all had to pay the price. We are here to right the wrongs this world has ignored." *John* raised the machete.

Maurice bared his teeth and charged, knocking him to the floor. His mind raced, and the tears blinded him. *She's dead*, he kept repeating in his mind. His sorrow was cut short as *John* grabbed him by the throat and squeezed. He could hear laughter from off to his left. The other two Beatle assholes were really enjoying this insanity. He landed a punch to the masked man's face and blood flew out from the mouth hole.

"C'mon, Mister *John*, let me at 'em!" Maurice heard the big man beg. It made him smile. He threw another punch, but the lanky man blocked it and squeezed harder with his other hand. Maurice knew he was a dead man, but he was sure as hell going to make these psychotic shitbags pay the price. He wasn't getting any air and knew he only had a few seconds left.

Maurice thrust his knee up and slammed it into *John*'s groin. *John* let out a howl and curled his legs up, which forced Maurice upwards, so Maurice pulled back and landed a blow to the writhing man's nose. He heard a loud crunch and blood poured from the nostril-holes in the mask, painting the chalky-white latex red. *John* went slack and his hand released Maurice's throat and *John* fell limply to the floor. He rolled off the unconscious man toward the overturned table, came up on one knee, and prepared for the other nut house rejects to attack.

The big man and much smaller woman stared down at their incapacitated leader and froze. Maurice could feel the adrenaline kick in. He could feel his heartbeat speed up, but his mind grew clear. He saw things in slow motion. It had been a long time since he'd felt that way. He'd missed it. He scanned the room and saw the body of the guy wearing the George Harrison mask. Blood covered him and the surrounding floor. Then he saw the shotgun lying in a pool of crimson, and he knew he had to get to it.

The two leather-clad murderers saw his intentions. They stared at Maurice and tensed. Maurice glowered back at them, then at the gun.

One... Two... THREE! He dove for the shotgun. They jumped toward him. A loud crashing noise came from behind Maurice and it forced the two assailants to pause. Maurice's hand found purchase on the wet shotgun and he rolled backward into the wall. A loud scream filled the room and all three of them looked for the source.

"God, *no...*" Maurice uttered, and chambered the next round.

Chapter 22
"Golden Slumbers"

"Ellen, NO!" Maurice shouted. She flung the cooler door open, saw the carnage, and freaked out. Ellen snatched a bottle of Jameson whiskey from the bar, shattered the bottom of it, and ran hell-bent-for-leather behind the bar, toward the exit. She didn't have a snowball's chance in hell, Maurice thought, and tears continued to blur his vision.

"I'll get the bitch! You tend to *Jules Winfield,* here," *Paul* ordered, and sheathed her shotgun. She pulled out her machete and headed on an intercept course toward the end of the bar.

"On it, luv," *Ringo* said, slapping the flat of the machete's blade against his gloved palm. His gigantic frame cast a long, wide shadow over Maurice, and he prepared for the worst. The big man slowly approached him and he raised the shotgun and stood up.

"Back the fuck up, *Magilla Gorilla,*" Maurice said. "One more step and you'll be fixin' a hole of your own."

"No need for violence now, mate." *Ringo* side-stepped toward the upright pool table. "We just had some rubbish we had to remove."

"Keep flapping your gums, big man, and your face is going to look like some of your goddamn bangers and mash." Maurice slowly stepped forward toward the big man, who was now leaning against the pool table.

"Well, the way I see it, you have the gun, so what can this lil' blade do to you?" The big man continued to slap the machete against his palm.

"You're not as dumb as you look, *Ringo,*" Maurice said, keeping his aim on his attacker's chest.

A piercing scream broke Maurice's focus, and he spun to see the lady dressed as Paul McCartney yank Ellen down to the ground by her long black hair. It was a move he never should have made.

Maurice found himself on the ground with the shotgun he'd just had in his hands pointed at him. Swallowing hard, he glared up at the behemoth standing over him. He whispered the Lord's Prayer and shot the big man a defiant stare. He had lost everything this vile night, but the last thing he would give up was his pride.

"Shoot me, you big shitbag. What are ya waiting for? Permission? You big pussy." Maurice spat. He heard Ellen's cries and the sound of a struggle, but knew he had his own death to deal with. He lifted his chin as *Ringo* tucked the cold barrel under it and pushed it up. "What? You need a woman to tell you what to do?" He knew it was a gamble, but it was all he had.

"Shut the hell up!" *Ringo* shouted.

The sounds of a vicious struggle behind him caused Maurice to jump underneath the aim of the big man's shotgun. A slight movement from behind the pool table caught his attention, and he tried to calm his breathing. There seemed to be one last hope in this cesspool of sorrow.

"I'm going to end this, right here and now. Say good night, *Gracie.*" The big man leaned down and shoved the heavy 12-gauge into Maurice's throat.

Ringo suddenly stood up straight, dropped his massive arms, and let the gun clank to the floor. His masked face stared straight ahead at the bar. He looked like a marionette as Maurice looked on. The big man collapsed to his knees as Daddy pulled the long blade of his Bowie knife away. The fresh, dark red blood caught the glint of the Christmas lights in its reflection and Daddy, too, fell in a heap on the floor of the bloody bar.

Maurice crawled over to Daddy and grabbed his limp arm. He rolled him over. "Hang in there, we're gonna be okay," he said, but he could tell by Daddy's chalky-white skin color that he'd lost too much blood. Daddy had saved his life. He felt the tears come again, but this time they were in shame for judging the man and all of Ashley's family. *No time for that shit*, he thought, and caught Daddy forcing a weak smile. Daddy motioned with a weak wave for him to come closer. Maurice leaned in and put his ear to the dying man's mouth. Daddy grabbed his hand, held it tight, and pulled him in close.

"Run, dumb ass…"

Daddy smiled, and Maurice caught a tear running down the burly man's bearded jowls. He looked back and saw *Paul* put a bullet in Ellen's head. He knew he had to go, and he did.

It wasn't until he busted through the blue tarp and scaled down the deck into the waist-deep snow that he realized just how fucked up he was. Blood was pouring out from the pulsating wound in his side. While it didn't penetrate and organs, it still hurt like a sonofabitch and blood ran from that wound as he sprinted, as quickly as he could manage, for his life. As much as his blood flowed from his body, it paled in comparison to the tears of pain and loss he shed with each labored step he took into the thick woods outside the Torchlight Inn. The storm raged on all around him as he staggered, and he made it a good twenty yards before the adrenaline wore off and he collapsed into a deep snowbank.

As the blood loss and fatigue overtook him, he could smell the bitterness of propane and burning wood. His tears never stopped as his eyes filled with darkness.

His heart wept.

Chapter 23
"Carry That Weight"

Maurice could barely breathe. The gaping slash in his side sent torrents of pain shooting through his entire torso. Agony tore through him with every breath he attempted. The flesh wound in his left thigh stung as if a million pissed off wasps had used it for target practice. His vision blurred and his body felt as if on fire. The smell of blood and burning wood filled his crusted nostrils. He didn't know how long he lay there, buried in the deep snow. All he could hear was the sizzling and crackling of a nearby fire and the crows cawing high above him amongst the tall pines and white birch trees.

"The bar!" He panicked as he realized the source of the smoky smells and crackling sounds. His heart raced and he tried to sit up. The snow covering him was heavy and wet. At least the bleeding had stopped. He dug himself out of the snowdrift. Every part of his body shot with pain from the many cuts, bruises, and burns. He caught a whiff of burnt hair and flailed his hands about his head. He groped at his hair and found a wide patch in the back, burned clean to the scalp. The skin burned with searing blisters, and he felt a sticky liquid oozing from them. As he felt down his back while struggling to stand, he found that the rear of his jacket had been burned through as well.

"God damn," he croaked.

The sky was calling for twilight and he could see the long path that led through the woods back to the bar. Not that he had to look that hard, considering the deep red blood trail that splattered the snow through the naked trees. He focused his eyes in the weak light and tried to remember what the hell had happened. He stumbled forward through the deep snow, following the path.

Dark plumes of black smoke and ash filled the sky directly at the end of the path. He cried with every step he took. It felt like a million small razor blades had made a crosshatch pattern over every inch of his beaten body. His heart sank as the thought of Ashley hit him like a ten-pound sledgehammer. He hoped that his eyes were playing tricks on him. Maybe it was all a horrible practical joke, or an alcohol-induced nightmare. Anything but what his heart spoke to him and his head agreed. He picked up his pace, ignoring sharp and agonizing pangs of pain, and made his way down the dimly lit path.

He followed the bloody path and realized, as his head spun, that it was his own blood that he was following. His stomach churned, and he felt bile burn all the way up his esophagus and into the back of his throat.

Leaving the woods, Maurice fell onto the volleyball courts that, in the summer, were filled with drunken participants. But now the courts lay buried in deep snowdrifts and pieces of burning timber and smoldering ash. He caught his balance and stared out across the parking lot of the burning bar. It looked like black wrinkled fingers jutting out from the snow-covered earth. Large tendrils of smoke and flames leapt high into the gray morning sky as if praying to the almighty for acceptance and begging for entrance to the heavenly resting place.

The Torchlight Inn was no more, just a charred black skeleton that belied the massacre that had occurred inside just a few hours before. The makeshift deck lay in a burning pile, and he could make out bits and pieces of bodies and limbs. They, too, seemed to reach out to heaven. The only thing left was the metal cooler; charred black and standing all alone, like a staunch statue in the smoldering debris. Its dark form appeared to be in mourning as it stood in sad contrast with the slowly lightening sky.

He broke free from the fire's hypnotic trance and jerked his head about, looking for Ashley. The parking lot was filled with snow. Ash covered cars, and he heard the roar of an engine and the blaring of music coming from the front of the burning bar. He shambled as fast as he could through the almost thigh-deep snow and the sheer pain racking his body.

He stepped through the snow and over burnt bodies, large chunks of timber, and pieces of the bar. As he rounded what remained of the entrance, he saw a white van fishtail in the slick snow and head south down the road. He could have sworn he heard the musical refrain of "Good Morning Good Morning" coming from the vehicle as it sped away.

"What the fuck..." he started, but interrupting his words, he caught a flash of movement and clanging of metal off to his right, from the flagpole in front of the remains of the bar. He stopped breathing. He had to squint to keep the morning sun's rays from blinding him as he tried to see what was dangling from the tall flagpole. The brutal Lake Ontario winds whipped across the open parking lot and sent a whitewash of snow to cover the entire area. He covered his head and cringed in pain as the cold burned his charred and blistered skin. He staggered closer to the object bouncing against the pole and stared up.

Maurice examined the thing strapped to the pole as it swayed in the strong winter gusts and his heart felt as if it would explode into a million fleshy shards as his mind tried to wrap around just what he was looking at.

Once he realized what it was, he wished he had died back in the frozen snowbank of the woods.

There, swaying in the early morning light and in time with the Arctic-like winds, was a body. Or what remained of a body. It had no arms or legs. Just a blood-soaked torso tied with nylon rope to the pole, like a disgraced sailor to his ship's mast. But this was no sailor.

It was Ashley.

Her once perfect body had been mutilated and destroyed. Her arms and legs were crudely hacked off, the bloody stumps cauterized. He stared in disbelief and horror as tears gushed from his wide eyes. He felt his knees shake and he let out a loud, baleful cry that sent the crows scattering from their woodland perches.

Her once brilliant brown eyes stared into nothingness. Her mouth hung wide open, and Maurice could see that it was a mangled mess; most of her teeth looked as if those monsters bashed them in, or ripped them from her bleeding gums. Her once soft, alabaster skin was now the color of crimson, covering yellow and blue brutalized flesh. He wanted to stop looking but found himself unable to turn away, even though his soul shattered more and more with each new gruesome detail discovered.

The cruel wind continued to batter Maurice's exposed skin, but he felt nothing but anger, sorrow, and loss. The tears that fled his eyes froze on his frostbitten cheeks as they made their escape. He wiped his eyes and saw something sticking out of her jacket pocket. He shook as he stepped closer and reached for her. He had to stop her body from swaying to reach the pocket. The touch of her broke him. His temples throbbed and he grit his teeth. His vision flashed white and he let out a primal scream that broke through the howling winds. It was at that moment his shaking hand found purchase on the object sticking out of her torn and burnt jacket pocket. He pulled it out and staggered backward, wiping more tears from his eyes as he examined the object in his quivering hands.

It was a book.

The deafening sound of several sirens filled the morning air, but he didn't even notice. He just stared, a frozen glare, at the book.

The torn cover read: *The Catcher in the Rye.*

It dumbfounded him.

Why? He noticed a bookmark jutting out from inside the book. The winds picked up and nearly yanked the book and the bookmark out of his numb hands. He held fast to them both and examined the folded-up piece of paper.

It was a birth certificate, along with a picture of Ashley. On the birth certificate, it read: *Julia Rita Chapman.*

Ashley's mutilated corpse swung like a pendulum in the harsh winter winds as the fire trucks and Wayne County Sheriff cars pulled into the smoldering remnants of the Torchlight Inn's parking lot.

Maurice collapsed into a heap in the deep, cold snow. He dropped the book and the worn piece of paper. The wind seized the bloodstained document and whisked it away southward.

He cried out and buried his head into the ash-covered snow.

Epilogue
"A Day in the Life"

"Well, that was a mighty fine night, if I say so meself," *Paul* quipped as she yanked off her blood-covered mask and chucked it into the large Wal-Mart bag sitting between her feet in the backseat of the speeding van.

"Aye, that it was, my dear," *John* stated. His voice was cold and monotone. He held the soaked bandage on his nose and swallowed a bit of blood.

"Check it off the list," he ordered, and stared straight ahead at the snow-covered road. The final chords of "Across the Universe" faded.

The redhead took the pen from her inside shirt pocket, perused the large binder on her lap, and checked off the section entitled *Lennon.* She flipped the pages over and rubbed her freckled chin. She fumbled with the pages, then finally came to rest on one section and smirked.

"What's next?" *John* asked as he removed his sweat-soaked mask in one quick movement and threw it to the redhead in the backseat.

She shoved the masks into the bag, cinched it up, and chucked it in the back. She went back to the large binder and chortled aloud.

"Ah, yes. Very fitting, I must say." The redhead smiled as she looked over the large binder on her lap. She paused, pulled a CD from one of the binder's pages, and handed it to the large man in the passenger seat. He accepted it and slid it into the CD player.

She placed the binder on the empty seat next to her, reached into the back of the SUV, and pulled out a box with the words *Jones* written in black Sharpie marker.

She opened the box, and her eyes grew wide with excitement.

"Hope you have your passports in order, boys, we are headed home." She laughed and handed the big man his new mask.

"Me? For Christ's sake, why do I always get stuck being the drummer?" the large man pouted as he stared at the gaunt *Charlie Watts* mask. He gripped his bandaged midsection and pain shot through his large frame. However, the promise of more carnage was better than any painkiller known to man.

The white van turned onto the New York State Thruway, headed east towards New York City, and disappeared into the snowstorm as the haunting tones of "Sympathy for the Devil" wafted on the cold wintry breeze.

Off Limits
Dean Harrison

Chapter 1

"So, you're my baby sister's new boyfriend?"

Shawn smiled and offered his right hand. Ellen bit down on her lower lip, fearing what would come next.

A smirk as sharp as a reaper's blade cut across Jack's face. "Well, welcome to the family, college boy." To Ellen's relief, he shook her boyfriend's waiting hand. The grip looked tight enough to break bone. "Want a beer?"

"Sure," Shawn said, lifting the suitcase in his left hand. "Just as soon as I get rid of this."

"I'll take it for ya," Jack said. "And give me yours, Ellie. They're goin' in your room, *right*?"

Ellen didn't like the emphasis he put on that word, nor did she like the malevolent gleam dancing in his cold blue eyes. He reached for her suitcase, brushing the top of her hand with his abrasive fingertips.

The touch sent an icy shiver spiraling down her back, rattling the foundations of her frame like a violent earthquake. *What was Jack doing home anyway?* she wondered in disgust. *Where has he been for so long? And why did he decide to show up tonight, of all nights?*

And what about Dad? What did he say? What did he do?

"No," Ellen said, trying to sound pleasant, "he's staying in the guestroom. Where's Mom?"

"Here I am," Christine called, appearing as if on cue from the door to the right of the staircase, a large goblet of red wine clasped in the bony fingers of her right hand. "I'm so glad you guys made it here safely. That drive on the Interstate can be absolute murder."

"Don't I know it," Ellen said, hugging her mother and accepting a small peck on the cheek.

Christine turned to Shawn. "And this must be the young man we've heard so many wonderful things about." With arms spread out like vulture wings, she glided across the floorboards and snared him into a spidery embrace. "It's so nice to finally meet you."

Shawn looked uncomfortable in the willowy woman's arms. "Uh, nice to meet you too, Mrs. Campbell."

Catching his startled expression, Ellen stifled back a chuckle. She warned him that might happen.

"Oh please, call me Christine. Why don't you kids go make yourselves comfortable in the living room while I gather up some snacks? Yes, Jack, be a dear and take their things upstairs and…could you bring your father down from his study, please?"

"Sure," Jack said, turning toward the darkened staircase. "Right on it."

Ellen caught the snide tone in her brother's response, the way his upper lip curled. She knew there was no way he would bother persuading her father down from his sanctuary, not after what had obviously gone down between them before she arrived just moments ago with Shawn. She could feel the electricity from that storm saturating the air and figured the fight had been a violent one, a category five monstrosity.

Thank God we missed it, Ellen thought. *But Jack won't get him down here. That'll never happen.*

She knew her mother wouldn't work any miracles either. So it was up to her to coax the bear down from his cave if she wanted him to meet Shawn tonight.

But not now. Let things cool down a bit. It's the only way to ensure–

"Shawn, would you like some iced tea?" Christine asked before turning away.

"Yes, ma'am. Thanks."

"I need to go check on dinner. We're having chicken parmesan. Ellen's favorite. Back in a jif."

As Jack climbed the creaking staircase, Christine scurried back towards the kitchen, swaying from side to side like a palm tree in a tropical storm, the wine sloshing around her glass like tiny waves.

Shaking her head, Ellen glanced up at Shawn, smiled and gestured widely with her hands. "Welcome to the family."

Shawn winked an eye, placed a hand on her back and began to gently rub it. "No worse than mine."

Ellen dropped her purse on the small table by the front door and stepped into the large paneled living room, where she collapsed into the brown leather sofa in front of the brown brick fireplace. "I still think we should've gone somewhere else for spring break...like the beach."

"Too late." Shawn flopped down next to her, thought for a minute, looked at her and said, "You hate the beach."

Ellen leaned her head back and groaned. "I can't believe this is happening. I swear he couldn't have picked a worse time to re-emerge from wherever the hell he disappeared to."

"You don't talk much about him, you know. I almost forgot you even had a brother."

"Not surprising," Jack said, startling them both as he materialized from the foyer like a suave, strapping phantom dressed entirely in black. "We never really got along after shit went south around here."

That was quick. And how the hell did we not hear him coming down the stairs?

"But I hope that can change." Jack eased into one of the plush burgundy armchairs flanking the fireplace, reached for the beer bottle leaking condensation on the redwood coffee table set in the center of the furniture arrangement, threw back a long satisfying swig and said, "Shit, I forgot. You wanted a beer, didn't ya, college boy?"

Shawn smiled tightly. "Don't worry about it. It can wait."

"Well, maybe later we can all go out for a drink. I know a really cool place called the Torchlight Inn. Been around Miller Falls for years. Got a helluva reputation for–"

"Maybe not," Ellen said, crossing her arms and legs, sinking beneath the weight of her brother's watchful eyes.

"It'll be loads of fun," Jack said. "Ain't that what spring break's all about? Good times? So, college boy, what's your major?"

"Criminal justice," Shawn said, slipping his arm around Ellen's waist.

Jack cracked a mean smile. "You gonna be a cop?"

"No. A lawyer."

"Impressive." Jack took another long pull from his beer. "Anyway, how'd ya meet my baby sister here?"

"We had an English class together," Ellen said, becoming annoyed with her brother's condescending tone. "I take it you couldn't get Dad down?"

Jack's smile took a sour twist. "Ain't no gettin' that fucker down. Not after the blows we shared."

Shit. Ellen rolled her eyes. Now she definitely had to go upstairs and use her *daddy's girl* powers to wheedle him out of hiding. She was about to ask Jack the one question nagging her mind when her mother appeared with a long wooden tray carrying two glasses of iced tea, a large bowl of Chex Mix, and another goblet filled to the brim with wine.

Ellen was amazed that she was able to hold the tray steady. She wondered how many drinks that made for her mother tonight, and how many more she planned to consume.

"Here we are." Christine placed the tray down on the coffee table, handed Shawn and Ellen their drinks, picked up her own glass, and took a seat in the armchair on the other side of the fireplace. "Isn't this nice?"

"Be even better if we had Dad," Ellen said. She placed her iced tea back on the tray, slid her hands slowly down her jeans, and rose from the couch. "Let *me* go up and get him this time."

"No, honey, I can–"

"No," Ellen interrupted, waving her mother back in her seat. "I better do it." To Shawn, she said, "Be right back."

"I'm sorry, honey," Christine said meekly, lowering her eyes with her wine glass poised up to her lips. "Be sure to knock. He's been working hard on his new novel."

And probably a bottle of scotch, too. Ellen took a deep breath, eyed Jack cautiously, and headed for the stairs.

Chapter 2

Almost every step moaned beneath her feet as she made her way up. Along the wall to her left were old family photographs. Ellen glanced over them as she slid her hand along the smooth mahogany banister.

Though it was dark in the stairwell, she could still make out the photos of her and Jack from back when they were younger, more innocent. Back when they were close. Back before, as Jack had so eloquently put it, "shit went south."

The second-floor landing was lit faintly by a rectangle of light spilling out of her bedroom. Peering in as she passed by, she noticed Shawn's old, tattered suitcase on the floor at the foot of the bed. *"They're goin' in* your *room,* right?"

Her brother wasn't trying to be funny by that remark, which was the reason behind the fierce knot twisting and turning in her gut like a very sharp knife.

What possessed Dad to let him back into this house? After what he pulled before he left.

She remembered catching Shawn rummaging around in her father's safe the day he ran away from home. He was eighteen, and she had just turned twelve.

"What're you doing?" she said sharply. *"If Daddy sees you–"*

Jack turned with a fistful of bills, looked down at Ellen with narrowed eyes, and said, *"Shit's about to go bad, Ellie. And you know what I'm talkin' about."*

"He didn't do it!" Ellen said; she was almost crying.

Jack only shook his head and brushed past her without saying another word. When her father got home later that night, Jack was long gone, and Ellen's parents had the biggest fight she had ever heard them have. The nightmares began soon after that.

Turning away from that treacherous path of memories, Ellen reached the closed door of her father's office at the end of the hall and knocked. "Dad, it's me, can I come in?"

Without waiting for a response, she opened the door (he never got around to putting a lock on it, not even after Jack had stolen all that money) and flinched. The pungent odor of cigar smoke and expensive liquor slapped her hard across the face, making her eyes water.

Jesus Christ, Dad.

Regaining her senses, she stepped into the office.

It was small, lighted by a green-shaded lamp, and lined wall-to-wall with dusty bookcases crammed tight with various reading materials and all other forms of miscellaneous junk.

There was also an oak gun cabinet in the corner of the room near the window. To this day her father never allowed her to peek within to see his dangerous toys, the little things that kill.

Reaching back behind her to close the door, Ellen glanced at her father, who was hunched over his laptop at his desk. She could barely hear the tapping of keys under the sound of Deep Purple's "Hush" playing on his iTunes.

And at the sound of the door clicking shut, Robert Campbell turned away from his work, smiled, and stood up from his swivel chair. "Hey, baby girl," he said, looming before her like a red, shaggy-haired giant from somewhere within the pages of Grimm's Fairy Tales. "Was wondering when I'd be seeing your pretty face around here."

"Hey, Daddy." Ellen wrapped her arms around his torso. As usual, her hands wouldn't meet when she reached across his back.

Robert placed a finger beneath her chin, tilted her head up, leaned down and kissed her gently on the lips. His copper-colored beard lightly tickled her skin. "How was the drive?"

"Long and boring."

"With the kind of education you're getting, I'd say it is well worth the trip, wouldn't you?" Robert sat back down in his chair, took Ellen's right hand and guided her into his lap. His dark brown eyes were warm yet lined with the telltale signs of guilt and regret. "Sorry I didn't call you ahead of time about your brother. He showed up right before you did."

"Yeah, I figured that. It's all right."

"No, it isn't." Robert sighed, glanced over at the laptop on his desk and clamped it shut.

Ellen never got a chance to see what he was writing. "Mom said it's a new book?"

"Supposed to be." Robert placed an elbow on the scuffed-up edge of the desk and rubbed his high, sweaty forehead. "Having a little trouble getting it started. Think I have writer's block."

"You'll get through it. You always do."

Robert reached for the small glass of scotch standing by his smoldering ashtray. "Wonder sometimes if I should've stayed a cop."

"You hated being a cop, and so did I." Ellen watched her father down his drink and asked herself: *Why does everyone in this family try to solve their problems with booze?*

Placing the empty glass down, Robert took a deep breath and let it out slowly. "So, I guess you want me to come downstairs and join the party. Am I right?"

Ellen bowed her head. "Well, it would be nice for you to meet Shawn. That's the main reason we came, you know."

Robert placed his left hand on her cheek and caressed it with his coarse fingertips. "Is this boy stealing my baby girl away from me?"

Ellen blushed. "It's getting pretty serious, I guess."

"Not *too* serious, I hope."

"Daddy!"

Robert slid his hand through her hair. "Guess I should've known it was only a matter of time before someone did."

Ellen's blush deepened. "No one's stealing me from you." With her hands clasped together in her lap, she looked over at the stack of books to the left of her father's laptop. She raised her eyebrows as she scanned the titles. They were all from the occult section of the bookstore, a section into which she never thought he would venture. They touched on such subjects as sorcery, witchcraft, and black magic. "Um, are you blending horror with your crime fiction now?"

Robert glanced down at the stack of books. "Maybe."

His demeanor changed. The warmth he exuded upon seeing her just moments ago dissipated like a wisp of fog and his eyes grew hard, distant, and focused on a point somewhere far beyond what anyone outside his troubled mind could see.

Ellen was sure it had something to do with the uninvited guest downstairs, yet still she tilted her head to the side and asked, "Are you okay?"

With another heavy sigh, Robert placed his left hand on Ellen's right shoulder and squeezed it tenderly. "Why don't you go back downstairs? I'll be down before dinner. I promise."

"Daddy, don't let him get to you. Don't let him ruin the rest of the week. Please. It's really important to me."

He touched her cheek again. Ellen leaned into his palm. "Go back down before your boyfriend starts to worry about you."

Nodding her head, Ellen gave her father one more hug before leaving his office and kissed him on one thick, hairy cheek. "Please don't take too long," she said, climbing off his lap and heading for the door. "I don't know how much more of Jack I can take on my own."

She felt her father's eyes following her as she exited the room. She wondered just how he would take to Shawn, who was the first boyfriend she ever had, and the only man besides her father that she could actually say she loved.

She remembered how he reacted when she first told him they were dating and felt a fresh sense of worry blossom like a rose of dread in her stomach.

Oh please be okay with this. Oh please, oh please...

When she made it back down to the living room, she saw Shawn relaxed on the couch and nursing a bottle of beer.

Fantastic. Jack's got his hooks in him.

She frowned as Shawn laughed along with Jack, who was snacking on a handful of Chex Mix, relating a story about how, when they were children, he convinced Ellen that she was adopted and that her real parents were leprechauns who were trampled to death by a crazed stampede of giants.

"It traumatized her. She cried for hours."

"Yeah, it was a clever trick," Ellen said, flopping down next to Shawn. She patted his leg. "I see you decided on that beer."

"Gave his arm a good twistin'," Jack said. "Wanted to loosen him up."

Ellen suddenly wished she had never left Shawn alone with her brother. She didn't expect them to get chummy, and God knew what else Jack had told him while she was gone. "Mom in the kitchen?"

Jack nodded. "Dad upstairs?"

Ellen glanced toward the foyer and listened for the creaking of stairs beneath heavy feet, but no such sound came back at her. Disappointed, she returned her attention back to Jack. "So what've you been up to all these years?"

With a small shrug, Jack downed a swig of beer and said, "This and that. You know. Tried to make my way in the world."

"Any particular reason why you decided to show up now? Do you need more money? Are you in any kind of trouble?"

Brushing a dark wing of hair back from his eyes, he said, "Money's always an issue. But I'm not in any trouble."

Leaning forward with her elbows on her knees, Ellen asked, "Then why are you home?"

"Just wanted to set things straight."

Ellen didn't know what to make of that, or the look on his sharp angular face, the secretive smile tugging at the corners of his mouth. It brought forth more questions. And fears.

Set things straight?

Her voice quivered slightly when she asked, "What things?"

Jack leaned in. His smile broadened darkly. "Everything."

From somewhere in the back, near the dining room, a musical voice sung out, "Dinner's ready!"

Chapter 3

Shawn had the feeling Ellen's father didn't like him. There was something unsettling about the look in the man's stern dark eyes and the close way he scrutinized him as he shook Shawn's outstretched hand.

The writer's grip was like an iron vise. Shawn tried his damnedest not to show how much it hurt him. "I really like your books," he said, hoping to abate the blizzard coming off the titan who was crushing his hand like an aluminum beer can. "Especially the Jim Turner series."

"Thank you," Robert said, glancing at Ellen, who was smiling nervously as introductions were made. "Glad you enjoyed them." He let go of Shawn's aching hand.

"Now that we're all here," Christine said, patting her husband's beefy arm. "Let's go eat before dinner gets cold."

Still without a smile on his heavily whiskered visage, Robert gestured for Shawn to move forward. Feeling the tension tightly winding the muscles in his back, Shawn nodded and followed Ellen into the dining room.

Jack was already seated at the table, which stood beneath what looked to be an antique chandelier. He winked at Shawn as he slid a forkful of pasta into his mouth.

Why is Ellen so worried about her brother? Shawn wondered. *He seems all right. It's her father I'm concerned about.*

But that's how it was supposed to be, right? The boyfriend should be apprehensive about meeting his girlfriend's father for the first time, should be concerned about making a good first impression, should be worried about whether or not dear old dad would accept him as a new part of his little girl's life.

But he seems to have made up his mind already. I can see it. He doesn't *like me.*

Shawn took the seat across from Jack. Ellen took the seat to his left, across from her mother.

Robert sat at the head of the table between the two women, and for a moment his ire shifted from Shawn to his son, the only one of the two Campbell men who seemed to accept him on the spot, offering his seal of approval with a nod and a beer.

Probably because no one else wants him here, at least not Ellen and her father. But what's so bad about the guy? After talking with him for a while, he seems cool.

Thinking this, Shawn recalled Ellen's reaction upon seeing Jack's old gunmetal-gray Ford Mustang parked in the driveway the moment they pulled up to the house. He remembered the gasp that raked her throat, the fear that turned her eyes to saucers, and the shock that drained her face of color. He thought about how she shook her head in adamant denial at what she was seeing, visibly quivering as her hands flew up to her mouth and she muttered, *"No, no, no, no, no."*

What could have possibly warranted such anxiety in her? As far as Shawn could tell, it was the family head that needed to be watched with caution. It was her father who inspired terror in the hearts of those around him. Except for maybe Jack.

But why?

Shawn decided to chalk it up to Jack's unexpected return home. He remembered what Ellen said about him picking the worst time to suddenly reappear and she was right. Had Jack not shown up tonight, perhaps things would have been different.

Maybe that's why her father's in such a bad mood. Maybe that's why he doesn't seem to care all that much for me. Other than the fact that I'm Ellen's first, and hopefully final, boyfriend.

Shawn considered that. Ellen *was* the baby of the family. And for the last twenty-one years (as far as he knew), no male occupied a place in her heart other than her father. And now that had changed.

Before he could mull over that any further, Robert Campbell began to speak. "So," he said, putting knife and fork to a hunk of chicken, "I understand you plan on attending law school after graduation?"

"Yes, sir." Shawn accepted the basket of garlic bread going around the table.

"What kind of law?"

"Criminal." Shawn took a piece of bread and passed the basket to Jack.

Robert took a moment to glare at his son. Then he looked back down at his dinner plate and muttered, "You're in good company."

"Shawn wants to be a prosecutor," Ellen almost pleaded. "He interned at the attorney general's office last semester."

"That's impressive," Christine said, helping her daughter lighten the mood. "Did you assist in any big cases?"

"Yes, ma'am," Shawn said. "A few."

"How exciting. I love *Law & Order*. Is it anything like that?"

Shawn smiled and shook his head. "Not near as dramatic."

"I could've told you that," Robert said, raising his glass of soda to his lips. "Real life's never as exciting as TV or books."

"Yes, sir," Shawn said, taking advantage of the gradual shift in temperament. "If TV portrayed the criminal justice system the way it actually works, no one would bother watching it."

"The public has all sorts of crazy misconceptions about police work, no thanks to crap like *CSI*."

"I liked *The Shield*," Jack said, with a string of pasta dangling from a corner of his mouth. "That show was the shit. Corrupt pigs and everything.

Showed how shit really goes down. And I know, because I seen it all. Even in this country bumpkin town. That right, pops?"

Shawn heard Ellen groan softly by his side. Robert knitted his eyebrows tightly, glaring again at his son.

With a crooked smile, Jack downed his beer and said, "I mean, you've seen some pretty shady shit back in the day. Tell the college boy here about your last case, about how you–"

Robert slammed a fist down on the table, rattling the plates and silverware and making everyone around the table jump in their seats. "*Enough*," he demanded, eyes flamed with rage.

For a minute, there was silence as father and son stared each other down. Shawn glanced at Ellen; she looked about ready to scream or cry. Christine grabbed the bottle of wine from the center of the table, replenished her glass, and began to drink.

"Sorry." Jack finally averted his eyes. "Too much beer, I guess. Didn't mean to cause any trouble. Guess I still need to learn to think before I talk." He looked up at Shawn and Ellen and grinned sheepishly. "Sorry about that."

"It's okay, honey," Christine said, placing her hand on Jack's shoulder. "We all make mistakes, you see. And we all know you're trying very hard to behave." She took another hearty sip of wine. "So, Shawn, tell us a little about *your* family. What are they like?"

Chapter 4

It came as no surprise to her that dinner would be a disaster. After one particular nasty skeleton peeked through the keyhole of the Campbell closet, Ellen's mother began to probe around for the ghouls that climbed the twisted boughs of Shawn's family tree.

Which failed, thanks to her Ellen's father, who immediately jumped in with inquiries about Shawn's favorite Jim Turner novel.

"*Evil in the Blood*, hands down. That one was definitely a turning point for Turner. You explored his dark side. He became more of an antihero in the end. I really liked that."

Brushing breadcrumbs from his beard, Robert nodded his head. "That one was the most fun for me."

Deep down inside, Ellen released a sigh of relief, for the dark cloud hovering over her father was now beginning to break, allowing sunshine in to liven up the atmosphere.

And other than Jack's clumsy remark alluding to the debacle that drove their father to lay down his badge forever, no other comments were made to lead the conversation down dark and shady avenues where roamed the grim and restless ghosts of the past.

That was until her mother, after her umpteenth glass of wine, began telling stories that made everyone at the table blush and shift uncomfortably in their seats.

She touched on every subject from the pain of childbirth to the strict teachings of the Catholic Church governing the laws of sexual activity. Whatever Jack told Shawn earlier while Ellen conversed with her father upstairs could *not* have been as bad as this. There was just no possible way.

Ellen looked around the table, gauging everyone's reaction to her mother's shameless babbling.

Jack slid down in his seat with his right hand covering his mouth as his robust physique shook with silent laughter. Shawn bit down on his lower lip, listening to the inebriated woman go on and on about the ghastly, hellfire perils of living in sin. God only knew what adverse thoughts and judgments were spinning around his mind. Ellen looked to her father for help.

Robert met her eyes. He was clearly just as irritated and embarrassed with the disastrous direction in which his wife had taken the conversation.

"Are you Catholic, Shawn?"

"No, ma'am. I don't really belong to any church."

Christine paused in the act of lifting her wine glass. The stark disapproval in her glassy eyes was just as grim as the thin-lipped frown on her withered face. "Well, no matter your beliefs, the Bible makes it quite clear that sex is a sacred act meant only for–"

"Christine," Robert finally interjected, "this isn't an appropriate time for such talk."

"What talk? I'm only saying that–"

"We know what you're saying, and we've heard enough of it. Understand?" Robert's knife and fork clanked as he dropped them onto his dinner plate. Lifting his napkin to wipe faint traces of tomato sauce from the corners of his mouth, he said, "Let's talk about something else. Ellen, how are classes going? You keeping that A average up?"

Ellen smiled appreciatively. "Of course."

"Good girl. I just know you're on the way to the top of the Dean's List."

"She sure is," Shawn said with an eyewink.

"She was always the smart one in the family," Jack said after finishing off his beer. "Always made me jealous."

Ellen and her father traded another meaningful glance.

"Oh, don't talk that way, Jack," Christine said. "You're smart too. And special. Very special. Right, Ro–"

"I'm finished here," Robert said, rising from the table with his dishes. "It was good to meet you, Shawn. Maybe later you can come up to my office and see some of my books, the rare editions. But I've got some work to get done tonight. I have a deadline to meet. Sorry to be rude."

"It was great meeting you too, sir," Shawn said. "And I would like to see those books you mentioned later. Good luck with your new novel."

Ellen wanted to protest, to order her father back down in his seat, to beg him not to leave her alone, not now. But the look he gave Jack made her keep her mouth shut. Sometimes she could persuade her father with her magical wiles, and sometimes she knew better than to jab her finger incessantly at the bear.

And this was one of those times. The look he gave her and her mother confirmed it. He was leaving, and there was not a damn thing she or anyone else could do to stop him.

"So," Christine said after Robert departed from the dining room. "What do you kids have planned for the rest of the night?"

"Remember I mentioned the Torchlight Inn earlier?"

"Yeah," Shawn said. "It sounded like a pretty wild place from what you said."

Christine polished off her wine glass and asked, "What's the Torchlight Inn?"

"It's a bar outside of town," Jack said. "I thought it'd be cool if I took Shawn and Ellen there and bought them a beer or two, have a little fun tonight."

"I don't know," Ellen said. "Maybe we shouldn't–"

"Aw, come on, Ellie. I told ya I wanted to set things right, and I meant it. I was a real asshole in the past, I know, and I want to make up for all I've done to cause a rift. I mean I know I can't do it overnight, but it's a start, ain't it?"

"I agree, honey. Your father's not ready to accept your brother's apologies, but I am. And you should too. It's the Christian thing to do, after all. To forgive the sinner."

Shawn watched Ellen fume in her seat. He could practically see the steam billow from her ears. Her chocolate brown eyes narrowed into dark slits as she glowered both at Jack and her mother.

"Just for an hour," Jack said, not fazed by the daggers being thrown his way. "I promise you won't be sorry."

Shawn snuck his arm around Ellen's waist. He felt tension building up inside her, tightly twisting her nerves into little knots. He knew how she got when put into situations such as this and it wasn't pretty. She would bottle up all of that emotional baggage simmering inside until one day, without provocation, she'd erupt in a blast of tears and hysterics, becoming inconsolable, which was when it was best to leave her alone. And Shawn hated to leave her alone.

But he also felt that her brother was authentic in wanting to reach out to his family, something with which he sympathized.

Jack had explained his motives to him in the living room before dinner. He wanted to get back into his family's good graces. He had enough of being the black sheep, enough of wandering from city to city and state to state, wasting his life away. He wanted his family's forgiveness. He wanted to be home.

And Shawn knew exactly where he was coming from. He was once in his shoes.

Back in high school, he had a long hard struggle with drugs and had run away from home on numerous occasions, drifting from place to place and sleeping in gutters, dumpsters, and crack houses, pissing his life away. But when he ran into one of his older brothers looking for him out on the street one night, he learned that his mother had cancer and was going to die. It was then that knew he had to be home, that he had to be there for her. He had always been her favorite son.

It wasn't easy. It took a long time for his family, his father especially, to accept him back into the fold. So Shawn identified with Jack. He used to *be* Jack.

And Ellen knew it. Which was why Shawn felt he could convince her to give her brother a second chance at the redemption he sought.

Leaning to the side, Shawn whispered in her ear.

Chapter 5

Ellen gave in, but only because of what Shawn said to her.

"Fine." She looked up at her boyfriend, wanting to choke the life out of him for being so damn compassionate and naïve.

Just tell him why you can't go. Tell him why it's a bad idea. Tell him why you just can't trust your brother no matter what he claims his motives are. Tell him about the nightmares.

She could not do that. Shawn would think she was being silly and irrational, harsh and cruel.

And what if Jack was being sincere? What if he was truly trying to change?

But what's your gut telling you, Ellie? Sweet, tasty Ellie.

It's telling you that Jack is the devil, and not even God forgives the devil.

But she knew what Shawn would say and what he would think if she didn't give the devil a chance. After all, he was once just as bad and had fallen just as far, just as hard from the edge of grace. It was possible that they'd even followed the same paths.

No. That's impossible. Things may have been bad for Shawn, but they couldn't have been as bad as whatever Jack had gone through.

Anything's possible, and Ellen knew it. After all, Shawn never told her *everything* about his past, about the things he did while living out on the streets, where it was survival of the fittest, where plenty of bad things happen, where not everyone comes out in one piece.

He could have been just like Jack.

The thought introduced her to a whole new level of fear, one that wrapped her entire body in ethereal sheets of bitter cold ice, freezing her all the way down to the marrow of her bones, making her consider things that taunted her endlessly in her worst nightmares, the ones about her brother.

Sweet, tasty Ellie...

She shivered in those cold, waif-like sheets.

...You're all mine now.

Shawn knew he could convince her. He also knew she'd be reluctant, which she clearly was. Her eyes told him so.

"I'll drive," Jack said, slipping into a worn, black leather jacket. "It's pretty hard to find at night."

"That's cool with me," Shawn said. "You got a nice set of wheels, by the way."

"Thanks. Maybe you can take it for a spin later. It drives like a bitch out of hell."

"Lovely," Ellen said, snatching her purse up from the table in the foyer. "Why do you need that jacket? It's not cold at all out there."

Jack brushed his unruly hair away from his eyes. "It's how I roll." He opened the front door and stepped outside.

Indeed, the night was a mild one, ideal for jeans and short sleeves. But a gentle wind rustled among the magnolias, azaleas, and surrounding pines trees, sending a ghostly chill nibbling down Shawn's neck as he crossed the front porch and headed down the steps.

Velvety clouds passed across the waxing moon. Crickets sung their mournful tune in the shadows of the thickets that bordered the Campbell's colonial-style home. Ellen stayed close to Shawn as they followed Jack down the redbrick path cutting across the lawn toward to the driveway.

Jack stepped around to the driver side of the Mustang, unlocked the door and swung it open. Shawn opened the passenger side door for Ellen, who pushed the seat forward and climbed into the back.

"Guess you got shotgun," Jack said. "Hop on in."

Shawn stepped in and swung the door shut. Jack stuck his key into the ignition and fired up the engine.

Pantera's "Fucking Hostile" blasted from the speakers. Jack leaned over the console and turned down the volume. "Sorry about that," he said.

"Nothing wrong with metal," Shawn said, catching Ellen rolling her eyes in the rearview mirror. "Dimebag was the shit."

"Got that right." Jack hit the headlights, shifted gears, and pulled down the driveway.

"Can we put something else on?" Ellen reached between the seats and handed Shawn a black CD case. "Anything but this crap."

"You never were into hardcore shit, were ya, Ellie?"

"No. And please don't call me that anymore."

"A'ight. Got some Maiden and Priest. Pop one of those in if you want."

"You're a Priest fan too, eh?" Shawn flipped through the contents of the case. "Ah, *Sad Wings of Destiny*. You've got the classics."

"Only the best."

"Sweet." Shawn ejected the Pantera CD. "My dad got me into Priest when I was a kid. He had all the good shit." He slipped the *Point of Entry* album into the CD player. "Ellen, I know you like this one."

As the first rock n' roll riff exerted its power through the crackling speakers, Jack shifted into drive and hit the gas. Shawn grinned and reached his hand back behind his seat. Ellen slipped her small hand into his.

It was cold and trembling.

Jack sped down the main road running through Piper's Cove, the swankiest neighborhood in Miller Falls. With his left hand gripping the steering wheel, he reached into the inside pocket of his jacket and extracted a Camel from the crumpled soft pack within. After sticking the cigarette between his lips, he went back in for his lighter, which he pulled out and ignited.

A bright orange flame flickered and flared, warming up his face. Breathing in the sweet, soothing taste of nicotine, Jack dropped his lighter back into his pocket, where it clicked softly against the wooden handle of his Buck knife. Cracking the window open for ventilation, he released a long funnel of smoke, plucked the cigarette from his lips, and said, "Anybody want a smoke?"

Ellen didn't respond. Her boyfriend declined.

Fuckin' pussies. Jack stuck the cigarette between his lips and dropped his free hand down upon the steering wheel. *Ain't gonna live forever. Might as well cut loose while ya still can.*

Because if things went his way tonight, his baby sister and her chump of a boyfriend would not live long enough to see the sunrise.

Jack momentarily took his eyes off the road and glanced into the rearview mirror. Ellen was staring out the window to her left, moonlight shining upon the delicate features of her small heart-shaped face. The pale light danced seductively in her worrisome eyes, turning Jack on like a blast furnace.

It was good she was worried. She should be.

Because tonight she was going to feel a whole lot of pain, and Jack was going to enjoy inflicting every bit of it.

He took a long drag on his cigarette and exhaled.

And that college boy, baby sister's lover man; Jack cracked a wide grin just thinking about what he was going to do with that little punk-ass weasel.

If only the old man could be there.

As smoke drifted over his face, Jack noticed how firmly Ellen's breasts pushed up against the clingy fabric of her blouse and thought how nicely she had developed over the years. The way her bubbly ass filled those tight jeans made his mouth water for the tangy fruit he knew she possessed between her slender thighs.

He knew they called this yearning unnatural. He knew they called it sin.

He also knew he didn't give a shit, because in the jungle of the human mind nothing is off limits. But Jack wanted more than just his sister's flavorful cunt. What he truly wanted was the main reason he had come home tonight. Taking his sister was just a delightful bonus.

Again he thought about the old man, and the smile on his face grew to impossible lengths.

Look what you've created, you sick bastard.

Jack couldn't help it; he burst out laughing, startling the other two occupants in the car out of their skins.

And as he sliced a path through the moonlit darkness with his headlights, Ellen and Shawn exchanged quizzical glances and mutual fears.

Chapter 6

Ellen had never heard of the Torchlight Inn before, but that wasn't much of a surprise. For most of her life, she had been sheltered from the seedier sides of Miller Falls and had therefore lived in blissful ignorance of the dark, forbidden things that lurked on the outskirts of town.

Which was exactly where they found themselves. Far out in the boonies, in deep desolate woodlands with rundown shacks, dilapidated houses, ramshackle trailers, and abandoned gas stations.

The further they went into the shadows, the more Ellen sensed they were making a colossal mistake. Their isolated surroundings and Jack's sudden, unprovoked laughter foreshadowed something very bad coming down the road. She felt it in her gut, and her gut never steered her wrong.

Then why not tell Jack to turn the car around and take them home?

"Here we are," Jack said, flicking his cigarette stub out the window. "Past the point of no return."

Ellen caught his eyes in the rearview mirror and shivered. The feeling that he was rummaging around her head, reading her thoughts, weighed in her gut as he turned onto a gravel parking lot occupied by a couple of motorcycles, rust-ridden pickup trucks, and other vehicles of various makes and models.

"This is the Torchlight Inn?" Ellen glanced at the small clapboard building and grimaced. It was a complete dive.

Jack rolled into an empty parking space beneath the gnarled branches of a moss-covered oak tree. "Well, whaddya expect, little sis? A fancy nightclub?"

Ellen shrugged as she scrutinized the Inn. The outer façade of the building was weathered and filthy. A beer light flickered faintly behind a dirty window screen, and the only source of outside light came from a mercury vapor lamp burning atop a telephone pole tilted slightly to the right amongst the weeds and overgrowth. How this place received any business was beyond Ellen's comprehension. It was located in a small, wooded alcove off a lonely country road far from the rest of civilization. Who in hell patronized a place like this, and did she really want to find out?

But maybe she was being too judgmental. Perhaps it was just another cozy country bar where a person could relax with a beer and shoot some pool while an old country ditty played from the jukebox. Perhaps Ellen was just being a snob, a characteristic trait she loathed in other people.

Or maybe she was just letting her imagination run hog wild. Maybe she was just being paranoid, letting her nightmares get the better of her. After all, Shawn seemed okay about going through with this, and he was good about evaluating situations, about sensing when potential danger was ahead. Perhaps everything would be fine.

But what's your gut telling you, Ellie?

"Let's go," Jack said, killing the engine. "Don't know about ya'll, but I could really use a cold one."

Gravel crunched beneath Shawn's feet like broken bits of glass as he and Ellen followed Jack to the entrance of the bar. A nocturnal cacophony of crickets and cicadas chirruped within the black-green shadows of the surrounding woodland, and a glowing Budweiser sign in the window hummed monotonously with it. As they approached the door, Shawn could hear the fist-pumping riff of Deep Purple's "Smoke on the Water" and the clacking of pool balls. The sounds grew louder as Jack pushed the door open and stepped inside.

The interior of the Torchlight Inn was as Shawn expected. He'd seen it in every small-town honky-tonk he had passed through: dim lighting, smoke-choked oxygen, the stench of stale beer and cigarette ash, and the underlying threat of violence hanging in the putrid air. It was grimly foreboding, yet he felt at home. He felt comfortable in this place with the old, crinkled one-dollar bills scattered and stapled all along the walls, and the grisly boar's head hanging over a broken-down arcade game in the dank corner by the restrooms. He felt in his element here with the underdog who sat alone at the end of the bar, weeping the blues into his beer. But he knew Ellen didn't, and so he held onto her hand and kept her close, and kept his eyes open for trouble.

He noted two burly bikers circling the pool table by the jukebox. One looked up as they walked toward the counter and pinned his dead yellow eyes right on Ellen. Tapping his tall, meaner-looking friend on the shoulder with the end of his pool stick, the beer-belly biker pointed their way. Keeping diligent watch from the corner of his eye, Shawn pulled Ellen closer, leading her to the counter.

There were a few older men sitting alone at different ends of the long, chipped-wood bar. They all held beer mugs and stared into them with glum faces. Shawn, Ellen, and Jack climbed three rickety barstools and sought the attention of the bartender, who was flipping through the pages of a magazine called *Taboo*. According to the Person-in-Charge sign hanging over the cash register, his name was Bobby. He had small, heavy-hooded eyes, a fat hound-like snout, and when he finally glanced up from his voyeurism and slapped the magazine down in annoyance, he leaned over the counter with thick, tattooed arms and grumbled, "ID's."

Shawn reached into his back pocket and pulled out his wallet. Bobby took his merry time looking over Ellen's ID.

"You sure don't look twenty-one," he said.

Ellen smiled. "I get that all the time."

Bobby grumbled something unintelligible, handed Ellen back her license and, without verifying Shawn's legal age or Jack's, said, "Whad'ya'll want?"

Jack spoke up before Shawn had a chance to open his mouth. "Three shots of Jimmy Beam and keep 'em comin'."

"No, that's all right," Ellen said. "I'll take a—"

"Aw, come on, Ellie. Just one shot to toast with, then whatever you want for the rest of the night."

Ellen rolled her eyes, looked at Shawn, and relented. Bobby poured three tumblers full of whiskey and then lined them up in front of his newly arrived patrons. Shawn took his glass as the others reached for their own.

"A'ight," Jack said, raising his shot glass in the air. "To new beginnings."

They all clinked glasses and tossed back their drinks. The amber liquid burned going down Shawn's throat, bringing tears to his eyes. He set his glass back down on the counter and placed a hand along Ellen's back. From the pained expression on her face, he could tell the whiskey didn't sit well with her. As Jack said earlier, she never was into the hardcore shit.

The track on the jukebox switched to Jimi Hendrix's "Hey Joe." Shawn glanced over his shoulder at the bikers who were clacking balls along faded green felt.

The shorter one with the beer belly looked their way. Shawn quickly averted his eyes and glanced into a murky corner of the bar near a set of dartboards. A small table was shrouded in a thin veil of cigarette smoke, and a small, scantily clad woman with long curly blonde hair, leathery skin, and a fat lower lip sat alone with a cigarette poised in the air. She caught Shawn staring and winked one bloodshot, lizard-like eye and grinned. She was missing a few teeth, and the ones that remained looked as rotten as driftwood.

Shawn shuttered in revulsion, turned away, and asked Bobby for a Bud Light.

Ellen ordered a rum and Coke, wondering where Jack got the money to throw around on drinks.

"Here ya go, girlie."

Ellen gave the leering bartender a tight smile and took her drink. Shawn smirked, rubbed the back of her neck, and took a swig from his bottle of Bud.

Jack tossed back another shot of whiskey, then said, "I'm goin' to the jukebox. Any requests?" Without waiting for answers, he spun off his seat and headed toward the jukebox.

Ellen leaned in and said in Shawn's ear, "Look around. Do you really think being here's a good idea?" She eyed the sketchy characters at the jukebox. "I don't like this place. It gives me the creeps. And look at the woman over there in the corner. You think she's a meth-head?"

"Looks like she had her fair share," Shawn said.

"And those biker guys are freaking me out. What if they come over and start trouble?"

"I don't think thcy will. Don't worry about them."

"I can't help it. They keep staring at us."

"So don't stare back."

"Why did we come here? How was this supposed to be fun? A pretty wild place, Jack said? Pretty shady is more like it. Dad always warned me about these kinds of places, which is why I always avoided them. Nothing good can happen here."

"Just relax. Nothing bad is going to happen. Some of these guys may look rough, but that doesn't make them evil." Shawn put his arm around

Ellen's shoulders and drew her into him. "It'll be cool." He kissed the top of her head. "I'll protect ya."

Ellen pulled gently away and sighed. Though she knew she was being stupid and stereotypical in her thinking, she could not help feeling that they could be in for some bad trouble.

And with Jack, there was always trouble.

She looked around at the men sitting at the counter. They looked harmless enough, though one kept glancing up at her with a reptilian smile on his crusty face, a predatory gleam in his hungry eyes.

Ellen shivered, picked up her drink and took a sip. Its soothing effect helped settle her nerves.

"I say we stay for a couple more drinks and then head off," Shawn said after a long swallow of beer. "Jack's heart seems to be in the right place. But I'm not really in the mood to get shit-faced tonight. Kind of tired, actually. Been a long evening, hasn't it?"

Ellen raised her eyebrows and chuckled. "You can say that again. Not exactly what I was expecting. Good God, the way Mom went on and on about premarital sex. I seriously thought I was going to die."

Shawn cracked a smile, bottle to his lips. "Yeah, that was pretty funny."

"Not to me."

An Alice in Chains tune started up on the jukebox. Ellen recognized it right off the bat. Jack used to blast that loud grungy music in his bedroom at night, pissing their father off.

"Got some good tunes lined up," Jack said, returning to his stool. "Hey, barkeep, I'll take another shot."

Ellen watched her brother take a cigarette and a lighter from an inside pocket of his jacket and light up. She remembered the way he laughed in the car before they arrived and wondered what had been on his mind at that moment. Jack met her eyes and winked. Ellen looked away and saw her terrified expression in the dirty mirror behind the counter.

Want to set things straight? How the hell could she have fallen for such bullshit? How could she have let Shawn persuade her to? She knew Jack well, he didn't. Shawn knew nothing of the sinister things that lurked in the darkness of her brother's mind, the trouble he had caused for her family. She wasn't old enough to comprehend the damage at the time, but she was now.

Ellen eyed Jack's reflection in the mirror. He watched her intently, a knowing smile on his face. It was then that a door in her mind creaked slowly open, releasing the memory of a hand sliding up her leg like a snake as she struggled to scream and cry out in the darkness of her bedroom.

The snake was long, hard, and throbbing as it slithered up her nightgown, whispering, *"Sweet, tasty Ellie..."*

Ellen drew in a long, harsh breath of air. Her brother had tormented her in the past, in the usual sibling rivalry ways, but this revelation... How could she have forgotten?

She remembered feeling as if Jack was rummaging around her head, reading her thoughts. Could he control her mind?

Was it possible that Jack made her forget those sick and repulsive things he did to her? But how could he? How was such a thing even possible?

The snake whispered in her ear, *"Bad magic, baby."*

Chapter 7

Each song he chose on the jukebox had special meaning, and Jack chose this one especially for Ellen.

It was called "Confusion," a tune off Alice in Chains' *Facelift* album, and it was significant to what he had planned for his baby sister tonight.

Remember when the blood first ran down your legs, Ellie? I'm sure you do now. Oh, it was so sweet. And you were only twelve.

Of course he blocked it all from her mind and made her forget it ever happened so she wouldn't tell their parents and get him in trouble. But with the blood staining the pale flesh between her thighs, and with Ellen insisting she didn't do it to herself, their mother began to have awful suspicions about what happened, and her prime suspect was her husband. After all, he had always been very affectionate when it came to Ellen, always had her sitting in his lap, always kissing her on the lips.

Christine had a little sit down with Robert at the kitchen table a day after she finally mustered the courage to speak with him about her suspicions, and the confrontation was awkward and tense, raucous and teetering on the edge of violence. Of course Robert denied every bit of it and blasted Christine for even accusing him of such a horrible thing as child molestation.

Ellen denied it happened as well, and Christine had no choice but to apologize to her enraged husband and let it go.

But then the next day, Jack told his mother a little lie. He told her how sometimes, late at night, he would see Dad sneak into Ellen's room, and then later he would hear Ellen whimper and say, *"No, Daddy, please don't...please don't."*

And his mother believed him. She *always* believed him. He was good at persuading her of such things, at planting seeds in her mind that would poison her perception of the truth, of her husband and his relationship with their daughter. Jack had just begun to learn of his powers by then, and he used them well.

What are these powers? he had asked himself at the time. *And why do they make me feel like a god?*

Robert never had a chance to confront Jack about what he told Christine because he had already left town with over a thousand dollars he stole from the safe in his father's office. He ran away from home in part to escape the wrath of Robert, a man who held back no punches, and in part to search for answers to all the questions he had about himself, explanations for the powers that were slowly growing in strength.

And he found them.

He wasn't who he believed himself to be. He was something much stronger, and over time he had *become* much stronger.

I am invincible! I am immortal!

I am a fucking god!

The old man was going to find out tonight, and when he did, Jack was going to bring the giant down.

Jack swallowed his fourth shot of whiskey and glared over at Ellen, at Daddy's little girl, as a much heavier version of Pink Floyd's "Another Brick in the Wall" started up on the jukebox.

You've always been his favorite, and I know why.

All the anger, lust, and jealousy from so many wasted years rotting in the boneyard of memory swelled and churned in his stomach like a wicked brew of something deadly. Bile burned black holes in his gut like boiling acid, raising the fury in his heart to infernal heights, fueling his desire.

Jack clenched his fists tightly. Had he known then what he knew now, he would've taken them all down simply by thinking it.

But that wouldn't have been as much fun as this was going to be, as what he had planned, as playing with them like puppets, pulling their strings for his own amusement.

And watching them suffer.

Hey, little sister, let's see how much you can bleed now.

The bikers were coming their way.

Shawn saw them first, and felt his heart kick up a notch. He could see by the brutal mischief on their hard, gritty faces that they weren't coming over to offer to buy their next round of drinks.

"Oh God," Ellen groaned. She saw them too, and began shaking like a leaf in a bitter cold wind.

Immediately Shawn rose from his stool, flexed and shielded Ellen from what he knew was coming. He'd seen it so many times before. He wished he still had his brass knuckles. He wished he still had his knife. They had come in handy for so many of these situations before, and he wasn't sure if he could take these two big guys alone with his fists.

But I'm not alone.

He looked over at Jack for help, and felt his heart seize up in his chest.

The son of a bitch was looking up at him and smiling, a knowing look in his eyes like he planned this whole thing from the beginning.

"Hey there, boy," the shorter, fatter biker with the full bushy beard said. "Got somethin' we want."

Shawn reached for his beer bottle on the counter, grabbed it by the neck, then raised and smashed it against the edge of the bar. Ellen yelped as the glass shattered to the floor.

With blood pumping and adrenaline racing through his veins, Shawn thrust the broken edge of the bottle out in front of him and snarled. "Back the fuck off!"

The bikers stopped a couple feet away from the weapon trembling in Shawn's outstretched hand. As Ellen began weeping, they grinned like bloodthirsty jackals creeping in slowly for the kill.

What's going on? What the fuck did we get ourselves into?

Shawn glanced over at Jack. He was sitting silently on his barstool, still smiling and enjoying the show.

Why are you doing this? You mother–

From somewhere behind the counter, Shawn heard the metallic click of a hammer being cocked and felt his blood solidify.

"Drop it," Bobby ordered. "Or I'll blow your damn brains out and make your bitch here eat up the mess."

"Shawn," Ellen whimpered. "Oh God… Shawn."

"Don't worry, Ellie," Jack said. "It ain't you they're after."

Confused, Shawn looked from Jack to the bikers looming before him. The taller one, the one with the long greasy hair and hard stubbly face, winked a diseased eye and said, "You sure are one fine piece of yuppie ass." He licked his cracked lips.

A seed of fear blossomed to full-blown terror as all those ridiculous, southern-fried clichés from the movies came to life right before his disbelieving eyes. "What the hell?" Shawn glanced over at Jack in shock. "The fuck is going on here?"

"I said drop it, college boy!" The command came from Bobby; he called him *college boy*? How the hell did he know he was in–

Ellen went from sobs to hysterics. She leapt up from her stool, but Jack snatched her back by a fistful of hair, pulled her into his lap, and pressed the serrated edge of a large Buck knife up against her throat.

All the other men at the counter suddenly stood up and began to form a tight circle around Shawn. Murderous glee shone in their eyes as they closed in, cracking their knuckles.

Shawn almost burst out with laughter. *I don't believe this is happening. What the fuck? Is this for real? Is this a joke?*

Somewhere in the back of his head, a voice belonging to a demon whispered, *"No joke, college boy. This shit's for real."*

In stark disbelief, Shawn looked again over at Jack, who was licking away the tears running down Ellen's cringing face, and said, "What the hell are you?"

Jack cracked an evil grin. "I'm the big brother," he said, lips unmoving. "And we're about to have us a little fun."

Shawn wanted to lunge at him. He wanted to bury the busted end of his only weapon into the sick bastard's throat. But he felt the threatening gaze of the bartender's pistol staring him down and looked helplessly at Ellen.

She opened her tearful eyes. Shawn's heart swelled and exploded at the sight of so much pain and anguish in someone he loved with so much passion and worship. Ever since the first day they met he knew she was the one, and now… *I can't save her, can I?*

"No," Jack whispered again in his head. *"And no one can save* you.*"*

Feeling the noose of hopelessness slip around his neck, Shawn let go of the broken beer bottle and closed his eyes against the impending flood of tears as everything he ever wanted in life – a brighter future with a beautiful woman who loved him despite his past, despite his former sins, despite everything – shattered to pieces on the dirty barroom floor.

Chapter 8

The moment she heard the glass shatter, Ellen closed her eyes and wished the world away.

"No, Ellie, keep them open, you're gonna wanna see this."

Jack yanked her head back by a clump of her hair. Pain shot through the roots embedded in her scalp. Another onslaught of tears jabbed at her eyes like sharp steely knives. Ellen opened her eyes to see a horde of drunken men beat her boyfriend bloody.

They punched him in the face, in the gut, smashed beer bottles over his head, and kicked him to the floor, then stomped on him repeatedly before lifting him off the floor and carrying him over to the pool table, where they leaned him over and pulled down his jeans.

"NO!" Ellen shrieked, horrified, closing her eyes again. "PLEASE DON'T! STOP! JACK! MAKE THEM STOP!"

"Mmmmm." Jack pressed the edge of his knife against her throat. "I remember when you first said those words to me. Only no one else could hear you but me. I'll never forget the way you tasted on my tongue, Ellie. And you smelled like honeysuckle."

Ellen groaned in anguish. Her mental block opened even further, allowing the memories to come crashing down upon her like a tsunami, tearing her fragile psyche apart:

Someone climbed into bed with her, waking her up. She could not tell who it was because the darkness of sleep still clouded her eyes and the curtains over the window were pressed tightly together, keeping out any natural source of light.

"Daddy?"

Sometimes when her father came home from his night shift, he would sneak into her room just to cuddle with her.

But then she remembered her father did not go to work tonight. That he went to bed early, complaining of a headache.

As the mattress sank with the weight of another warm body snuggling up to hers, she surmised that it could still be Daddy, that there was nothing to worry about. Maybe he couldn't sleep. Maybe his head was still bothering him.

She was about to ask him when the covers were pulled down from her body.

A twelve-year-old Ellen wondered what was going on. She was beginning to feel very cold and very scared. What in the world did her Daddy think he was doing to her? This wasn't right!

One hand slithered past her waist. Ellen cringed and tried to cry out, but no sound would come from her mouth. It was as if her vocal cords had been sliced in half.

"That's right, baby. You can't make a sound. Now lie still, and be good for Daddy."

Ellen's eyes grew wide. He called himself Daddy, but the voice definitely did not belong to her father.

Her mind screamed. Her body tried to move, to struggle, but she quickly found she couldn't. She was paralyzed. And it didn't seem like it was only her brother holding her down.

Ellen grew cold and stiff, her flesh creeping along her bones. She had heard stories about family members who abused each other in the worst, most unthinkable ways. Her mother watched those kinds of stories on Lifetime on a nightly basis. But of course Ellen never believed it would actually happen to her.

"Please, Jack," *she tried to cry out.* "No! Don't! Please STOP!"

"Mmmm." He licked her face, nibbled at her ear, kissed her neck. "Ellie... Sweet, tasty Ellie..."

Jack shifted, groaned, and shuddered on top of her. Tears streamed down Ellen's face.

"Ooh yeah... You're all mine now."

This time when Ellen tried to scream, she succeeded.

"Yeah, that's right, baby," Jack said. "We had plenty of fun during those nights, didn't we? But you just couldn't keep your mouth shut about the pain, about the bleeding. Good thing you could never remember exactly where it was all coming from."

Tears seeped through Ellen's tightly clamped eyelids. She recalled a lot of terrible things attributed to her brother's mischief, like those times she almost died: the day she nearly drowned in the pool; the day she tumbled down the stairs. Jack had always been nearby with a devious smile on his lips. But he had always told her it was an accident, and she believed him.

Why did he debase and violate her in that way? She had always loved him as a child growing up. She had idolized him and worshipped the ground he treaded upon. Why would he hurt and victimize her? Why would he do such a cruel and disgusting thing?

"Because I hated you," Jack whispered into her ear, "just as much as I loved you. And I wanted to know how you tasted."

Ellen opened her eyes to the sight of a long, throbbing cock slipping in and out her boyfriend's tight, hairy ass.

"Oh no." Her face crumpled like a paper bag as she squealed, *"Oh GOD!*

"There is no God," Jack said. "There is only me."

Ellen shut her eyes again and tried to deafen her ears to the screams Shawn made as he was sodomized by a big, toothless man with a fleshy pink dildo sticking from black leather pants.

"Don't worry." Jack nibbled on her earlobe. "His suffering won't last long. And your time will come." He licked her face and kissed her neck, making her skin crawl all over again.

"By the way, Ellie, how were things at home when I left? How long did it take for Mom to figure out that Dad was never the one hurting you? How long did it take for her to realize it was all me, the unfortunate son playing his pranks as usual? Or did she ever?

"And what did that do to her relationship with Dad? What did it do to *your* relationship with Dad? Fucked ya'll up pretty bad, didn't it?"

Ellen shivered. It was all true. In fact, that's when the drinking began, the fighting, the tension. Her mother was a staunch Catholic, so divorce was never an option for her. Still though, she used the bottle to escape the horror Jack created in her mind, as did her father.

"And what about you, Ellie? Did you begin to think that maybe it was true? That maybe Daddy really was the one touchin' you? Were you afraid of him? Or did you push it all back?"

Ellen shook her head. "I never believed it! None of it!"

"Liar. But you did end up telling them that you did it all to yourself, in your sleep. You were scared, but you didn't want Mommy to blame and hate Daddy, so you lied to protect him. Did she believe it?"

"You're evil, Jack! You *are* the fucking devil!"

"Now how long did it take for you to figure *that* one out?"

Closing her eyes, Ellen pushed herself to a place where her brother couldn't find her. A place he could no longer hurt her.

"Oh, I'll find you, Ellie. Haven't I always?"

Yes, he had. He was like a demon creeping into her nightmares, showing her the terrible things a man was capable of once stripped of the moral bounds that society uses to distinguish man from beast. Once he learned of his true nature, once he was back in the jungle of the savage, free from the leviathan, free from the philosophy governing civility, he began to commit the most awful crimes imaginable. And he did it all with a blood-lipped smile.

"I'm a wanted man in almost every town in the South, but no one knows my true identity. No one knows my true face. I never let them see it."

Ellen felt herself slowly slip from consciousness.

"But you knew I'd come back. Deep down, you must've known I'd be back to finish what I started."

And when the darkness closed in, its embrace was warm and welcoming, just like her father's arms.

Before Shawn got knocked around like an inflatable clown and then hauled off to the pool table, he flashed back to a time when he first held Ellen in his arms. When he first smelled her soft auburn hair, and touched her smooth youthful face, and kissed her tender pink lips. When the horror of this night was inconceivable.

It was his special place, the memory of the night he spent in Ellen's dorm room, and he desperately wanted to be there now:

They had just gotten back from seeing a lousy movie at the theater. Shawn had walked Ellen up to her dorm room where she invited him in for a beer from her hidden stash in the fridge. Soft rock music played on the radio as Ellen stretched out on her bed, placed her beer down on the side table, and propped herself up in an overtly provocative pose. "You are a bashful one, aren't you? Will you make a move already?"

Shawn just stood in the middle of the room, beer to his parted lips, too stunned to speak.

"We just went out on our third date. I can't wait forever."

He didn't know what to say. He hadn't expected this, at least not from her. He had sensed that she was skittish when it came to intimacy, and so all this time he told himself to take things slowly with her. She was special and he didn't want to ruin things by rushing her into something for which she was not ready.

But here she was, splayed out on her bed with her chest thrust out, her hair tossed back, and her lips pursed into a slight pout. Apparently, she was tired of him taking his time. She was tired of waiting. She knew what he wanted, because she wanted it too.

"It's okay," *she said, sneering sweetly.* "I don't bite."

"I'll remember that." *Shawn set his beer down on the table near the kitchenette and walked over to her bed.*

She cocked an adorable, crooked smile. "That a boy."

He eased down onto the mattress, wedged himself between her and the stuffed animals she kept up against the cinderblock wall for cushioning, and shifted into a more comfortable position by her side.

He then slipped one arm beneath the girl he had never been able to keep his eyes off of during British Literature II, and felt the stirring in his loins churn more rapidly as she moved closer to his side.

"Who would've thought it'd take you so long?" Ellen snuggled into his chest. She took his hand and kissed it.

"Didn't want to scare you off," Shawn said. "I was afraid I'd lose you."

"You have nothing to fear but fear its–"

Shawn held out the hand she kissed, warding off the cliché. "Don't finish it, please."

Ellen giggled and looked up at him with brightly beaming eyes, the kind in which a man could easily lose himself.

Shawn ran a hand through her long straight hair. It was as fine as silk and smelled of lavender and vanilla. His impending erection was no longer impending.

"You're cute when you're nervous," Ellen said.

Shawn raised an eyebrow. "Nervous? Why?"

"You're about to kiss your favorite writer's daughter."

His hard-on shriveled back a bit. "Okay, you just killed it for me."

Ellen giggled again. "Well, let's see if I can bring it back to life." Playfully biting her lip, she lowered her eyes and began to unzip his pants. "I sense a pulse," she said, slipping her hand into his fly.

Shawn's heart began to beat rapidly in anticipation of her touch. His breathing quickened as Ellen fondled his penis. Her hand was soft and smooth. She lifted her eyes as he hardened in her gentle grasp. "Lazarus is back from the dead."

"Giving him a name now?" Shawn touched Ellen's face, tilted her tiny chin up with one finger, and then kissed her lips, took in her tongue, swallowed her down.

It was better than he had ever imagined it in all his wet fantasies.

Once they got their fires burning, they peeled off their clothes and clung to one another, letting their mutual passions get the best of all rational thought.

They did not have sex. They did not fuck. Shawn had fucked before and it was nothing like this.

They made love, or at least what Shawn felt love really was like, and it felt good.

It was also Ellen's first time, as he had come to discover.

And that meant a lot to him. It meant she had given him a sacred part of herself that she could never get back. She had given him a gift, a trust, and with that Shawn knew he could never let her down.

But he was doing it now. He was betraying her by not saving her from this nightmare. Yes, he could fight these five lunatic drunks closing in on him, but he knew he couldn't possibly win, not alone.

And with Bobby pointing a pistol in his direction, and Jack holding Ellen back by the hair with a knife to her throat, he knew it was all over but the dying. He had failed Ellen.

"I'm sorry, babe," he said, looking at her, his heart breaking at the torment twisting her beautiful face, right before a fist rammed into his jaw.

He never got a chance to tell Ellen he loved her.

And he never would.

Jack watched as the gang of men tore into Shawn like rabid dogs on a kitten. Holding a whimpering Ellen close to his body, he reveled in the way they ripped at his flesh like buzzards on roadkill, and sunk their teeth into the meat on his bones.

He had expected this cannibalistic feast to commence after they were done shooting their load off in every possible orifice they could find. The animal hunger in them was there all along, bubbling below the surface, ready to break the leash holding it back. Jack saw to it. It was all part of the plan.

The moist sounds of teeth tearing, ripping, and crunching muscle and flesh were muted by the violent surge of Guns n' Roses' "Welcome to the Jungle" ricocheting off the walls like bullets.

The blonde-haired slut with the swollen lip was clapping and jumping up and down and cheering the dogs on as if it were some morbid pep rally.

Jack smiled, amused, and glanced over at the bartender. He was once again flipping through the pages of his magazine and smoking a cigar as if nothing out of the ordinary was happening in his bar.

Ellen was no longer in hysterics, no longer screaming Shawn's name. She simply cringed in Jack's lap and whimpered as he lovingly stroked her hair with one hand and held his knife to her breasts with the other.

Soon, it will be their time. Brother and sister. But first, he had to be sure that Shawn was all the way dead.

It can't be too long, Jack thought. *There can't be much life in him to hold onto. He's not that strong. I can sense it.*

Shawn had stopped his screaming right about the time the men – now dogs – began to feast on his unconscious body. Jack was almost certain that there was not much life for the ol' college boy to cling on to. With what was happening to him now, Jack was certain that whatever remained in that butchered body was on its way out.

He looked back toward the gorging, at what happens to humanity when all their foolish laws and morals tumble down. When man gives in to what is taboo in the eyes of society, but natural in the heart of the savage in the jungle.

Jack remembered, at the age of fifteen, witnessing the neighbor's two Dalmatians (both males, one father and the other son) humping each other in the flowerbed. He was fascinated by the incestuous spectacle, fascinated that animals, unlike their human brethren, knew of no bounds. For them, anything was up for the taking, nothing was off limits.

That is the way of the jungle, and aren't humans in a sense animals too? What distinguishes man from beast? What is man's true nature, and from where did he originate?

Where does man truly belong?

"In the jungle," Jack sang along with Axl Rose. And in the jungle, it was survival of the fittest. Jack learned that lesson well on the streets, and he was about to teach it to his little sister, a girl not used to the evils of man.

Shawn was dead, and so the men who mauled him – those dogs, those growling puppets – were no longer needed.

Jack yanked Ellen's head back by a clump of hair, forcing her to scream. Tears flowed down her wet, rosy cheeks. His erection throbbed eagerly against her bottom as she trembled in his lap. His heart hammered against his chest as he breathed her in (she still smelled sweet, like honeysuckle). He was ready to take her like he had always wanted to. He would go all the way with her, and then, he was sure, all else would fall into place.

"Stand up," he said, knife still to her chest.

"Fucker," Ellen spat, though her voice was shaky and small. "Son of a bitch, why'd you let them kill him?"

"Them?" Jack waved his knife around the musty air, smiling wickedly. "Who?"

This time when she opened her eyes, her scream hit a banshee crescendo.

Chapter 9

Robert Campbell shut down his laptop, sighed heavily in exhaustion, and poured himself another glass of scotch. He knew he should probably slow down on the booze, but tonight had been a terrible night and he needed the numbing escape of hard liquor, though it wasn't doing him a shitload of good.

Because he still felt sober, and still felt guilty as hell.

Robert poured the liquor down his throat and slammed the glass back down. He then reached across the desk for the silver-framed photograph of his daughter and drew another sigh. This time the sigh was one of profound sadness and regret.

The picture in his hand was Ellen's senior portrait from high school. She was seventeen, wearing a black dress, and looking just as beautiful as ever with her wide expressive eyes smiling at the camera and her long auburn hair spilling down her slender shoulders like silk. She was quite a vision to behold, with her little freckled nose and cheeks. Robert was very proud of the beautiful young woman she had become.

He was also very worried about what might happen to her now that Jack was home, a circumstance in which Robert played an unfortunate hand. He should not have allowed Jack back into the house.

Christine had nagged him to do so. She had gone on and on about forgiveness, how Jack was their prodigal son, and all the other Biblical rubbish she had spouted off for the last twenty-six years. But the nagging had quit working long after Jack stole his money and ran out of town. No, Christine had nothing to do with Robert's decision to invite trouble back into his home.

However, she did have something to do with that trouble being in existence…

NO! Robert set the photograph of Ellen back down and told himself not to go there, it was no longer worth dwelling on. He knew better than anyone that you cannot go back in time and change the past. Such a concept was for those who dealt in the realm of science fiction. He dealt in the realm of reality.

Crime was what he knew best. It was what he spent most of his life fighting. From real life as an investigator chasing down murderers and drug dealers, to fictional life where he battled his own demons through a detective named Jim Turner and banished them every time.

But he couldn't banish them in real life, not forever. Robert had learned that all too well over the years.

Demons always come back, no matter how many times you stabbed them through the heart.

Robert poured himself another drink.

Christine still had her suspicions about what happened to Ellen when she was twelve years old. She still suspected he was responsible for their daughter's bleeding and bruises, for her nightmares, even though the phenomenon, which Ellen had claimed she did to herself, had stopped well after Jack left the house. After he pulled his little stunt, purporting to having seen him sneak into Ellen's room and–

Robert pushed the thought away before it got him worked up. It didn't matter anymore. He decided to leave it be once he was sure that he would never hear from Jack again, as did Christine, who only assumed the problem with Ellen ended because she had kept Robert under close surveillance, which didn't last very long, unlike Ellen's nightmares.

They came at her once a year.

A year to the day Jack disappeared.

Ellen claimed never to be able to remember her nightmares after waking up screaming in bed, sweating and shaking all over. Robert was sure she had been lying, but he never pressed the issue. Because it was obvious that whatever happened in those dreams, whatever vivid images haunted her impressionable mind, was overly traumatizing, because she would never allow herself to fall back to sleep until the frightful effects of those night terrors had passed, and that would sometimes take days.

Robert and Christine took her to a shrink, who ran tests and put her on medication to try treating the problem, but the dreams continued coming for Ellen like a ruthless and immortal killer in a B-horror flick. And they always came on that fateful date marked on the calendar, the date that marked the anniversary of the great family rift.

Robert downed his drink and brought his attention back to the stupid, selfish thing he did this evening, the thing that could possibly hurt his daughter all over again.

They say a vampire can't harm you unless you invite it into your home, and Robert had regrettably done just that.

And you call Jack the trouble with this family. You call him *the villain.*

Robert rubbed his aching forehead and thought yes, there was a villain here and a crime had been committed, but this time the usual suspect was not at fault.

Tonight, it was Robert's turn to play the bad guy.

Ellen's senior portrait continued to smile sweetly back at him, but he couldn't return her gorgeous gaze. The thought of what he had done, the guilt for allowing it to happen all over again, weighed down on him like heavy chains of steel, chains he could not shake off.

Or could he?

There was still something he could do, wasn't there? There was still a way he could make things right, turn everything back around.

A knock came at the door just as he began rising from his seat. If it was Ellen, he would tell her that everything was going to be fine and not to worry. That he planned to get rid of Jack right now, even if it cost him a few thousand dollars more from his safe, and that he wished she and that Shawn Farris boy well. He seemed like a very nice kid, and all Robert wanted was for her to be happy.

But when he told the knocker at the door to come in, he saw it was his wife and dropped wearily back down in his seat. "What is it, Christy? I'm very busy."

Christine stepped meekly into the office and Robert looked her over with a grimace. She used to be a beautiful woman. She used to have a long flowing mane of dark hair that he would delighedly run his fingers through, a smile that lit her eyes with so much light they were blinding, and a graceful figure that once fit warm and lovingly into the crook of his arm.

But now her hair was cropped short, her eyes vacant and lost, and her body shriveled and cold. If ever he tried to hold her, she would stiffen apprehensively in his arms as if afraid that he would crush her bones into powder if he squeezed too tight. He could not remember the last time they made love or even the last time he *told* her that he loved her.

And vice-versa.

Whatever romance and passion they once possessed was long dead, buried and left to rot, and the putrid stench of that festering love was what remained of their marriage.

If it were not for their strict Catholic beliefs, they would have gotten a divorce around the time that Ellen left for college. Then again, Robert was not sure how much faith he had left in the Church, in God.

Christine smelled heavily of wine. She never used to drink so much, but then, neither had Robert. Everything went to hell around the time the drama with their children began.

"I just want to apologize for dinner," Christine said, not looking directly at Robert. "The things I said, I... I'm sure I embarrassed our Ellen."

"Then it's her you should apologize to," Robert said, reaching for his near-empty bottle of scotch. He splashed a little of the liquor into his glass. "Why are you telling me?"

"Because... I just wanted to thank you for not giving Jack such a hard time...for letting him stay and not...turning him back out to the streets. I know we've had our problems with..."

Robert rolled his eyes as he drank.

"It would be great if we could try to be a happy family again, Robbie. Don't you want us to be happy again?"

Robert was about to ask her when it was that they were last happy, but thought better of it. He did not want to have this conversation, and Christine always got in these sad, sentimental moods when she was inebriated. She would weep, whine, and wonder what ever happened to steer this family in such a horrid state of deterioration, and Robert would tell her Jack was born.

That was the start of it all. The kid was a problem child to begin with. The only saving grace was Ellen's arrival into the world, but still Jack managed to cast a dark shadow.

Robert thought about all the accidents Ellen used to have as a child. Jack was always right around the corner when they happened. And though there was only circumstantial evidence that Jack was responsible for what had happened with Ellen when she was twelve, the boy always seemed to have it in for his little sister and Robert had never been able to figure out why.

Is it possible that Jack could be up to no good even now?

Robert was sure of it. Why else would he have let him back into the house if he did not think Jack would create some kind of scene to scare that boy away from his little girl?

"I have to talk to Ellen," he said, standing up from his chair with a grunt. "She still downstairs?"

Christine wagged her head and looked down at the floor. "No, no. They went out with Jack, to some place called the Torchlight Inn. I've never heard of—"

Robert wasn't sure he heard right. "Wait a minute, what?"

"The kids went to some bar called the Torchlight Inn." Christine looked up at him quizzically. "Robert, are you all right?" She moved toward him, concerned. "You're growing pale."

The shock of what he had just heard knocked him right back down into his chair. His heart began to race, and his pulse hammered in his head as he tried to wrap his mind around this absurd and unexpected turn of events.

Christine hurried over to him, placed a hand on his shoulder, and leaned down as he began to breathe heavily in panic. "Dear God, Robert! Is it your heart?"

Robert held up a hand, warding her off. "The Torchlight Inn? Christine…"

"What? Lord have mercy, Robert, you're beginning to scare me."

Robert glared up at his wife and just for a moment, one fleeting moment, he wanted to wrap his hands around her skinny neck and strangle the life out of her.

But he defused that impulse quickly and said, as calmly as he could, "Christine, the county shut the Torchlight Inn down years ago. It's empty!"

Christine drew back slightly, confused. "What are you talking about?"

"The fucking bar!" Robert bellowed. "It no longer exists! It's home to rodents and cockroaches! What the hell are they doing there?"

"I…" Christine raised a hand to her lips. "I don't understand."

"Shit." Robert looked away, thinking of the worst possible scenarios. "What the hell have I done?"

His eyes turned toward the gun cabinet in the corner.

Could it really be as bad as that? Could it?

"Oh no," Christine said, seeing where his train of thought was headed. "Oh, Robbie, no."

Chapter 10

Darkness was all that Ellen could see. She thought for a moment that she was dead, that her heart had stopped beating, and that the grim reaper, draped in black, had harvested her with his sharp shiny blade of serrated steel, slicing her into oblivion, to hell, or someplace worse.

But then she heard her brother snickering, felt the fiery pain in her head as he pulled her back by the hair, and felt the edge of his knife lightly caressing her breasts.

She was breathing, she was alive, but she still could smell the rancid odor of death, of rot and mold, of waste and ruin.

The air was stale, dry and musky, and as her eyes adjusted to the darting shadows, she saw flickering orange lights dancing at different corners of her vision.

Candlelight provided weak illumination upon their dismal surroundings. "Where am I?" she said.

The answer came to her quickly, nudging her closer toward the brink of insanity as she observed the layout of the gloomy room.

"Holy shit!"

Jack's hideous laughter bounced off the blackened walls of what was once the Torchlight Inn. The sound drove an ice pick of fear further into Ellen's heart as she gazed around with wide, incredulous eyes.

"That's right, Ellie," Jack said gleefully. "Look and see. We're all alone here."

And he was right. There was no one else in the ramshackle room, no sign of life, nothing but overturned tables and chairs, boarded-up windows with moonlight seeping through the cracks in the warped two-by-fours. Animal feces, cigarette stubs, and other such rubbish littered the gray, rotting floorboards.

"It's just you and me, baby... Well...and that."

With his knife, Jack pointed in the direction of the pool table, which was covered in dust and cobwebs. On top of it lay Shawn's body, on its side with no sign of the brutal mauling it had suffered at the claws of inhuman savages.

"SHAWN!" Ellen shrieked. "SHAWN, HELP ME!"

He didn't respond. He didn't even move. His eyes were clamped shut, and his mouth was twisted into a rictus of agony.

"SHAWN, PLEASE! WAKE UP!"

"He can't, Ellie... He's dead."

"No," she began to whimper. "No, no, no, no, no."

"Yes, honeysuckle. Yes, yes, yes, yes, yes."

Ellen couldn't believe it. *It was an illusion. It was all some crazy phantasm. None of it was real! How? And how could Shawn be dead if it was all–*

"I have powers, baby. Black fucking magic powers. Not sure where they came from. Maybe God, maybe the devil. But whoever granted them to me, I've been damn thankful, 'cause I like 'em. They started around the time I turned eighteen. I can control people's minds, make them see, hear, and feel things that aren't real, but I'm sorry to say it was all too real for him, Ellie. It was so real that it killed him. All his fear, all his terror; it was all too shocking for his poor heart to take."

Ellen's lips moved frantically around words she could not speak, incredible thoughts she could not utter.

"You remember how you felt right after waking up from all those night terrors you had in the past – the sweat pouring from your body, the rapid beating of your heart, and the prickling of your skin? That's what happened to pretty boy over there. It was like a night terror times ten, and it was one in which he died. And you know what they say about dying in your dreams…"

Ellen shut her eyes, but the tears flowed anyway.

"But I didn't want that to happen to you. I have something else in store for you, little sister."

"What are you?" Ellen spat, anger now building up inside and overriding her fear as Jack led her over to the pool table. "Son of a bitch, you're not my brother…you're not fucking human!" She opened her eyes and cringed at the sight of Shawn's pale, rigid body.

"But I *am* your brother," Jack said, dragging her by the hair, knife still in place. "We're of the same blood, no doubt about that. But you're kind of right about that not being completely human part."

Ellen couldn't bear to look at Shawn. She struggled to look away, to close her eyes, but Jack wouldn't let her. He wrenched her head back, began cutting at her blouse with his knife, and demanded that she keep looking.

"Pull him off," Jack said. "And then climb up on the pool table. But no funny business, you hear? I'd sure hate to fuck a corpse. That ain't ever any fun."

The grisly hand of revulsion plucked at Ellen's nerves like broken fingers on an out-of-tune guitar. The vulgar discord sent a harsh wave of tremors all throughout her body as the fear once again gained the upper hand.

"Oh my God, you are sick…you are the dev–"

"Pull him off! Let's get this show on the road."

Chapter 11

"What're you doing with that gun, Robbie? What are you thinking?"

Robert ignored Christine as he holstered his .38 caliber revolver and then shut and locked the gun cabinet.

"This is crazy! You must be mistaken. Why in the world would Jack want to hurt Ellen? He's trying to change... He wants to be part of the family again... He wants—"

Robert was already out of the office and heading toward the stairs. Christine was in pursuit, still flapping her gums about forgiveness, repentance, and...

And murder.

Robert didn't want to hear any more about it. He had enough of her lecturing him about God and murder. That argument was the start of all this mess. Had he not caved in to her years ago, none of this would be happening now.

Should've killed the damn seed before it grew!

"Robbie!" Christine screamed as he marched down the stairs. "Are you listening to me? Robbie!"

Before he reached the front door, Christine grabbed his arm and pulled at him with all her might, shouting: "You could never love him, could you? You heartless bastard! You've always hated him! Always resented him! And all because he wasn't of your Godforsaken sperm!"

At that, Robert wrenched his arm away, swung it around, and backhanded his wife square across the face.

With a startled yelp, Christine snapped around on her heels and toppled to the floor like a useless sack of bones.

Stunned by his reaction, Robert turned to look down at the damage he caused. Never before had he struck a woman, let alone his wife. Yet there she was, slouched on the floor, looking up at him with wide astonished eyes and a trembling hand over her gaping mouth.

He could see small drops of blood hitting the floorboards. For a moment there was only shocked silence between them. They both knew a line had been crossed at that moment. The rift torn between them had widened. But, as usual, it would be Robert who would pay the price.

"I'm sorry, Christy," he said softly. "Sorry it has to be this way." Turning away from his fallen wife, his fallen life, Robert threw the door open, stepped outside, and slammed it shut.

Chapter 12

Ellen did as she was told.

"Lift with your legs," Jack said, standing behind her with the tip of the knife at her back. "He's dead weight."

"I'm sorry, Shawn," Ellen whispered as she pulled him off the table.

He fell to the floor like a sack of sand, splayed out.

Staring down at the empty shell of the man she loved, Ellen felt a sharp pang of guilt in her heart.

But the tip of the blade against her spine was sharper.

"Enough of this sentimental bullshit, Ellie," Jack said. "Now climb up and lie down on your back."

Jack stood back a step and smiled as Ellen hoisted herself up on the pool table and lay down flat.

The helpless signs of resignation on her tear-streaked face excited him. He loved a damsel in distress, loved to watch them cower and cringe beneath his overwhelming power and strength. It was sweet.

But a bitch that knew when to submit was even sweeter.

I have conquered, I have captured, and now I will enjoy the forbidden fruits of my labor.

Forbidden? Nothing was forbidden. This lust he felt, this yearning, was so natural, so pure. And how could something that felt so good be labeled as bad, as taboo? Fuck taboo! This was not unnatural. This was the true nature of man. Animalistic, depraved.

Sheathing his knife in his belt, Jack approached the table. "Don't resist," he said. "Not that you could."

Ellen shut her eyes and whimpered as Jack unbuckled her jeans and pulled them down her legs. She cringed and stiffened as he ran a hand along the smooth-shaven surface of her pale and trembling thighs. She wore baby blue cotton panties. Jack licked his lips and slowly began to pull those down as well.

"Damn, Ellie," he said with a snicker. "You've shaved every damn place I've been, haven't you? Nice. It's like you're twelve years old all over again. Mmmmm, hope you're still a virgin."

Chapter 13

Christine didn't try to stop him once he was out the door. He thought perhaps she would try to phone the police, and that was something he didn't need.

This was a family matter, this was personal, and this was a long time coming; cops would only get in the way.

Robert climbed into the cab of his Dodge Ram pickup truck, started the engine, and pulled down the driveway. As he pressed the accelerator, he switched on the radio, which was tuned to a classic rock station, just so he could drown out the words that Christine shouted before he smacked her to the floor.

"All because he wasn't of your Godforsaken sperm!"

No, Jack was not of his seed. They'd never found the guy who shot *that* cursed bullet. But whoever that son of a bitch rapist was, Robert was certain that his bad genes were passed down to his bastard son, branding him with the mark of the beast, of Cain, of the devil.

It was the only explanation Robert could fathom for why Jack was the way he was: he inherited his biological father's criminal traits. It was an old theory of criminology into which Robert put whole-hearted stock...at least in this case.

Jack was in no way a product of the healthy conservative environment that Robert and Christine provided for him. He was a product of the primitive nature passed down to him by the blood of the man who raped his mother. And despite the Catholic Church's firm stance against abortion, Robert found that it would have been a service to society had they terminated the pregnancy the moment it was discovered.

But Robert still could not understand how Jack managed to fool Ellen and her boyfriend into following him into a vacant building. What kept them from fighting once they discovered what they were getting themselves into? Did Jack have a weapon? What possessed them to–?

What possessed *him* to bring the gun?

Because he had his suspicions, and his suspicions were almost always correct.

He swung left out of Piper's Cove.

Chapter 14

Jack used his knife to cut away Ellen's blouse and baby blue bra. After tossing the tattered garments away, he took a moment to admire her firm, ample breasts.

They were soft and warm in the palm of his hand. Feeling the stirrings of arousal in his loins, he bent down to have a taste of one pale boob.

He could fit half of it into his mouth. He sucked on it greedily as Ellen wept and whimpered helplessly. She did not try to resist. Except to shudder and cringe with revulsion, she did not move a muscle. Jack wondered why.

He was not using his powers to hold her down. Nor was he keeping her from screaming out for help. He wondered if she was doing it on purpose; if she knew exactly what he wanted and was now fucking with *his* mind, subtly turning the tables on him.

"Always said you were the smart one," Jack said, knife in hand, as he unzipped his pants. "But I have ways of making you scream." Pulling out his member, he leaned over to lick away a tear that traveled down Ellen's right cheek. He whispered into her ear, "We're gonna have company soon. So I'm gonna make this quick."

He placed a hand on her boob and squeezed violently. Ellen squirmed around in pain, but bit down on her lower lip to keep from crying out.

Stubborn bitch.

Though Jack's frustration was nearing its breaking point, his penis was as flaccid as a deflated balloon. If Ellen didn't start singing, it was going to be difficult for him to plunge his way into her, to break her, to conquer her. That was now the only goddamn way he could get it up!

Frowning with deep displeasure, Jack clenched a fist and rammed it down into the breast he had been viciously fondling.

This time Ellen couldn't keep it back. The shriek from her throat was like a banshee wail, as sharp and clear as shattering glass.

Jack's penis slowly stiffened and rose like a serpent from the bristly thicket between his legs. With a mischievous sneer, he dug his hand into Ellen's hair and began twisting a large clump of auburn tresses. "That's more like, honeysuckle," he said. "That's how Daddy likes it." With the edge of his knife, he traced the delicate line of her jaw.

Ellen's face was clenched tight in pain, but her eyes and lips remained clamped shut. Jack tapped her chin with the point of his blade and said, "I'll cut it open myself, Ellie."

As Ellen opened her mouth, Jack leaned down for a kiss.

Ellen bit down on his tongue.

The pain was so keen it shot up his spine and into his skull, making his shoulder hitch up and his muscles grow rigid. His penis went limp right before Ellen thrust her knee into his crotch.

Jack shrieked like a rabbit being skinned alive. His eyes bugged from their sockets as blood leaked from his lips. Ellen took the advantage once again and slugged him in the jaw.

It was like punching granite, but Ellen couldn't let the pain in her knuckles distract her. She had to act fast if she wanted to escape.

With all her might, she shoved Jack off her, off the pool table, and right on top of Shawn.

"BITCH!" she heard Jack holler in a weak, mousy voice. "YOU FUCKING BITCH! I'M GONNA GUT YOUR FUCKING ASS ALIVE!"

As quickly as she could, Ellen scurried off the pool table and rushed for the exit as Jack scrambled to his feet screaming, "GET BACK HERE, BITCH! YOU'RE NOT GOING ANYWHERE! GET BACK HERE!"

Ellen grasped hold of the mottled brass handle of the large wooden door and pulled, but it didn't give an inch. It was stuck tight to the jamb. That didn't stop her, however, from tugging at the handle and banging on the door with her aching hand.

"GODDAMN CUNT!" She heard the frantic shuffle of footsteps coming up behind her. "YOU'RE MINE, ELLIE! YOU FUCKING BELONG TO ME!"

She spun around and took a swing, but Jack caught her fist as it sliced the air and slashed his knife across her chest.

Clutching her bleeding breasts, Ellen fell to her knees with a shriek. Seething with unquenchable rage, Jack punched the top of her head, grabbed a knot of her hair, and dragged her back towards the pool table.

"Ooooh, you're gonna pay for that," he growled around a bleeding lip as his balls pounded in hellfire agony. "Fucking HELL, you're gonna hurt!"

Reaching the pool table, he yanked her head back, slugged her in the face, and gathered her up in his arms. She was about as limp as a rag doll. The blows she suffered nearly knocked her unconscious and she was bleeding badly. Jack tried not to cut her too deeply (not yet), but he must have underestimated his own anger, his own strength.

Nevertheless, he heaved her back onto the pool table, spit a wad of blood onto the floor, and wiped the sweat from his face with the back of the hand holding the bloody knife.

He was no longer able to even consider fucking her now. The damage she'd done to his ego and pride was just as bad as what she did to his testicles. But he could still ruin her further than he already had. He could still fuck her up inside and out.

Breathing heavily, he glanced down at his knife and thought about all those Halloweens he used to carve pumpkins with Ellen. He remembered how they'd scrape the insides of the hollowed-out pumpkins with their little kitchen knives and scrape away pulp and seeds from the rough and wet surface. He remembered the sound it made.

Looking from his knife to the space between Ellen's legs, he wondered what kind of sound *she* would make, and what kinds of things he'd find scraped away at the most hallowed region of her body.

Chapter 15

Robert swung into the parking lot of the Torchlight Inn. His headlights brushed across Jack's Mustang as he slammed on the brakes and came to a halt in front of the entrance to the abandoned bar.

He remembered the horror stories surrounding this bar, and the terrible crimes that were committed within. If anyone asked him, the county had waited far too long to shut it down. It had become a slaughterhouse by the time the cops finally kicked open the door, locked and loaded. However, the damage to the town had already been done.

So many dead. So many innocent civilian lives taken by the hands of human monstrosities. It made Robert sick thinking about it – all the people they could have saved from inhumanity.

And now his daughter was here with her brother, a human monstrosity himself.

Robert killed the engine and hurried out of the truck.

From outside, he could hear Ellen screaming louder than he ever thought possible. Extracting his revolver, he reached the building's entrance, grabbed the door by its crusty handle, and swung it open with ease.

Despite all the screams revitalizing Jack's libido, he was aware that the old man had arrived.

Right on time, he thought as he pulled the knife from Ellen's bleeding vagina. *Let's wrap this little family reunion on up now, why don't we?*

Jack leapt off the pool table and slapped Ellen hard on the ass as she curled into a shuddering fetus, blood streaming down the inside of her legs.

"JACK!" he heard the old man holler. "The FUCK is going on in here?"

He could have used his powers of mind manipulation to bring the giant to his knees. He could have assaulted him with all sorts of ghastly, grotesque visions that would surely drive him insane. But he knew that what was lying behind him on the pool table, forever scarred and traumatized by what he had done to her, was enough to kill the bastard.

It was enough to wrap around his heart and squeeze until it stopped beating. To have his pride and joy, his blessed child, raped, violated, and turned into a weeping shell of a woman was as far as he needed to go to finally set things straight between them.

Between them all.

Robert had the black eye of a Smith & Wesson staring him right in the face as he stepped into the candle-lit darkness. Looking from Jack to Shawn's dead body, and then finally to his precious daughter, his red face went as pale as raw bone. His eyes grew wide and his whiskered jaw nearly swept the floor as it fell open.

"My God," Robert whispered, shocked and astonished. "What have you done?"

"What I always wanted to do, Pops," Jack said with a sneer. "How does it feel?"

Robert lowered the hand holding the gun as he stepped further in. He could not take his eyes off his daughter, who was still shaking and weeping in a pathetic ball of bloodied flesh.

Still conscious? Fuck it. Jack was sure the shock of what her body had gone through would soon take over and drag her down into the darkness of never-ending sleep.

But what if she lives? Jack smiled. *Doesn't matter.*

Robert stopped right in front of him and just stared. The look on the old man's face made all of this worth it.

Ellen's breathing was rapid and short, and for a moment she broke through her sobbing to groan weakly.

Jack's smile broadened and his eyes narrowed into slits as Robert raised the gun up against his head.

"Do it," Jack said.

It took a moment for Robert to find his voice, and when he did, he said softly, "Why?"

"Because you never loved me." Jack snarled bitterly as all the rage and envy he had clung on to his entire life rose like Cain from the pissed-on ashes of his soul. "Not even once."

Robert stared at Jack in perplexity. "Why would I?" he said, after a brief stretch of silence. "You're not even my son."

Those startling words were akin to a violent jab in the gut, knocking the breath from his lungs. *Not his son*?

Tears welled in Jack's eyes and stung like a dozen yellow jackets as he gripped the handle of his knife firmly. He wasn't expecting that answer from his father, and he sure as holy shit wasn't expecting the water works and the pain he felt.

But that didn't matter. It was all over now. All over but the dying.

"If that's how you've always felt," he said through clenched teeth, "then I'll just finish what I started."

Spinning around, he raised the knife and lunged for Ellen, intending to plunge it straight through her throat.

But before he had the chance to even break the skin, to kill his sister, the girl he always loved and hated, a loud firecracker pop deafened his ears and shut out his lights.

And the last thought that ran through his mind before it was blasted away: *Did he really mean it?*

He would never know for sure, but it no longer mattered.

What he'd come home to accomplish had been accomplished.

His family was now as broken and fractured as his life had ever been. He had gotten his revenge.

Second Shots

Bartender, Please
Ty Schwamberger

Erin raised her weary head off her chest and looked through blurry eyes at the figure stepping through the doorway. She hoped it was anyone but Gabe, but as he came closer to the pillar she was chained against, she knew her luck hadn't changed. Yes, it was him. Gabe. Or, as he now liked to be called – T-Bone.

"Well, what do we have here?" T-Bone said, stopping a few feet in front of his capture. He had a macabre grin stretched across his bearded face. "Did you rest well, my dear?"

Erin choked down the few drops of saliva that were in her mouth. They felt like sandpaper going down her throat. Her eyes fluttered a few times, still trying to clear her vision. "Yeah, I guess."

"What?"

"Yeah, I guess I slept okay," Erin said again.

"And?"

Erin closed her eyes, trying to understand what Gabe meant. Then she remembered how he always wanted to be addressed.

"Sir."

"Ah, much better. Now, what would you like to do today? Maybe a little sucky-sucky or a little sticky-sticky? Or better yet, how about a little more slice n' dice? I know how much you love when I go to work on you with these tools T-Bone so graciously left behind for me."

"Whatever," Erin mumbled in reply.

"What was that?"

"Nothing. Never mind…Gabe."

At the sound of his former name, he ran up and head-butted Erin. She screamed out as fresh blood starting to pour out of the wound. She started coughing, unable to breathe. He screamed in her face. Erin could feel the rancid spit flying from his mouth with every hateful word.

"You're a real fucking piece of work, you know that don't you, bitch? You should be happy you're even fucking alive. I could have easily gutted you like a fish like T-Bone did to Alan, but no. Instead, I figured if I kept you alive, you'd realize what a dick tease you had always been back on campus and maybe one day grow to learn some fucking respect for people that love you."

Erin couldn't believe the things that her former best friend had just said to her. She had always known she was a bit of a tease to guys, including Gabe, but never thought it was to the level that would warrant how she was now being treated. Gabe, er, T-Bone was treating her like she was a piece of trash, not his best friend. They had once been able to have fun together and talk about whatever was on their minds, but not now. Oh no. Now he was acting like he never liked, cared, or loved her as a best friend should. He had turned from a sweet, happy-go-lucky person to a thoughtless, horrible person that she barely recognized anymore. Erin had no idea why he was acting like this; whether he had always felt this way about her and their friendship, or if the events that had unfolded during their time at the Torchlight Inn had pushed his sanity over the edge. Whatever the reason, Erin knew she couldn't survive the emotional and physical abuse – from the medical instruments lying on the table behind Gabe or from the tool between his legs – much longer. Something had to give. Whether it was going to be her own sanity or her life, she did not know. But the pit in her stomach told her that she would find out soon enough.

"Yeah, 'cause this sure *feels* like love," Erin finally said.

"What? What was that, bitch?"

"I said, 'Yeah, 'cause this sure feels like love,' T-Bone."

"What the fuck is that supposed to mean, Erin?"

Erin's eyes widened at Gabe's stupid remark. She couldn't believe his mind was so far gone to not know what he was doing was wrong, that someone claiming they love you should never treat you like he was treating her, that there should always be respect, above all else, where love is concerned. He obviously didn't get it, and Erin now realized that it probably wouldn't matter what she said to Gabe, that he was probably going to keep her chained to the pillar in the basement of the bar until her mind snapped or he outright killed her. She decided to go for broke and give him what he wanted the most – her love. Erin closed her eyes, took a few deep breaths, and hoped against hope it would work. Then she let the words fly.

"Bartender?" Erin said in her sweetest voice possible.

T-Bone, who was now a few feet away and busy looking over the various instruments of death that were lying on same metal table that the former crazed bartender used, didn't hear the voice from behind him. His mind was elsewhere, somewhere that sane people can't understand or even think about venturing. Erin said the word again. This time her voice must have snapped him back to reality, as he turned around and faced her again. Erin looked down, and although she couldn't quite make out what type of surgical tool he was holding, she could see the flickering light coming from the burning torches at the ceiling bouncing off it.

After not getting a reply from Gabe, Erin finally said, "Can I *please* order something to drink? My mouth is surely parched, and I'd love for it to be nice and moist for the next time we kiss. I already enjoy it quite a bit, but it'd be so much better for *you* if I had some moisture in my mouth, ya know? Then my tongue wouldn't feel like it's got kitty litter stuck to it." Then she smiled and chuckled a few times. Erin hoped that joking like they had always done in the past would somehow bring back some small part of her best friend, but it didn't seem to have the intended effect. Instead, Gabe just glared back at her, expressionless.

Finally, he said, "Oh yeah? And how do you intend on paying for this drink, miss?"

Erin smiled; he was playing right into her plan. "Anyway you want, T-Bone. I mean, I know we've technically already had sex and all, but with me always being chained to this pillar I really can't pleasure you like I want to, ya know? So, I was thinking, if you'd be kind enough to get me a drink, and let me drink it myself this time with my own two hands, afterward I'd be glad to give you the time of your life and really show you just how much I do, in fact, love you."

When Gabe didn't reply right away, Erin figured he was thinking of the next hurtful thing to say or do to her. She looked down to the hand holding the pain-inflicting instrument, and watched as Gabe twisted it around and around in his palm. Erin was sure he was thinking of how to hurt her next, so it made her heart skip a beat for the good when he next spoke.

"Hmmm… Well, I guess that'd be okay. I suppose even if you never really loved me back at college, you never lied to me. Well, at least not that I know of. So there really isn't any reason why I can't trust what you're telling me now is the truth. " Erin shook her head back and forth, indicating that he could believe her once again. Then Gabe said, "All right, I'll fetch you a drink. Whatd'ya have, miss?"

"A beer would be fantastic, T-Bone. Thanks a ton," Erin said, smiling from ear to bleeding ear.

"You got it, miss. I'll be back in two shakes of a lamb's tail. Now, don't you be going anywhere till I get back," Gabe replied, then laughed.

He turned away from Erin, gently put the tool he had been holding down on the metal table, and started walking towards the door. As he was shutting the steel door, Erin thought about asking him to unchain her now, but thought better of it and instead yelled out, "Thanks, T-Bone. You're the best!"

Erin couldn't tell from the distance between the pillar she was chained against to the steel door whether Gabe was smiling or not, but the flutter of her heart told her he was.

Gabe came walking through the door a short time later. In one hand he was balancing a large plate that had two frosty mugs of beer on it, and in the other hand he was somehow carrying two flat-topped stools over his shoulder. He walked up to the large metal table that didn't contain the cutting instruments and set down the plate. Then he walked over to Erin and placed the stools a few feet apart from one another. Erin smiled down at Gabe, but he didn't look up. Next, he walked back over to the tables, transferred the tools onto the bigger of the two, then picked up the plate and small metal table and walked back over to Erin. He set the table down in between the stools, then carefully placed the mugs an equal distance apart. Erin looked on in amazement at just how much pride her former best friend seemed to take in his new job as owner and bartender of the Torchlight Inn. She didn't know whether to keep smiling or frown at what Gabe had become. He had once been the nicest guy she'd known. When she really thought about it, she did fancy him over Alan the first time they had all met, but it was Alan that had made the first move on her. That was the main reason she had ended up with Alan, and not the new maniac that she was now about to have a drink with and, eventually, try to kill.

"All set," Gabe finally said, finished setting up an intimate table for two. "You finally ready to get down from there and be an obedient little girl?"

Erin smiled and said, "You betcha, T-Bone. Sitting at our own private table, having a drink together with no one around to bother us is gonna be great."

For the first time since Gabe had taken over as owner of the bar, he flashed what looked like a genuine smile at Erin. She kept smiling back at him. So far her plan was working perfectly. She hoped it lasted until…

"There ya go," Gabe said, keying open the padlock that secured her to the pillar. "I hope your wrists aren't in too bad of shape."

Erin stepped away from the pillar and brought her hands around to the front of her body. Her wrists were bloody, but the cuts didn't seem deep enough to need any immediate medical attention. Erin knew if she could pull off her plan, she'd have all the time in the world to go to the ER and get patched up. But right now she had more important things to deal with.

She slowly walked over to the table, picked up the cold mug, and started to drink. The cold beer tasted bitter but wonderful, flowing into her dry mouth and down her scratchy throat. She used her college drinking skills to chug the beer even before Gabe could make it from behind the pillar to the table.

As Erin heard Gabe nearing, she quickly slammed down her empty mug, screamed, "Bartender, I need another," then snatched up his mug, twisted around, and threw the beer in his face. The cold beer stunned Gabe, and he screamed out and started pawing at his face, trying to clear the liquid from his eyes.

That's when Erin made a break for the metal table that held all of those horrible instruments that Gabe had used on her time and time again.

She picked up a macabre-looking medical saw, then twisted around and charged back towards Gabe, who was just now wiping away the last of the beer from his eyes.

The next to last thing T-Bone saw was his own tool of torture, as Erin reached out and slashed his throat. Blood from his carotid artery spurt out onto Erin's bare chest as he clutched his throat and started falling backwards.

As Gabe lay on the dirt floor in the basement of the Torchlight Inn, he smiled at all the things he'd ended up doing in life, watching the torches on top of the pillars continue to burn bright.

August 16, 1977
(The Death and Birth of the King)
Thom Erb

Make the world go away.

The young boy sat cross-legged on his cramped bedroom floor with a radiant smile on his distorted face. A defect of birth left him with an abnormally pronounced cleft palate, and his left eye extruded enough that it seemed like it would pop out and bounce off his blotchy cheek. The small room's walls were covered with posters of the Beatles, the Rolling Stones, Buddy Holly, and all other manner of rock n' roll royalty. However, the most precious moldy real estate was reserved for his favorite, the *King*. The soothing comfort of the soft scratching of the needle on the vinyl record filled his happy ears. Elvis crooned, lamenting the dark life of living in the ghetto.

He sat surrounded by stacks of record albums, high enough that they almost touched the yellowing ceiling. The colorful albums created castle walls of vinyl, and he was king within the sonic sanctuary. Inside, the only things his long-dead mother left him: her massive record collection and his best friend, the *Stereophonic Music Master-1000* record player. They offered sweet sounds and audible promises of a better place where he wasn't different and laughter was because of true happiness, not his dreaded deformities. Elvis and the Beatles offered him an endless ticket on a bus to a world where he wasn't considered a monster when he went outside. That was, *if* his father allowed him to go outside. He knew the old drunk was embarrassed of him. He could live with that. What he was growing increasingly intolerant of was his ignorant father's hatred for the only thing that mattered to the young boy.

His love for music.

The old man never understood his *"monster-son's obsession with his bitch of a mother's music,"* and his hatred for it all seeped incessantly from the old man's beer-soaked pores. The bitter old man constantly tried to toss the young boy's records into the dumpster behind their dilapidated tenement. The young boy had kept the stinky bastard at bay so far, but he worried daily that there would come a time where he wouldn't be able to stop the vile attempts. His gigantic head throbbed with anger, and his taut limbs twitched with anxiety at the thought.

Over my dead body, the young boy repeated under his breath for hours until he eventually fell asleep to the low tones of his own determined mantra. But today was a good day. The crotchety old man was a few blocks away at a bar, watching a Red Sox double header with his alcoholic, slack-jawed beer buddies. That meant the young boy could sit in his room, drink his grape Kool-Aid, and raise the drawbridge to his cardboard-and-vinyl castle and lose himself in a symphonic euphoria.

The vast record collection sat stacked five-boxes high, meticulously organized alphabetically, and he knew it by heart.

What will it be today, Mom? he asked into the thick air, fingering the collection and walking the perimeter of the room, sipping from his large plastic mug. The magical *Stereophonic Music Master-1000* blasted "Mother's Little Helper" as he continued his search for his next sonic salvation. He did not know what time it was. The E section of the record collection blocked the only window, blotting out the light. He never cared much for time, anyway. The ticks on the clock to a young boy essentially locked in his own bedroom held little merit. He measured time in the length of 45s and 78s. Those records were all that mattered to him.

He walked the square of music, waiting for its usual *Voice* to speak to him. Waiting for musical inspiration. He'd grown close to the soothing *Voice* that made his life bearable and, combined with the record collection and the record player, the ever-present *Voice* completed his circle of friends. He grew more anxious and distraught as he walked and the *Voice* was silent. His heart skipped beats and sweat poured down his face. The *Voice* had never let him down. It had always kept him company. Had always told him what to listen to. There was a time he thought it was his dead mother, but once he started reading the Bible and accepted Jesus on the throne of his heart, he realized it would be painfully difficult for her to speak to him. He would be drawn and quartered in the fiery pits of hell. Suicide was a sin; while he loved his mother, he knew it wasn't her, and that left him wondering about the true source of the *Voice*.

The deafening silence of the missing *Voice* stole his breath. A bit of afternoon sun splintered underneath the bedroom door and the only sound in the dark room was the hiss and repetitive thump of the tone arm on the record player, waiting impatiently for its next selection.

"Oh, my dear friend. Where did you go? Tell me. Please tell me what to play next," the young boy pleaded, draining the rest of his drink.

"Danny Boy," the usually soothing *Voice* shouted into the young boy's mind. He fell to the matted and stained shag carpet floor, dropping the cup and staring wide-eyed.

"Danny Boy," the *Voice* kept repeating. The young boy jumped to his feet and ran to the exact spot where the album sat, jutting out bizarrely an inch beyond all the other records on the makeshift shelves. Waiting.

The young boy pulled the record from its jacket and placed it on the record player. He carefully placed the Stones album back in its jacket and put it in its correct spot on the shelf. The *King* sang sweetly of Danny Boy and the calling pipes. It felt good. It felt right to the young boy. He watched the vinyl spin around and closed his eyes, lost in the lilting chorus, and tears surprised him as they raced down his clammy face.

An ear-splitting screech from the record needle filled the room and dropped him to his knees. The music died with it. The song stopped mid-chorus, leaving only a painful ringing in his ears. What little light that once creeped underneath the door became blackened out as the young man's body and soul jolted with unbelievable pain and sorrow.

It took a few pain-filled moments for him to shake his head clear of the constant noise. The *Voice* was mumbling, but he couldn't make out the jumbled words. He got to his feet. His knees shook like leaves on a tree, but he kept his balance. The *Voice* was distant and speaking one word.

Murdered!

Murdered!

Murdered!

The word bore into his temples. He felt it pulse through his defective body. It wouldn't be denied.

The *Voice* suddenly fell silent as a pounding came at the door.

The door was kicked open and the young boy's father staggered into the doorway. A large bottle of vodka hung slack in one hand; in the other, a burning cigarette.

"Well, well, mama's boy, I got sum news fer ya." The slurring was hard to decipher, but the young boy had gotten proficient in drunken-ese.

The young boy recoiled against the far wall of records, spreading his arms out, covering them.

"Yer gonna love this, ya lil' tittie baby." The father pointed at his startled son.

"Leave m-m-me alone." The young boy's voice came out garbled and weak.

"Shut the hell up, ya little freak. This is *my* house and I'm tired of takin cur' of yer sorry ass. You gonna love to hear that yer preshus *King*, Elvis, is fuckin' *dead*! How ya feel 'bout that, huh?" His father staggered like a zombie into the bedroom, grabbing the record shelf to balance himself. He chortled and took a swig from the bottle and let the brown liquid pour down the front of his already-stained white t-shirt.

"Wha…what? NO!" The young boy's mumble exploded into a shriek.

"Oh, you bet your sorry little ass. The piece a' shit, popped too many pills 'n they found 'em dead as a doornail on the shitter. All hail the mighty *King*." The drunk laughed and grabbed the record shelf and pulled it down, sending the entire wall of vinyl crashing onto the floor.

"STOP!" the young boy screeched.

'I'm tired of all this shit, music'n all this…this hero worship shit. I am gonna smash these fuckin 'records. It done didn't stop yer whore of a mother from killin' herself, and I've done had it with yer shit too! They're ALL fuckin 'outta here, ya hear me, boy?" the father said, and stomped on all the records, now spread out on the floor.

"Papa, NO!" The young boy leapt down on top of the shattered vinyl.

The father yanked the young boy back by his long brown hair, tossing him against the right wall, causing the shelves to cave under the attack and sending the contents spilling onto the floor, joining the other crushed remnants of his mother's precious collection.

The young boy's hysterical torrent of tears soaked the once beautiful artwork of Janis Joplin's *Pearl*. When he rolled over, whole chunks of soggy, colorful cardboard came up with his cheek. He stared up at his lilting father with a burning hatred that filled every inch of his frail body.

"Now, don't ya look 'et me like that, ya lil' shit. Stop yer damn cryin', ya big pussy. I'm gonna give ya som'n to cry about!" The father kicked his sprawled son in the ribs and stepped over him to assault the last wall of useless records. He tripped over the *Stereophonic Music Master-1000,* causing him to drop his bottle.

"Motherfucker!" He caught his balance and stared down at the silent record player. "Goddamn tired of this piesh a shhhit blaring that shit all hoursss uh the damn nigh'." He stomped down with all his weight and his steel-toed Wolverine work boot made short work of the old tone arm cobra. Dozens of pieces of plastic, metal, and vinyl filled the air. The young boy tried to stop his drunken old man, but his body refused to respond.

The father stared down at the young boy and jerked back in a belly laugh. Then he caught himself from falling and remembered his fatherly job wasn't yet complete. He spit a huge snot-filled gob onto what remained of the record player and smiled. He fell onto the last shelf and pulled out the Beatles' *Sgt. Pepper's Lonely Hearts Club Band*, shot his frozen son a look of disdain and disgust, and held it out for him to see.

"See, thessse damn hippies and stonrs are pure evil, ya dumb sumbitch." He looked at the cover and shook his sweat-covered face. "Goddamn garbage 'n ya can bet yer boney little ass that these losers'll prolly join that fat ass Presley in hell befur too lung. Ya can bet yer messsh'd up face." He knelt down, pulling the record from its sleeve, and smiled wide. His yellow and black teeth smelled as bad as they looked.

"This shit right her isssh the damn reason yer mama put a bullet into her damn brainpan. Brainwashin' bullshit from fake ass rich bassstards that just smoke refer, snort cocaine, n' shoot all that oth'r shit." The young boy jerked his head away from his teetering father.

*Don't let him get away with this, Graham. Reprehensible, jealous sycophants like your father are responsible for my death and many others. You **MUST** stop him!* The *Voice* returned with a deafening blast. It startled the young man, for it never had used his name before.

"Don't turn away from me, boy. Ya gotta see this. I'm a-gonna make a damn man outta ya, even if it kills me." The father smashed the record over his son's head and laughed. He fell down on one knee, still laughing, holding the shards of the album in his hands.

It is time to act, Graham. Stop his abuse, the *Voice* commanded, and the young boy felt the words in his heart. They felt...true and righteous.

"Guess I'm gonna have to just start usin' my fists on ya, boy, once I'm done with all these goddamn records." The father's laughter echoed inside the destroyed castle walls as he stood up and loomed over his prone son.

"But first, I need to drain the main vain. Ya don't mind, do ya, boy?" The father unzipped his dirty work pants and yanked his pecker out, and a golden flow of piss arced out and onto the pile of smashed records. The old man laughed and bounced up and down, turning it into a game as he tried to find an Elvis album. His mocking laughter echoed louder as he located the *King's* Christmas record.

"Hot damn, that wass yer mama's favorite. This one's fer you, Peggy Sue." Urine splattered on the youthful face of Elvis, soaking it through. The old man ran out of piss, zipped up, and turned for the door.

"Ya better have all thisss sshit picked up by the time I get back. If ya don't, ya might wanna go look fer yer bitch of a mama's gun." The father laughed again, kicked the young boy in the thigh, and stumbled out the door.

The only light was coming from the kitchen windows, where the old man staggered and nearly fell while fetching another cold beer.

Anger sprang through Graham and he felt as if he were about to explode. He felt a renewed strength overtake him. Every muscle in his thin body tightened. It felt like a thousand volts were pulsing through him, and the *Voice* urged him on.

It ends today, Graham. It ends NOW.

Graham's once trembling hand, now filled with vibrant energy, snatched up the bottle of whiskey and he leapt to his feet. He had never felt so invigorated or so...alive. He liked it. He loved it.

The *Voice* was right. It ALL ends NOW!

DO IT!

He bolted toward the old man, who was hunched over inside the fridge. The drunk must have heard the floor creak, because he turned around in time to see the Mr. Boston bottle coming crashing down upon his head.

Shards of glass sliced into the father's forehead and one large piece popped his left eye like a ripe tomato. He fell to the cold floor in a heap.

"Wha...wha...the fuc, I kill ya...bas..." The father grabbed at his eye as a ribbon of blood flowed from it.

End it, Graham. End it now...my avenger!" the *Voice* rang in the young boy's mind.

"You will hurt no one ever again." Graham held the jagged neck of the bottle in his blood-slathered hand. With one wide eye and a deformed smile, he spent the next nine hours slicing and dissecting his father, whom he let linger on the doorway to death just so he could fully experience the pain he'd put the young boy through for ten dark and sorrow-filled years. A thick layer of blood caked and coagulated in the grain of the old wooden floor and the room smelled of copper, feces, and freedom.

Graham stood up and stared down at the butchered remains of what used to be his biological father. He smiled, slipped in the gore as he pulled the pitcher of grape Kool-Aid out of the open fridge, and took a long swig. He dropped the empty Tupperware container onto what he only could assume was his father's liver. He couldn't be sure, but it *was* the biggest organ inside the diabolical man's body, after all.

You've done well, Graham. But we have much work to do. This is just the beginning of many wrongs that you must right. Are you ready, my avenger? Are you ready, my son? the *Voice* beamed inside Graham's mind and it made him smile.

"I will never again let any injustice go unpunished. On this, I swear!" Graham shouted into the dark apartment. Sharp shadows cradled the horrific scene as he headed to his bedroom and packed some clothes, a few cassettes, and a *John Lennon* mask his mother had bought him for Halloween last year.

Good, my avenger... Now that you are ready, let us begin.

"What now? What's next?" Graham asked. He had a big backpack over his shoulder and held his father's pistol, which he found under his parents' bed.

Graceland, the *Voice* commanded.

And the *Voice* would be Graham's constant companion for the rest of his days.

Six Shots
By Dean Harrison

Robert Campbell stepped inside the Torchlight Inn, unable to believe it was back in business after all the horror that had taken place within its walls.

Maybe it's all a dream, he told himself, glancing around the grim establishment, moving slowly toward the bar. *Maybe none of it's real.*

A fresh-felt pool table gleamed in the spot where he killed his son Jack. Robert felt a cold lump of dread twist in his stomach as he passed it. He wondered if Jack's ghost was somewhere around, watching from a dark corner with a smile of triumph as Robert pulled up a barstool and ordered a shot of Wild Turkey.

The tired-looking bartender poured his drink. Robert stared at his glum reflection in the mirror across the counter...

And saw Jack standing behind him with a glass of whiskey raised in greeting.

Robert twisted around in his stool, mouth agape.

He saw a small group of old men playing cards at a smoke-enshrouded table near the jukebox, which cranked out an old Johnny Cash tune. A young biker couple shot darts in the corner by the entrance. Jack was nowhere to be seen in the haunted gloom.

Shaking his head, Robert turned back around. His first shot of the night was set down before him.

"Keep 'em coming," he muttered to the bartender, staring into the amber liquid that filled the tiny glass, seeing his daughter's face staring back at him with accusatory eyes.

Drawing a heavy breath, Robert snatched up the glass and downed the whiskey before those eyes spoke. He knew what they would say, had he waited to listen.

"Another," Robert said, slamming the shot glass back down on the counter.

They would have said it was his fault, that he failed, that he was a terrible father.

And they would've been right.

Had he not been so stubborn about her boyfriend and Jack, the beautiful life Ellen led would have never been shattered.

Robert tossed back his second shot, knowing exactly how this would end. He called out for another and thought about his daughter.

Ellen was never the same after what her brother did. Robert suspected a big part of her died that night, leaving the rest to fall along shortly, in a bathtub full of bloody water, after she opened up a vein to see if she could still feel.

Robert cursed his damn negligence, swept up the new glass, and poured it down his gullet.

"Another," he demanded.

Christine filed for divorce. She could have it, too, for there was nothing left of their marriage to hold onto. They stopped loving each other long before Jack darkened their doorstep.

Glancing back up into the mirror, Robert wondered again if this was all real or just another vision left over from Jack's nefarious bag of tricks. Watching the reflected images of the few patrons who were sitting behind him, he wondered if they were really there or if they were all just phantoms manifested by a black magic spell. If so, why was he summoned here? Hadn't Jack taken enough? Ellen, his pride and joy. His life.

If Jack was here and he was listening in, he gave no sign. Robert did think he heard a distant peel of laughter, but that could've been in his head.

After the Johnny Cash tune ended, the jukebox switched to "The End" by the Doors.

Robert drained his fourth shot of Wild Turkey and wondered which of the five rednecks in the bar would have picked such a song.

A chill ran down his back as he listened to the psychedelic music, and he wondered what exactly possessed him to come back to the Torchlight Inn after learning it was taken over by new management. Was he seeking closure? Answers? Or did he just enjoy punishing himself?

He thought again about Ellen.

She'd struggled so hard to rise above the pain and trauma she suffered, but found she couldn't. And after a year went by and her grades started slipping, she dropped out of college, moved back home, and began sinking into a deep depression. After therapy failed, she sunk even further into a bottomless pit of despair, locking herself away in her room, never socializing with anyone except the ghosts in her head.

Last week, after reasons failed to surface for her to carry on, she'd stepped into a hot bath and slit her wrists. They buried her a few days after. Robert wondered what her last thought was before she released her hold on life. He hoped it was pleasant.

The bartender set his fifth shot down before him and Robert took a good look at the man for the first time since straddling the barstool. He seemed somehow familiar.

When it finally dawned on him who he was, Robert's heart froze up in his chest.

It was Ellen's dead boyfriend.

"I admired you once upon a time, Mr. Campbell," said Shawn Farris as he scrubbed the wooden counter with a white dishrag. "But not anymore. You're a pretty awful person. I mean, look at what you let happen to your own family. You killed them."

Robert opened his mouth to speak but found he had nothing to say – no protests, no denials. The ghost was right.

"You're a failure of a man. You should've been the one who died. Not us."

Dropping his eyes in shame, Robert reached for his fifth shot. Would it do the trick to numb the feelings of guilt and regret from continuing to weigh down on his soul? He doubted it.

"You know what you have to do now, Mr. Campbell. Don't you?"

Nodding his head in sorrow, Robert lifted his final glass, poured the liquid down his throat, and then pulled out the revolver that was tucked in the waistband of his jeans.

"Okay, you get one more shot, and then you have to go. It's closing time, Mr. Campbell. You don't have to go home, but you can't stay here."

Feeling the eyes of all the restless departed in the gloomy bar watching and waiting for him to join their fold, Robert slid the barrel of his gun into his mouth. The steel tasted bitter on his tongue. So did the tear that ran down his face.

"This is the end," sang Jim Morrison's haunting voice as Robert closed his eyes, cocked the hammer back, and pulled the trigger.

Afterword
Ty Schwamberger

From left to right: Dean, Thom, and Ty.

I don't have the exact dates, but I first met Dean Harrison and Thom Erb online in 2009. I don't remember exactly how it came about. I'm guessing that Thom was through Brian Keene's website, while Dean might have been through Jack Ketchum's then-running message board. In any event, we were all beginning writers and looking for some friendship in this crazy business.

Thom and I first met in person at Context, a speculative fiction convention in Columbus, Ohio, in August of 2009. I believe I first met Dean in person a few years later at the same con. In any event, it was shortly after first meeting online when we started talking about collaborating on a project together – one with a common theme. After tossing around ideas for a few months, I sent the following email to Jessica Weis of the now-defunct Wicked East Press.

On Wed, Jun 16, 2010 at 10:34 AM, Ty Schwamberger wrote:

Hi Jessica.

I wanted to write and gauge your interest on a complete novella collection that was written by me, Tom Erb and Dean Harrison. Basically, we took the common theme of 'three college kids walk into a bar' and then each wrote a novella, taking the stories in our own directions. A synopsis for each story is attached.

Having said that, I wanted to inquire if you would be interested in reading the anthology for possible publication.

Please let me know your thoughts on this when you have a moment.

Thanks,
Ty

Thirteen days later, we had a contract in hand for an anthology of stories we called *Twisted Tales from the Torchlight Inn.*

Needless to say, the three of us were ecstatic. The book was released in trade paperback and eBook in January 2011. Thom even did the cover art for the project. It looked fantastic…on the outside, anyway. As we received our contributor copies and started reading through them, we noticed another common theme running throughout the book – ERRORS! And lots of them. It was obvious that the edits we had supplied to the publisher never made it into the final version. We were devastated. But, because we were troopers and this was one of our first books, we pushed ahead and promoted the thing. We even did a promotional giveaway for the book where each of us wrote a "what happens next" short story and packaged it into a PDF that readers would receive if they purchased the TPB or eBook of TTFTTI. We called it *Last Call*. Get it?

Unfortunately, because of a few poor reviews (let's face it, no one knew any of us back then) and the publisher not really giving a damn, the book never sold very well. After a few years, we ended up pleading with the publisher to let us have our rights back, which we ended up receiving at the very end of 2012. I don't believe Dean ever did anything with his novella, but I know Thom ended up getting his published through Crowded Quarantine Publications shortly after I told him Adam Millard was going to be publishing my novella.

Fast forward 10 years, and it brings us to the edition you are now holding in your hands.

It's funny how things work out.

The three of us have always thought about working on another project together.

But that's a story for another day.

Until then, go grab a cold brew and dive into these nasty, twisted little tales.

We hope *you* enjoy it.

Cheers.

About the Authors

Ty Schwamberger is an award-winning author & editor in the horror genre. He is the author of a novel, multiple novellas and collections, and editor of several anthologies. In addition, he's had many short stories published online and in print. Two stories, "Cake Batter" (released in 2010) and "House Call" (initially released in June 2013, then picked up for worldwide distribution in 2020), have been adapted to film. He is currently working with several other filmmakers for additional film options. He is an Active Member of the International Thriller Writers. Learn more at http://tyschwamberger.

Thom Erb is a genre fiction writer exploring all shades of darkness and light and the varying definitions of heroism. Refusing to pigeonhole his writing, Thom strives to craft tales that blur the lines of horror, fantasy, thriller, weird Western, science fiction, etc, for both adult and young adult audiences. You can learn more at www.thomerb.com.

Dean Harrison is a life-long fan of horror fiction. His published works include the novels THESE UNQUIET BONES and NYMPH. He's also had a handful of short stories published in various horror anthologies. He lives in Mobile, AL, a port city teeming with ghosts.

www.ingramcontent.com/pod-product-compliance
Lightning Source LLC
Chambersburg PA
CBHW020646260626
47157CB00008B/2924